ON BONAIRE

On Bonaire

A Lyle Cooper Story

Anne Bennett

CALYPSO HOUSE PUBLISHING

Cover design: Lynn Andreozzi
Interior design: Danna Steele
Author photo: Amanda Cramp

ISBN (paperback):979-8-9864896-3-6
ISBN (eBook): 979-8-9864896-2-9

"From birth, man carries the weight
of gravity on his shoulders. He is bolted
to earth. But man has only to sink
beneath the surface and he is free."

~Jacques-Yves Cousteau

One

The apartment was quiet except for the voices of the news reporters coming from the television. Lyle Cooper lounged in her most comfortable clothes: jeans and a Greenpeace sweatshirt, frayed at the cuffs. Sitting on her sofa with her bare feet up on the coffee table, she fished the last few kernels of popcorn out of the ceramic bowl balanced on her lap and threw them into her mouth. One hit her lip and rolled down the front of her sweatshirt. She picked it up, blew on it, and popped it into her mouth. She glanced at the clock: eleven thirty.

Her alarm was set to wake her at five. If she was going to have any energy to run before work in the morning, she needed to get some sleep. She pointed the remote control at the television. The voices fell quiet, and the screen went dark.

Near the door sat two suitcases, packed and ready to go. Tomorrow after work, she was leaving for a two-week vacation with four of her closest friends. She brightened at the thought of escaping her small, lonely apartment and spending time with friends under the warm Caribbean sun.

Right, left, right, left—the steady beat of Lyle's footfalls kept time with the music in her ears as she flew over the pavement. It was early and the air was still cool. Sunlight started to brighten her path as she ran through the residential area nearby. She admired the well-manicured gardens bursting with colors and freshly mown lawns.

She was scheduled to work a full day at the dental office. She planned to change her clothes and leave directly from there to the Raleigh-Durham airport. As she thought of her vacation destination, she momentarily lost the rhythm of her run. After a few awkward strides, she went back to listening to her music, keeping time with the beat and moving swiftly.

It took her thirty minutes to complete her route. She felt the familiar burn in her legs that she expected after a run. Sweat beaded on her face and neck as she slowed to a walk and stretched her arms over her head. She twisted right and left as she approached the stairs to her apartment. She took them two at a time to the second floor and unlocked her door. She was right on schedule and would have plenty of time to shower before leaving for work.

After pulling her long brunette hair into a high ponytail, she added some blush and mascara to her face, satisfied with the minimal makeup, then chose a pair of turquoise scrubs from her closet. The color brought out her eyes—the left one was light green and the right blue. She had heard comments about them all her life.

With her coffee mug in one hand and a packed lunch in the other, Lyle struggled with her key to open the back door of the dental office. The first to arrive, she flipped on the lights as she made her way through the office she loved, where she had worked as a dental hygienist for the past seventeen years. She applied immediately after college graduation. Twenty-five years ago, himself just out of college, Dr. Patel opened his practice. Once hired by Dr. Patel, she never looked back. She couldn't imagine a better boss. He had been her constant through her adult life.

In the center of the office were two desks for the administrative staff and a free-standing fifty-five-gallon aquarium—the main attraction. Dr. Patel had presented the aquarium to Lyle two years previous, in celebration of her fortieth birthday. As she came into the office that day, Dr. Patel and her coworkers stood by the tank and sang "Happy Birthday." The aquarium was the perfect gift. It combined Lyle's love of the ocean with an entertaining exhibit for both patients and staff.

She dropped brine shrimp into the tank and took a minute to watch as the fish darted about, gobbling up their morning meal.

It was her last day at work before vacation, and she had a full schedule of patients to see. She was cutting her flight a little close.

Bonaire, a tiny island off the coast of Venezuela, was a scuba diver's paradise. Lyle and her friends visited there for two weeks each summer and chose the same accommodations. They would dive early in the morning to midafternoon. The only downtime came in the late afternoon and evenings when they would enjoy a good meal, adult beverages, and a perfect view of the ocean.

Before leaving the office, she changed out of her uniform and put on a pair of jeans and a white blouse. She laced up her shoes and clasped an aquamarine necklace around her neck.

She was the first to arrive at the airport and waited for her friends at their gate. She was lost in her book when she heard Victoria's voice: "We made it and with no time to spare."

"Bon dia halo!" Lyle greeted her friends in Papiamento, the local language of Bonaire, with one of only two phrases she knew.

"Impressive." Victoria dropped her carry-on with a little force. She wore dark jeans with a blue top and high-heeled sandals. Her shoulder-length strawberry-blond hair was pushed back behind her ears.

But Lyle's eyes went immediately to the man walking up behind her. Rick MacLean still took her breath away. The previous year he and Lyle had been in a relationship and traveled to Bonaire as a couple. They were in the inseparable stage of the relationship and shared a room at the resort. Lyle was in love. She thought Rick was too. She was heartbroken when he broke up with her. As plans began to form for this year's trip, he was naturally included.

"We would've been here sooner, but Victoria's heels slowed us down." Rick bent down and kissed Lyle on the lips, a habit they never broke. She had to remember not to close her eyes.

Rick was perfect as usual. His shorts fell to just above his knee and had a crease in them. Lyle would bet money he had just picked them up at the dry cleaner's. His shirt was open at the collar, showing a little chest hair. His short dark hair was brushed straight back. The slight graying at his temples only added to his attractive appearance. He kept himself in top shape and, at age forty-five, could easily put a much younger man to shame.

He had an old-fashioned, gallant quality about him that Lyle found refreshing and more than a bit rare. Her thoughts drifted to last year's trip. She remembered the romantic evenings they spent together and wished she could be back in that heaven. She wanted to be back in his arms, back in his bed.

"I can walk fine in these sandals. We just kept getting stuck behind slow-moving people." Victoria flashed a grin at Lyle as she took a seat next to her. She touched her phone screen. "I'm going to call home for one last goodbye." She spoke with her husband and teenage son. After leaving thorough instructions on homework and frozen dinners, she said goodbye and dropped her phone into her purse.

Soon after, they started boarding. The red-eye wasn't the easiest flight, but it would get them on the island early enough in the morning to allow them a day of diving.

The flight passed uneventfully, and soon Lyle could feel the plane begin its descent. She watched out her window as the familiar island came into view below. The plane landed at Flamingo International Airport. She grinned at the terminal painted a bright flamingo pink, lest travelers forget where they've landed. The atypical color was a warm reminder of this island and welcomed her back again.

Lyle handed her passport to the customs officer, who opened the book and stamped on one of its pages. The pink flamingo stood on one foot over the word *Bonaire*.

They headed to the baggage claim area.

Victoria grabbed her bags off the carousel. "I'm going to call home and let them know we arrived safely." Lyle raised her eyebrows at her. "I know, I know, we've agreed to be unplugged this entire vacation. This will be my last call. I promise."

The friends had a rule that was agreed upon last year: while on vacation on Bonaire, there would be no phones, no emails, no internet, or any outside influences. They wanted the two weeks of vacation to truly be a time they could get away from it all, to enjoy one another and the beautiful surroundings undisturbed.

Rick and Lyle spotted their bags. As they dragged them off the conveyor belt, Lyle scanned the crowd of people gathered there. "I think Dottie may be here. She's coming with students from the university to do some research in the mangroves."

"Dottie's coming to Bonaire?" Rick asked, at the mention of Lyle's longtime friend.

"I should've asked her where she's staying," said Lyle. "Maybe we could all get together for dinner one night."

Victoria rejoined them, and they walked toward the minivan that would take them to the resort.

The sun was almost completely up as they traveled over the main road. The resort's minivan was full. The guests sat shoulder to shoulder as they were jostled over the bumpy road. It was only a short ride from the airport to Bon Adventure Resort. Lyle sat quietly and watched the landscape pass by. Bonaire was a hidden treasure for scuba divers. The island offered over sixty dive sites, most of which were accessible from shore. The Dutch island sat fifty miles north of Venezuela, with a mild and predictable climate year-round, making it a true paradise.

The beaches on Bonaire were not all blanketed in ankle deep sand. Many were covered with sparkling white coral. The coral was sharp and unforgiving underfoot. But it was that very coral that brought scuba divers to the island. Bonaire had the foresight to legally protect their coral reefs. This simple act kept the underwater environment pristine.

The sun was fully up when the minivan pulled into the main entrance of the resort and stopped in front of the reception desk. As with most things on Bonaire, reception was a permanent, open-air setup. Guests stretched and yawned as they made their way out of the van. Rick offered Lyle his hand as she climbed down the single step. The resort staff began unloading the mass of luggage from the back of the vehicle.

"Let's see if they're expecting us," said Rick. He led the way toward a smiling young woman standing at the desk. She checked them in and handed them their room keys. She also assigned them two pickup trucks, which would get them to the dive sites.

They agreed to settle in their rooms and get back together for lunch. They left a message with reception for Steve and Angela, two more friends joining them on this vacation, letting them know where to meet them.

Lyle was familiar enough with the layout to find her room on her own, in a two-story building at the center of the resort. She would have no ocean view, but there was less foot traffic to deal with and she liked the privacy the balconies offered. She carried her large roller bag and gigantic scuba-gear bag up two flights along the outdoor stairwell. A blast of cool air hit her when she walked into the bright room. She checked the temperature setting on the air conditioner and moved it up five degrees. She didn't like to be cold.

In keeping with the island theme, the room was furnished with white wooden furniture. The queen-size comforter was Caribbean blue and had white starfish embroidered along the border. A framed print of red flowers hung on the wall above the headboard. A welcome basket filled with treats sat on the coffee table. A club chair and matching love seat completed the room.

Lyle rifled through the basket and fished out a small tin of mixed nuts. She poured a generous helping into her hand and tossed them in her mouth.

She had to give the sliding glass door an extra pull to get out onto the balcony. Leaning on the railing, she looked down at a tree-covered pathway leading to the resort's restaurants, dive shop, and oceanfront. The coral bean trees, higher than the building, were almost close enough to touch. She listened for the parrots that would sing from the trees, but the birds were quiet this early in the morning.

She took a few minutes to put away her clothes then placed her toiletries on the counter in the bathroom. The overnight flight left her exhausted, so she took a long nap and woke again just before noon.

She put on a pair of shorts and a tank top and went to meet her friends at the resort's entrance. They walked across the street to a small restaurant. The outdoor tables were surrounded by a small white fence, the only thing that distinguished the dining area from the sidewalk out front.

As the three walked into the restaurant, they heard a familiar male voice: "Hey guys, over here!"

Steve and Angela were already enjoying cool drinks at a table under a large umbrella. Steve Williams waved at the group. His hair was light and curly, and he let it fly any way it chose. His nose was peppered with freckles, and his light blue eyes stood out against his rosy skin.

They exchanged hugs and smiles and joined their friends at the table. Rick shook Steve's hand and smiled at Angela. "Welcome to Bonaire. How was your flight?"

"The best thing I can say about the flight is that it's over." Angela smiled and sipped her diet soda. At twenty-eight, Angela Knight was the youngest of the group. Her pin-straight dark hair fell to her chin. She was always in full makeup, wore heels to the grocery store, and had a standing weekly appointment with her manicurist. Her Instagram often included pictures from weekend trips to Las Vegas, bachelorette parties at the beach, and social events with her sorority sisters. She was sporting a new tattoo today: a lifelike shark circling her ankle.

Victoria took a long drink of her ice water. "When did you get in? Your flight must've been ahead of schedule." She picked up the menu.

"We arrived on time. We just dropped our stuff in our rooms and headed over here. I'm starving. Just peanuts and soda on the plane." Angela smiled at Lyle. "I think we're neighbors. I'm in 2B just next to you."

"I'll try to keep the noise down," Lyle said with a grin.

"I guess I really scored. My room is oceanfront," said Rick. Balled-up paper napkins bombarded him as he did his best to ignore them while glancing at the menu.

As they finished their lunches, Steve leaned back in his chair. "Is everyone over their jet lag and up for some afternoon diving?"

Angela perked up. "I brought some new gear I can't wait to try out."

"How about a dive at the resort?" Rick said. "We can postpone using the trucks until tomorrow. We'll keep it shallow and easy, just enough to get our gear wet. After we've all had a good night's rest, we'll start the deep dives."

Lyle placed her napkin on her empty plate. "I'm in, but all my gear's still in my room. I have to move it down to my locker at the dock." She placed a bill on the table. "I'll meet you all down there."

She walked back to her room to start the tedious task of getting her gear organized. She opened her bag and began removing and organizing the contents. Just having the basic dive equipment meant having enough gear to sink a small ship. Her buoyancy compensator, or BC, was an inflatable vest, with air pockets to make a diver float and other pockets that held lead weights to make a diver sink. She put the BC to the side. The resort supplied the air cylinder that would be attached onto the back of it while diving.

She lifted and untangled her regulator. It contained a series of uncontrollable hoses that moved the air from the cylinder to the diver's mouth, enabling them to breathe underwater. Next, she took her dive computer out of its box. She tested the battery and put it on her wrist. She would rely on it for information such as depth, dive time, how much air she had, water temperature, and the amount of nitrogen absorbed in her body. She pulled her large fins, boots, mask, snorkel, and wetsuit out of the travel bag.

Lyle packed as much of the gear as she could fit into a large mesh bag. The bag had nylon straps she could fit over her shoulders and carry like an oversized backpack. The gear that wouldn't fit would have to be carried separately.

She put on one of the five bathing suits she had brought, a simple red one she bought at a sporting goods store. She covered her face and neck with sunscreen—the rest of her body would be covered by her wetsuit and protected from the sun. She trembled and adjusted the air conditioner setting up a second time.

She searched through her drawer and threw on a white T-shirt that fell to her thighs. She fished her phone out of the jeans she had worn on the flight. The unplugged rule was in effect, so she would only use her phone as an alarm clock and to play music. She said a silent farewell then placed it on the nightstand.

Two

The sun momentarily blinded Lyle when she opened her door. She balanced the heavy bag on her back and awkwardly cradled her wetsuit, fins, and mask in her arms. She carefully descended the stairs and then followed the tree-canopied path that wound between the resort's buildings. A fine sheen of sweat broke out on her forehead.

She soon left the shady cover of the path and walked toward the waterfront. The sun beat down on her. She stopped and readjusted the gear in her arms and pushed her sweaty hair off her forehead, her T-shirt stuck to her back.

With her gear rebalanced she continued on and soon the ocean came into view. At the oceanfront, she walked down several steps to the dock. She stopped a moment to admire the vast blue ocean and to catch her breath.

The water sparkled. It tempted Lyle to jump in and rinse away the sweat that now saturated her bathing suit and T-shirt. Her hair had given in to the humidity and floated in wisps about her head. A slight breeze blew in off the water. She closed her eyes and let it cool her.

A voice from the dock caught her attention. Captain Maartin, the head of dive operations for the resort, was leading some guests along the dock. He took it upon himself to give first-time visitors a tour of the dive center, making sure everyone knew where to find equipment and any other gear and supplies they might need.

The group of three, two men and one woman, listened attentively as Captain Maartin explained dive procedures. They nodded as the captain gestured toward the dive shop. One man sported a baseball cap pulled low on his forehead. The woman wore a wide-brimmed straw hat with a navy-blue silk ribbon around the crown that blew in the breeze. She held the hand of the second man as they strolled along the dock.

Lyle wasn't surprised to see Calypso, Captain Maartin's loyal dalmatian, tagging along with the tour group, as she had the run of the resort. Guests often received a greeting from Calypso—she'd pause just long enough for a scratch on her head.

A strong gust of wind came in off the water. Lyle dropped her chin and squinted her eyes. She heard a surprised cry come from the touring group after the young woman's hat was taken by the wind and tumbled over the dock toward the water. Her hands were full of gear and her mesh bag was cutting into her shoulders, but Lyle instinctively shuffled forward to try and stop the hat. She stumbled nearer as she watched it roll closer to the dock's edge. She caught up to the runaway hat before it fell to the water below. The gear on her back shifted, throwing her off balance. With her arms full and only her feet free to stop it, she lifted her foot and stomped on the delicate straw, trapping the hat under her foot. She couldn't stop her forward momentum and her second foot caught on the hat. It was drug along the dock until she was able to regain her balance and stop herself.

She slid her bag off her shoulders and let it fall to the dock where it landed with a thump. She picked up the flattened hat and looked toward the tour group. One of the men was coming toward her with an annoyed expression on his face. She haphazardly tried to contour the hat back to its original shape. The navy-blue ribbon was dangling off, and the brim lay flat over the crushed crown. Gravel from her shoes was embedded in the weave, and bits of straw stuck out in random directions. She tried to move the ribbon back in place and worked to straighten the bent brim. The man stopped in front of her and shook his head at her futile attempt.

"Yours?" asked Lyle.

He grimaced and snapped, "Great job. This hat is a Bortolino. It cost more than you make in a month." He flagrantly assessed her from her shoes to her frizzy hair. "Two months, probably."

Bright hazel eyes shone above chiseled cheek bones. His square jaw was covered with several days' growth. The ends of his blond highlighted hair blew in the breeze, struggling to escape his ball cap. He stood less than six feet tall, and his strong arms were showing the effects of being out in the sun too long.

Lyle recognized him easily. She had seen several of his films—romantic comedies and tragic love stories. Most recently he received accolades for his portrayal of a real-life American hero named John Magnum. The face Lyle was looking at littered the tabloids and evening gossip shows. They reported stories about what actress or model Michael Miller had on his arm of late. He was the current American heartthrob, and his face on the cover sold magazines.

"I may have been a little over aggressive trying to catch it." She handed him the mangled hat. "Maybe with a little work it can be restored to its original splendor."

"A little aggressive? You completely ruined the thing. We may as well hold a damn burial. Your super-sized clown feet did a lot of damage."

Lyle looked down at her feet. She didn't think they were particularly large.

"I don't know why you tried so hard to save the damned thing. It's no good now." He scowled at her. "What was the sense in stopping it when you completely messed it up in the process? You should've let it fall in the water. Then it would only be wet, not totally demolished."

Steam billowed up Lyle's neck. She was sticky with sweat, and her back and shoulders ached. She snatched the hat out of Michael's hand and clenched her teeth. She threw it like a Frisbee, sending it flying off the dock. They watched as it sailed to the water below. "Happy now, jackass? Now it's wet."

The hat bobbed up and down with the waves.

"Did you just call me a jackass?" he asked, clearly indignant. "Do you know who I am?"

She ignored the question and began to pick up her heavy bag. He grabbed her arm to stop her, but she pulled away and whipped around to face him.

He held up his hands in surrender. "Whoa now, settle down."

Lyle lifted her bag and awkwardly draped one of the straps over her shoulder. It was much too heavy to carry that way, but her adrenaline had her feeling stronger, and she wanted to get away from the disappointing star.

He watched the hat as it floated out to sea. "Nice throw. I may need to call the coast guard to get my sister's hat back."

She walked away.

He called after her, "Hey, I just got off a very long flight and I haven't had any sleep in two days."

Lyle was willing to listen. She stopped and faced the actor. She would hate to find the Hollywood good guy was, in real life, truly a smug ass. She squinted and waited for him to apologize.

"I was only joking about the big feet. Don't make a PR thing out of this."

Lyle remained silent. She didn't hear an apology.

Captain Maartin's group started to move along the dock. Michael jogged to catch up to them, and Lyle watched as he rejoined the group. She felt betrayed to have found that the popular star had such an air of arrogance about him.

She left her gear on a bench and walked to a large thermos with a cone-shaped paper cup dispenser attached to it. She helped herself to several cups of icy water while watching Captain Maartin's group continue their tour. Michael Miller pulled his hat down low on his forehead again, trying to avoid recognition.

After finishing her water, she assembled her gear.

Her friends arrived, and soon the five were entering the water. Standing chest-deep in the sparkling ocean, they put on their fins and checked that everyone's air cylinder was turned on. They could hardly wait to make their first descent.

Victoria gazed at the open ocean. "I've been looking forward to this day ever since we left the island last year. Two weeks of diving, relaxing and sleeping in. Nothing can ruin this vacation."

"You may change your mind about that when you hear our dive plan for tomorrow," said Steve.

Lyle took the bait. "Okay, what's the dive plan for tomorrow, and why aren't we going to like it?"

"Rick and I were thinking, and don't respond until you've given yourselves a minute to think about it." He hesitated. "Pre. Dawn. Dive."

"Why?" Victoria's voice had gone high. "We can dive anytime, anywhere. Why do we want to dive before the sun comes up?"

"Good job with the thinking about it for a minute, Victoria." Steve rolled his eyes. "Think of it as doing our night dive early in the morning. We can see the reef as it was all night long. It'll still be dark outside, so the nocturnal life will be active. We can see the reef before it wakes up and still be the first in line for the breakfast buffet."

Victoria cocked her head. "Is this plan all about your stomach, Steve?"

Angela grinned at Victoria and waited to hear her friends hash this one out.

"Okay, I've actually let the idea sink in," said Lyle. "I think it's a good idea. We always had to stay up and wait for the sun to go down before starting our night dives. By the time we're done diving, cleaning our gear and putting things away, it's close to midnight. If we dive early in the morning, before the sun comes up, we can avoid all the late nights."

"It's settled then," said Steve. "Set your alarms for four thirty."

Victoria looked from Steve to Angela to Lyle, then Rick. She felt like she missed out on the punch line. "Four thirty? We're really going to do this? Dive before the sun comes up?" When no one replied, she reluctantly agreed. "Whatever."

Rick couldn't help but notice Angela's new equipment. "Angela, I think a bubble gum factory exploded all over your new gear."

"Hey, do you know how hard it is to find hot pink fins? I lucked out. I got these at my dive shop in Raleigh. It was the last pair they had." She floated on her back and lifted her feet up out of the water. Two neon pink fins waved in the air.

"Great. We aren't going to see anything on this trip." Steve put his mask in place. "The fish will see Angela's feet coming a mile away and head for the coral."

"You think my fins are bad?" She lifted her mask and snorkel out of the water. "I found these to match."

Lyle placed her regulator in her mouth and took a strong breath to make sure air was flowing freely. They each made a fist with their right hand and pointed their thumbs down: the signal to descend.

Three

The phone alarm woke Lyle. She had had a fitful night and was now tangled in her sheets, unable to move. Her nightshirt had worked its way north as she slept and was wound tightly around her chest. She pulled at it and kicked the sheets.

"Fuck me."

She worked herself free, fumbled for the phone on the bedside table, and shut off the resonating beep. She lay back in bed and held the phone directly over her head. She squinted into the bright light: 4:30 a.m.

"Damned overachieving dive buddies."

The room was black. She was up before the sun and quietly cursed herself for agreeing to Steve's predawn dive plan. She sat on the side of the bed and placed the phone back on the table. She stretched her arms up over her head and assessed how her back had done on the commercial mattress. She leaned to the left and twisted, then leaned to the right, twisting again.

"Pretty good."

She opened the curtains to the balcony. Just as she thought, the resort was unnervingly dark and quiet. There was no sign of any movement, human or otherwise.

"The fish are in for a rude awakening."

She brushed her teeth and hair and put on a swimsuit. She covered up with a pair of blue board shorts and her Bob's Crab Shack T-shirt. She grabbed several underwater flashlights and illuminating tank markers and left her room.

Steve, Rick, and Victoria were at the dock and had already begun assembling their gear. The only light came from a security spotlight from the restaurant above. Lyle opened her locker and pulled out the gear she had stowed there the day before. The four of them worked in silence for several minutes. When they finished, they sat on the bench to endure the arduous task of putting on wetsuits. They were made of neoprene, they slid on about as easily as a pair of pantyhose that were two sizes too small.

Lyle broke the silence, her voice still scratchy with sleep. "Where's Angela?"

"I'm here." A voice came from the darkness. "I haven't had my coffee yet, and I'm seriously reconsidering who I'll vacation with in the future, but I'm here."

They were in the water by five. Being in the ocean seemed to wake their senses. It was eerily dark and quiet as they checked each other's equipment with their underwater flashlights. Illuminated red, green, and blue markers hung from each tank, making them visible to each other in the darkness. The five of them had dove together so often, they were immediately on the same page. They completed their checks and floated about, anxious to get started.

When diving as a group, they appointed one person the leader in order to keep everyone together. There would be no natural visibility this morning. It would be easy to lose someone in the opaque water.

Getting down to business, Victoria asked, "Who's going to be our dive leader this morning?"

"I'll lead us," said Lyle. "We'll swim slowly and stay in a group." She dipped her head in the water, wetting her hair so it would stay back and out of the way. The sky was full of stars. Tiny bright lights on a black velvet background. She took a moment to search for any constellations she knew but found none.

She placed her mask on her face and her regulator in her mouth, and the others did the same. She made a fist with her right hand, thumb facing down, and in complete silence, they descended into the dark water.

Lyle watched the illuminated computer on her wrist. The displayed numbers steadily increased as she sunk deeper. When it read forty feet, she stopped her descent and waited for her friends to catch up. The group kept their depth relatively shallow in the more dangerous darkness. The surrounding blackness put them on full alert. They advanced unhurried, knowing they would see more ocean life if they quietly snuck up on it. A leisurely pace would use less of their air and allow them more time to dive. The black water was strangely warm and calm. Narrow beams of light broke through the murk.

They swam over the reef and directed their lights down at the coral. Lyle spotted a sea turtle partially hidden under a rock shelf. The air breathing animal was known to be able to sleep for several hours underwater. She repeatedly tapped her tank to alert the others of her find. In silence, they floated over the sleeping turtle.

Lyle led them farther along the reef and spotted a large piece of coral with her flashlight. Several fish were taken by surprise by the flash of brightness. The small fish swam away quickly, trying to avoid any danger.

The divers moved along weightlessly through the pitch-black water. The only noise was that of exhaled bubbles passing over their ears. Lyle glanced behind her and counted four light beams searching the reef, her only assurance that they were all still together.

Suddenly, something side-swiped her. It flashed a beam of light at her as it sped by then disappeared into the darkness. Startled, she inhaled sharply. The creature was enormous but moved passed her like a shot out of a gun. Her heart raced as she waited to see if it would return.

She looked to her dive buddies following behind her. It was impossible to know if her friends had seen what it was. She again counted four beams of light. They were all still together.

They had seen the six-foot-long tarpon several times before and at some point, named it Charlie. The silvery scales of a tarpon can reflect the light from a diver's flashlight, creating a flash when they swim past in total darkness. Charlie had perfected swimming with divers. He kept just out of sight and waited for a small fish to be blinded by a curious diver's flashlight beam. He then torpedoed from behind, passing very close to the diver, and made a meal of the stunned fish.

Lyle knew the tarpon living on Bonaire were not shy or even frightened of people. After all, swimming alongside divers made hunting fish easier for them. Charlie had probably been swimming with them since they descended. Lyle knew the gigantic fish would most likely stick with them until they left the water. He would hide in the shadows and wait for his next victim.

Four

The sun was up when the divers emerged from the water and walked in their heavy, dripping gear to the benches on the dock. The sky was clear, and the humidity wasn't going to be a problem today.

"I forgot how big that tarpon is," said Angela. "Swimming along with us, Charlie had a hearty breakfast this morning." She slid her arms out of her BC. "Let's get this gear off and get some breakfast ourselves."

Lyle stood in her bathing suit and rinsed her BC with a hose, removing all the salt water from the delicate valves. Despite her attempt to dodge it, the cool water bounced off the equipment and splashed all over her legs.

A voice yelled down to them from the restaurant patio above. "Good morning! Done with a dive already? I'm still on my first cup of coffee."

Lyle saw a man grinning down at them. He was unshaven, and his hair was still disheveled from his night's sleep. He leaned on the railing and held his coffee mug in his hand as he watched.

Rick glanced up at him. "'Morning. Save some of that coffee for us. My friend Angela here is ready for a few cups."

At hearing her name, Angela glanced up at the man. She then caught Lyle's eye and gave a subtle wink.

Rick pulled on a T-shirt and spoke to the man. "You're welcome to join us tomorrow morning."

"Thanks for the invite, but I prefer my diving after the sun comes up." The man waved and walked back to his table.

The group towel-dried and put their clothes on over their damp suits. The resort was casual and diver friendly but had a strict policy of no bathing suits or wetsuits in the dining areas.

They went up the stairs to breakfast, where it smelled of freshly brewed coffee and sizzling bacon. Each table had a vase full of mini-Gerbera daisies. A slight breeze rippled at the edges of the white tablecloths and kept the patio cool.

Victoria and Angela went straight to the coffee bar, while Lyle, Steve, and Rick filled their plates at the buffet. Lyle couldn't wait to enjoy the assortment of food on her plate. An omelet stuffed with mushrooms and two pancakes covered in warm maple syrup left little room for anything else. She placed her sizeable croissant directly on the table. She wasn't shy about filling up at breakfast. The day ahead was sure to deplete any calories she would consume.

As she listened to the quiet conversation of her friends, she glanced around the restaurant at the other guests. Her attention landed on a man seated at the next table. Leaning on his elbow, he used his fork to shovel eggs into his mouth. His stomach brushed against the edge of the table. His arms and legs, although long and lean, lacked any muscle tone. What caught Lyle's eye was his *Dive Roatan* T-shirt. She had been toying with the idea of a trip to Roatan and wondered what the man had thought of the diving there. He wasn't especially handsome, but she had to admire his hair. It was long and blond and flowed in soft waves past the man's shoulders. It sported natural highlights that women would pay a fortune for. She wondered what kind of conditioner he used.

As they ate, they watched several staff members hose down and sweep the dock below. Other staff loaded full air cylinders onto the boats for the divers who would be going out diving with them that morning. Lyle had scheduled some boat diving when she sent her deposit in for the room. Tomorrow morning, she was scheduled to go out on Bon Adventure's *Mi Dushi*, the largest of their fleet.

Glancing down at the crew, Victoria saw a few familiar faces. "Captain Maartin is still here, and there's Francesca."

"I saw him on the dock yesterday," said Lyle. "He was giving guests a tour."

Angela sounded excited when she said, to no one in particular, "I am the luckiest woman alive," holding her forkful of eggs halfway to her mouth. "This vacation just got one hundred percent better."

All four turned to see what had caught her eye.

"Stop looking!" she snapped. "Eat your breakfast." She looked at her own fork suspended in midair and put it down on her plate. "Steve, please stop looking. Everyone, just eat your breakfasts."

Steve obediently turned his attention back to his toast.

Angela spoke so softly it was hard to hear her. "See that guy at the table over there?" The four swiveled their heads. "Don't look over there!" They looked at her and tried to hold in their laughter. "Michael Miller is having breakfast just two tables down from us."

"I'm obviously supposed to know who Michael Miller is," said Rick. "But it escapes me at this moment." He waited for an explanation, but Angela was so starstruck she hadn't heard him and continued staring at the actor.

"I have two teenage daughters at home. They're huge fans of his. My wife is too," said Steve. "He started his career playing the lead on *Greener Pastures*."

Hearing the name of the short-lived television show, Angela turned her attention back to her friends. "That show was like a zillion years ago. He was just a teenager then. He makes movies now. He's starred in a bunch of stuff." She glanced back over at Michael Miller's table. "He just played Lieutenant John Magnum in the movie." She looked at Rick for any hint of recognition. "You know, the movie is based on the book, about Lieutenant Magnum's real-life experiences overseas. It's a huge hit. It's still in theaters, and he's getting all sorts of praise for his performance. They're talking Academy award nomination."

Lyle had read the book Angela was referring to but hadn't seen the movie yet. Magnum's story was fascinating, and his bravery in battle and selfless acts made him a true American hero. When it was announced the book would be made into a movie, the hubbub in Hollywood was who would get the prized role of portraying Magnum on screen. The announcement that it would be Michael Miller was bigger news than the movie itself.

"I saw him on the dock yesterday," said Lyle, unimpressed. "He was taking the resort tour with Captain Maartin."

"What?" whispered Angela. "You knew Michael Miller was staying at our resort and you didn't tell me?"

Lyle glanced at the star's table. He was seated with the same woman and man who were with him on the tour yesterday. He had pulled his ball cap down low on his face and was slumped a bit in his chair, trying to escape notice. She felt a little sorry for him. He was now on Angela's radar, and Lyle had a feeling Angela wasn't going to let this fish get away.

Victoria poked Angela with her finger. "You should go over there and introduce yourself."

Angela looked down at her plate and pushed her dark hair behind her ear. "I can't do that."

"When will you ever get this chance again?" asked Steve. "He's a single good-looking movie star. They don't come a dime a dozen."

Angela looked over at Michael's table and ran her hand over her damp hair. "I really shouldn't."

"Go over there," said Lyle. "Ask him for an autograph. Maybe get a picture."

"Today's not a good day," Angela said, sounding defeated.

Four voices together asked, "Why not?"

Angela put her hands on her head. "My hair's a mess. I just got out of the water. I don't want him to see me like this."

Rick stood and tossed his napkin onto his plate. The others followed his lead and began getting up. He waited for Lyle as she pushed her chair in under the table. He surprised her by placing his hand on the small of her back and gently running his thumb in circles as they walked together toward the exit. Perhaps it was simply out of habit, Lyle wouldn't read anything into it.

They retrieved their gear from the dock and placed it on the grass just beyond the restaurant entrance.

"Lyle and I'll go get the trucks and be back here in ten minutes," said Rick. "We'll load up and head out."

Bon Adventure's pickup trucks were dual cabs, spacious enough to fit up to four people, with enough space in the bed to haul all their gear. The group had reserved two trucks for their use. Today they would leave the resort and dive the reefs at the south end of the island.

Five

Rick and Lyle searched for corresponding license plates among rows of matching white trucks. They found their assigned vehicles and drove them over the bumpy gravel road that ran through the resort.

The trucks pulled up, and Victoria, Steve, and Angela loaded their equipment into the back.

"Same setup as last year?" Victoria asked. "Boys in one truck, girls in the other?"

"Sounds good to me. I'm not crazy about Rick's driving." Angela winked at Rick and placed her pink fins in the rear of the girls' truck.

Once everyone's stuff was loaded, Rick spoke from his driver's seat. "Why don't we drive down to Aquarius? We can start there and then work to the north." Aquarius offered an easy area to enter the water. The site names were as global as the guests on the island, some Dutch, some Papiamento, and others English. Each site on the island was marked by a painted yellow rock, the bright color easily visible from the road, with the dive site's name printed in large black letters.

Lyle yelled from the driver's seat: "See you at Aquarius."

Victoria sat shotgun, and Angela in the center of the back seat. Lyle threw her sunglasses on and shifted the truck into first gear. The tires spun with their hasty departure.

Most of the vehicles on the roads were dive trucks owned by the many resorts on the island. The two trucks slowed while traveling through the town of Kralendijk. Markets, gift shops, ice cream parlors, and restaurants lined the narrow streets. No building was taller than two or three stories, and most were painted in cheerful, alternating vibrant colors.

As they left town and traveled south past the airport, the landscape changed. To their right, the road ran just yards away from waves crashing onto the white coral. On the left were the sea salt beds. They were a surprise to anyone who hadn't seen them before. The huge mountains of white salt resembled the great pyramids of Egypt. Next to those, fields of harvested ocean water glowed bright pink. Brilliantly colored fields of ocean water as far as the eye could see. The unexpected color was created by the algae that flourished there. It was the same algae that gave the local flamingos their wonderful hue. The white salt mountains and pink seas were impressive to the first-time visitor but something Lyle and her friends were accustomed to. They warmed Lyle's heart and made her feel at home on this idiosyncratic little island.

As they drove, the girls listened to the radio. They swayed along to the beat and Lyle played drums on the steering wheel. They rolled the windows down, allowing a cool breeze to blow through the truck.

Victoria turned down the music. "Truth or dare, Angela?"

Angela rolled her eyes in the back seat. "Truth."

"Okay, good. Truth, let's see. Let me think of a good one." Victoria looked out the side window for a minute. "Got one." She turned to Angela. "When you were dating that guy Alex, the banker, how did you manage to get along in the bed? What I mean is, how did you have sex?"

Lyle glared at Victoria. "That's disgusting, I don't want to know the answer to that."

"Yes, you do. We were just talking about this the other night while we were waiting for Angela at the movie theater."

"You guys are sick," said Angela. "My sex life is private. Mostly. Except for all the stuff I've already told you. Victoria, I had no idea you were so crass. Besides, you're playing it all wrong. You're supposed to ask the question first and then I decide truth or dare."

"Too late," said Victoria. "You already picked truth."

"It was just innocent curiosity," Lyle said. "We were wondering if his build made having sex difficult. He had a very large belly, and the possibility of it getting in the way during sex, well..." She let the thought trail off. "Then we were trying to figure out how you'd position yourself with that guy. If he's on top, you suffocate. If you're on top, it would be like finding a needle in a haystack."

"Here we go," said Angela. "Perfect ladies out in public, but in this truck, we're as foul-mouthed and classless as they come."

"Why were you dating him anyway? The man had very little to offer in the personality department. Lyle and I just figured he was good in bed. Then we had trouble imagining how that might work." Victoria waited for Angela to come back with a smart answer but she never did.

Then Angela yelled from the back seat: "Pull over! Stop the truck." Lyle slowed down, but she got even louder. "Lyle, I said pull over! Stop the damn truck!"

"Angela, what the hell?" Lyle slammed on the breaks, and the truck slid through the gravel to a stop on the side of the road. She was sure Angela was having a medical emergency or had found a critter in the back seat with her. She put the truck in park and whipped around to face her friend. "What the hell?"

Angela sat up straight and looked out Victoria's window. All urgency gone she stared in awe. "It's Michael Miller." She glanced at Lyle and out the window again. "He's diving here."

Once Lyle realized there was no emergency, she took a breath and slumped in her seat.

They watched the three divers assembling their equipment just yards away. Their truck was parked on the white coral beach near the water. "We told the guys we'd meet them at Aquarius. We're going to dive here later."

Angela's eyes were huge as she gawked out the window at the attractive star.

Victoria couldn't find it in her heart to disappoint her friend. She turned her gaze back to the divers on the beach. "Change of plans. Pull the truck in, Lyle. We're officially stalkers now."

Lyle had no desire to see Michael Miller again, but the wonderment on Angela's face convinced her to pull in. The white coral crunched under the tires as they advanced over the bumpy terrain. She carefully maneuvered around a third truck that sat empty on the beach, its doors left wide open. In the back were T-shirts, shoes, and several empty beer cans. Clearly, these people were in the water already.

She turned the truck around and backed up as close to the water's edge as possible. They could put their gear on and walk just ten feet and be in the water. "Watch for the guys," she said, looking toward the road. "They should be just behind us. Maybe they'll see us as they drive by."

Angela came out of her starstruck state. "I can't believe my luck. I'm diving at the same spot as Michael Miller. Damn it. I don't have my phone. You know, without a picture it never really happened." She pulled off her T-shirt and climbed out of the truck. With one eye on the actor and one eye on her task at hand, she assembled her gear.

Lyle and Victoria joined her at the back of the truck. "We all agreed," said Lyle. "No phones no internet, no work. We're all unplugged for the next two weeks."

"I know, I know, unplugged, I agreed. But a picture would be nice. Everyone back home would be so envious." She removed her shorts and stood in her red bikini. It was a cute suit but completely impractical for diving. Her breasts tested the limits of the strings tied around her neck.

"Angela, did you somehow know this was going to happen?" Lyle gestured at her red suit.

"Hey, you never know and you can never look too good." She grinned mischievously.

The ocean was as blue as the sky above. A light breeze swept onshore, keeping them cool as they worked with their equipment. They had just attached their air cylinders to their BCs when they heard it. A very loud pop followed by a long hiss echoed across the beach. Any experienced diver would know that sound. The pitch of a blown O-ring was coming from Michael Miller's truck. Lyle watched as he quickly turned the leaking cylinder off and stopped the hissing noise. He fiddled with something then turned the cylinder's valve back on, but the hiss of pressurized air reverberated over the beach again.

Victoria asked Lyle. "How long until we save Prince Charming?"

"Oh, he's no Prince Charming. I ran into him on the dock yesterday. He's an arrogant snob if you ask me. We're not helping him."

"Arrogant or not, we'll let them try it one more time."

"He should be able to fix his own equipment," barked Lyle. "We don't need to go over there. Let's get our gear on and get in the water. It's hot out here."

"Lyle, he needs our help," Angela pleaded. "We can't just leave him there with a broken tank. He won't be able to dive." A thought occurred to her. "OMG, I'll go help him, you two, stay here."

Lyle tilted her head. "When was the last time you changed an O-ring without breaking a fingernail?"

Once again, the sound of high-pressure air escaping the cylinder blasted from the back of Michael's truck.

"Damn you, Lyle," Angela said. "Okay, you can come with me. We better go now before that tank doesn't have any air in it left to save."

Lyle pulled her emergency repair kit from the back seat of the truck. Changing a blown O-ring was a basic repair. Any beginner could do it, but you had to have the parts and tools. "I'm doing this for you, Angela. Not for Mr. Rude Miller."

They were just yards away from Michael and his friends when all three heads turned to watch their approach. Lyle was wearing her baggy board shorts and faded Bob's Crab Shack T-shirt. On the back it read *Eat and get the hell out*. The shirt was over six years old. Last year she had cut the sleeves off and the neck out. Understandably, all eyes went to Angela in her red bikini.

Lyle touched her hand to her chest. "Hi, I'm Lyle Cooper." She gestured toward Angela. "This is my friend Angela Knight. Sounds like you may need a repair."

The back of their truck was filled with the newest and most expensive dive equipment. Lyle noticed their fins didn't have a scratch on them.

Michael lifted his chin toward Lyle. "Don't make this one mad. I've seen her temper." The wind blew his hair and it kept landing in his eyes. Annoyed, he continuously swept his hand over it, pushing it back over his head, willing it to stay out of his face. He was sporting a bronze, even tan. Lyle noted he still hadn't shaved. His piercing eyes were hazel. His build was right there on display. Strong arms and chest and a muscular, flat stomach.

The petite, blonde woman next to him said, "Hi, I'm Natalie. This is my brother, Michael, and my boyfriend, Diego. We have a leak or something." She had a pleasing smile and warm personality. She wore a tank-style suit, and her designer sunglasses sat atop her head.

Lyle ignored Michael's remark and spoke directly to Natalie. "Sounds like a blown O-ring. Do you have a repair kit?"

Michael cut in. "No, no repair kit. I'm guessing you do?" His eyes dropped to the small neon orange box Lyle held, the words *Save a Dive Repair Kit* emblazoned across the top.

Lyle lifted the box. "I was a Girl Scout," she said, making air quotes with the fingers of her free hand. "You know, be prepared."

"I'm pretty sure that's the Boy Scout's motto." Michael challenged.

"Well, either way, you didn't grasp the concept." She put her box on the tailgate next to the malfunctioning tank. Michael jumped in the truck's bed and stood the tank up on end so Lyle could reach it easily. He knelt on one knee and held it still. She searched through her little box for what she needed, surprised by his helpfulness, and got to work.

Michael, just inches from her, noticed her gemlike eyes. One blue, the other green. They were so bright, they glowed from her lightly tanned face. He flashed a tentative smile. "Mind if I watch? Apparently, this is a skill I should have."

Lyle answered flatly. "No, I don't mind, and yes, this is a skill you should have." She began prying the frayed O-ring out of the valve and spoke without looking at him. "Basic diver skills. Diver 101. Let me guess, you were sick that day?"

He ignored the question and eyed the many replacement parts in Lyle's box. "With all those spare parts, you'd think you were performing brain surgery or something."

"It may as well be brain surgery for how unprepared you are," Lyle snapped.

She held the broken O-ring up and dangled it in front of him. He held his hand out, and she dropped it into his palm. She then fished several O-rings out of the neon orange box.

"We need the right size," she said.

She had spread the tiny things out in her palm and was searching through them with her index finger. Michael began to sift through them too. He was so close to her, she could feel his hair brushing against her. She wished he would leave her alone and let her finish instead of getting in her way.

He picked up an O-ring. "What about this one?" asked Michael. "This looks about right."

She ignored him.

"Hey, Professor Gadget, I'm only trying to help."

She rolled her eyes. "Let's try it."

Michael watched her as she deftly completed the repair.

"Hand me the regulator."

He straightened out the hoses of the regulator and handed it to her. She finished by putting the regulator on the tank and turning it on. A round of applause went up at her success.

Michael was unimpressed. "Well, that was easy."

"Next time, fix your own equipment! I'd be in the water by now if you had a tiny clue how to work your fancy new dive gear." She closed the box and turned to leave. "What an arrogant jackass," she murmured, but everyone heard.

Angela, horrified at the way Lyle was talking to the star, tried to calm the situation. "Your tank's all set," she said, overly cheerful. "I hope you have a good day of diving. Maybe I'll see you at the resort later. Alone. I mean." She glanced at Lyle. "Just me."

"So, Lyle Cooper, you save the day again. Yesterday it was my sister's sunhat and today my tank. Although the hat may never be seen again." Michael jumped down from the tailgate. "Is there no end to the number of inanimate objects you're sworn to serve and protect? Maybe you should wear a superhero suit. It could have a cape, and you could fly around the island rescuing helpless tourists."

Angela looked out at the ocean. "Oh shit. Here we go."

But to her surprise, Lyle ignored the comments. She had noticed Diego looking pale. He had been standing in full gear the entire time. "Diego, you should get in the water," Lyle said. "You'll overheat standing out here like that."

He wiped the sweat from his forehead. "Great idea. I'll wait for you guys in the water." He patted Natalie once on her butt and headed off. He called over his shoulder, "I'll meet you in the shallow end."

Victoria, also ready to go, was walking toward the water.

"Thanks for the help, Lyle. We're kind of new to all this." Natalie flushed when she asked, "Would you mind terribly if we tagged along with your group? I promise to keep my brother in check."

"That would be great!" said Angela. "We'd love to have you join us."

Lyle shot daggers at Angela, but she struggled with her conflicting feelings. She was worried that three new divers would be entering the open ocean with what seemed to be little training. At the same time, she didn't want to ruin her morning of peaceful dives. She remembered others who willingly helped her in her early years of diving and she knew she had to take the high road.

"Have you set up a dive plan? What are you planning to use for navigation?" She wasn't interested in their answer. She wanted to see their reaction to her questions.

"We just arrived on Bonaire yesterday," Natalie said. "This is our first dive off the resort. We don't have much experience. Michael learned a little bit for a movie he made." She lightly punched her brother on his arm. "They taught him just enough to film some underwater scenes."

"*Summertime Love.* I saw that movie twice." Angela began to explain the premise to Lyle: "Michael had to save his girlfriend from a sinking sailboat. She was trapped in the hull." She eyed Michael. "I think it was the best movie ever. I saw it twice."

Michael put on a pleasant smile. He spoke with a kindness that surprised Lyle. "Thank you. I'm glad you liked it. It was a lot of fun to make. My costars did a lot to really bring the film together." He reached around his back for the tagline and zipped up the back of his wetsuit. He then put his tank and BC upright and slid his arms into the vest.

Natalie continued, "Diego and I took a weekend class so we could dive with Michael on this vacation." She turned to her brother.

"Michael, I think it would be smart to dive with these guys. At least until we get the hang of it all. I don't want to get lost out there."

Michael scanned the wide expanse of the ocean. "If we were to get lost, my agent would miss me a bit, and the money I make for her considerably more." He turned to Lyle. "That is, if you'll have us."

She really didn't want to take on the responsibility of partnering with new divers. Michael was arrogant and still hadn't thanked her for the repair. She dug deep and buried her feelings. "Please dive with us. The crabs and eels are well fed. They don't need the three of you for dinner."

Victoria, in the water with Diego, shouted, "Lyle, what the hell?" She was running out of patience.

Lyle yelled back, "Just making some new dive plans." She turned to Michael and Natalie. "We're burning daylight."

Six

The group floated in the water as Lyle spoke. "We're an even number, so we can pair up." She gestured to each individual as she said their name. "Victoria and Diego will buddy up. Angela and Michael, you two stay together. I'll dive with Natalie. We're going to surface swim to that buoy." She motioned toward a buoy fifty yards away then spit out the water that had splashed into her mouth. "We'll descend the buoy line to the reef."

Victoria called out, "To the buoy!"

The group swam leisurely on the surface, enjoying the warm sun and blue sky. Lyle swam on her back, paddling lazily with her arms and kicking gently with her fins. She heard some splashing next to her and turned to see Michael.

"Now that I know how to change an O-ring, what else can you teach me?"

She held her arm over her eyes to block the sun. "Slow down, movie boy. You don't want to burn yourself out on the surface swim."

"Why did you buddy me with Angela?" He maneuvered to swim on his back like Lyle was doing. "I didn't know they made dive gear in hot pink. I'd learn more diving with you. You're like the Jacques Cousteau of Bonaire, only a little younger and slightly better looking."

Lyle deepened the strokes with her fins and powered her arms. She flew past him on the way to the buoy, leaving him in her wake. Now he was making fun of her age and looks. One dive. One dive and she would be rid of him.

When they all arrived at the buoy, they placed their masks on their faces.

"We're diving as buddies," Lyle said. "This means we're each responsible for keeping an eye on our partners. Check that your buddy's air is fully turned on." Each pair took turns checking each other's air cylinders.

"Everyone have air?" she asked.

All the divers nodded and waited for further instruction.

"We'll decide our direction when we get down there and check the current." She made a fist with her right hand and pointed her thumb down. Regulators in mouths, the six divers descended together.

Lyle sank into the salty water, watching her wrist computer for depth readings. At ten feet, she released air from her BC to aid in her descent. At twenty feet, she exhaled and cleared her ears. At thirty feet, she double-checked her air pressure. At forty feet, she looked around to be sure the others were descending safely. At fifty feet, the colorful reef below her grabbed her attention. At sixty feet, she leveled her body and slowed her descent. At seventy feet, she marveled at the spectacle revealed before her.

The current was so gentle, they let it move them along. The sun's beams broke through the water and lit up the coral like a shower of fireflies. The coral was buzzing with life. Lyle and Natalie glided over the reef. They took their time studying what they saw and searched for hidden treasures Lyle knew were there.

She spotted an arrow crab balancing on the tip of a piece of coral. It stood less than an inch tall, with big bug eyes and eight long legs. Its pointy head looked comical, and the way its body swayed with the water made it look like it was dancing. She moved out of the way and motioned for Natalie to come closer and watch the funny little crab bopping in the water.

Only a few minutes later, Lyle again motioned to Natalie to come see what she had discovered. It was a sizable white lettuce leaf slug moving along a piece of branch coral. It looked like a half-foot-long piece of ruffled lace. Had it been any bigger, a woman might consider wearing it as a decorative collar on an expensive blouse. Natalie approached and nodded at Lyle when she saw the pretty laced creature.

They continued on moving over the reef.

Natalie spotted a colorful fish swimming between her and the reef. She excitedly pointed it out to Lyle. The butterfly fish darted in and out of the coral. The fish was only six inches long, but its coloring was an eyeful. Its flat, circular body was mostly yellow but faded to white at the fins. And its two black stripes—one over the eye and the other just before the tail fin—looked like a child had drawn them with a black crayon. The scales reflected light so well the fish appeared to shimmer in the sunlight. Delighted with her discovery, Natalie stayed there to admire the butterfly fish.

Lyle floated behind her and tapped on her shoulder. When Natalie turned toward her, Lyle pointed out to the open ocean. There, a school of hundreds of butterfly fish were swimming, lined up like an army of soldiers marching across a field. They created a shimmering wall, like stained glass reflecting the sun's rays. Natalie's eyes grew huge as she watched them swim by.

Lyle was surprised at how much she was enjoying introducing the living reef to Natalie. She sensed she was sparking something in Natalie that may encourage her to become a lifelong diver.

Seven

As the six divers walked out of the surf, they noticed the occupants of the third truck had also finished their dive. Two men were sitting on the tailgate, drinking beer. They had removed their gear and wetsuits and wore just their bathing suits and flip-flops. Lyle immediately recognized the blond-haired man from breakfast, the one she wanted to ask about Roatan. Seeing him drinking beer at ten in the morning squelched her curiosity. The second man looked as though he would be more comfortable belly up to the local bar than on the beach. Lyle wondered how he got his wetsuit on over his protruding beer belly.

As they approached, the blond man raised his beer. "Welcome ashore!"

The group passed him and continued to Lyle's truck. The girls removed their gear and unzipped their wetsuits while they discussed the reef with the three new divers. Lyle put on her T-shirt, to cover up against the sun's rays, then grabbed her ball cap and pulled her ponytail through the back. She dug in the back seat of the truck and found a bottle of water that was now warm but would have to do, then she rejoined the group.

Natalie's face was beaming. "You've got to tell me what those crazy creatures were. They're awesome, and so small. How'd you find them?" She turned to her brother and Diego. "Lyle was finding the tiniest, most unusual things. I didn't know what I was looking at."

"Maybe we could buddy up sometime." Michael mimicked his sister's excitement and raised his voice. "I'd love to see the tiniest, most unusual things."

Lyle ignored his irritating comments. He sounded like a spoiled kid when he teased his sister like that. Everything this guy said annoyed her. She turned her water bottle up and took a long drink. She finished the last drop and wiped her chin with the back of her hand.

"Anyone can find the big stuff," said Lyle. "It'll come to you. I have some waterproof fish identification cards if you'd like to take them with you on your next dive. The cards are an easy way to learn what you're looking at." She went completely still. Did she just say that? Waterproof fish identification cards were the diver's equivalent to a pocket protector. She went back to the cab of the truck and yelled over her shoulder, "You can share them with your brother. I doubt he knows what he's looking at down there."

Michael's eyes narrowed at Lyle's comment. Victoria tried to hide her smile, and Angela's eyes shot a stern warning at Lyle.

Lyle rifled through her dive bag for the cards. She returned and handed them to Natalie. "It makes it more fun if you can put a name to the fish you're looking at. When you get good, you'll be able to tell male from female in some species and juveniles from adults in others."

Natalie thanked her for the cards, and the three of them headed back to their truck to remove their gear.

Victoria pulled out a bag of fresh fruit and offered it to her friends. "I stole these from the breakfast buffet. I hope the resort doesn't mind." The pineapple tasted delicious. It was so juicy the girls had a hard time handling the chunks with their fingers. Lyle couldn't believe she was hungry again so soon after her enormous breakfast.

Movement caught her eye as she saw the two men from the third truck walking toward them. "Yuck. We've got company."

"Hi girls. Need any help with your gear?" The blond man smiled as he looked at each girl with an appraising eye. He wore swim trunks but no shirt. His erection could be seen pushing against the fabric.

His friend's breath was labored from the short walk over the coral. They both held beers in their hands and stood grinning like schoolboys.

Victoria spoke sternly in an attempt to dismiss the men. "We don't need any help. Enjoy your day."

"We've got some ice cold brewski in the truck. We'd be glad to share. We're very generous that way."

Victoria repeated her dismissal to the two men, "No thank you. We're just leaving."

The blond man fixated on Angela in her red suit. "Now that's a pretty color on a very pretty lady." He moved toward her and stood too close.

"Hey, I was going to ask you how the diving was on Roatan," Lyle jumped in and tried to draw his unwanted attention away from Angela. "I saw your T-shirt at breakfast this morning. I was thinking of a trip there."

"The diving was good. We also took time to sample the local flavors. We're hoping to sample some new ones this week." He put his bony hand on Angela's shoulder and ran his thumb over her clavicle. "What do you say, honey?"

Angela tried to back away, but the man followed along with her. She backed up against the side of the truck and had nowhere else to go. "Get your hands off me!"

Michael and Diego heard Angela's cry and started a brisk jog toward the group.

Lyle moved quickly to put herself between the man and Angela. He towered over her. She had to reach up to put her fists on his soft chest. She anchored her feet in the coral and shoved him backward. He staggered several steps back, his arms waving in the air as he struggled to regain his balance. As his momentum slowed, his face turned red. Lyle charged at him and rammed her forearms into his chest. The blow sent the man backward again, and he landed hard on his ass.

"Back off!" Lyle screamed. "Leave! Now!"

The blond man scrambled to his feet and seemed to contemplate furthering the confrontation but saw Michael and Diego quickly approaching and decided against it. The two men lumbered back toward their truck.

Michael realized the man was going to get away. He picked up his pace and ran after the blond man with rage pouring out of him. His body language spoke volumes as his arm muscles tensed and his hands balled into fists. He stared at his target as the blond man continued toward his truck, unaware of the approaching threat.

Diego caught up to Michael and wrapped his arms around his chest. He pulled him to a stop. "No, Michael, not here. Not now. Look man, they're leaving. Let it go, buddy."

The blond man turned back to the girls. "Crazy fucking woman!" The men threw their empty beer cans in the back of their truck and sped off.

Michael's fury ebbed, and he composed himself. Diego released him, and they walked toward the girls.

Victoria had her arm around Angela, trying to comfort her. Michael's eyes were wide as he looked at Lyle in amazement. She found his expression funny and couldn't resist teasing him. "What? Did you come over here to save us?" She grinned at Victoria and Angela, surprised to see they were also looking at her in wonderment. "Come on guys, snap out of it."

Having seen the men drive away, Natalie joined them. "What was that all about? Are you all okay?"

"Just a couple of drunks overstepping their boundaries," Lyle said casually.

Diego draped his arm around Natalie. "Damn, Natalie. Did you see Lyle put that guy on his ass? He went down hard."

"Diego, she could've been hurt." Michael turned to Lyle. "That was a stupid thing to do. That son of a bitch was drunk. There's no telling what he may've done to you. He could've turned on you and beat the shit out of you."

Lyle had no response for Michael. Her friend was being manhandled by a creep. She reacted without any thought as to what harm may come to her. She looked at him as he shook his head. She was having a hard time keeping up with the ever-changing personalities of Michael Miller.

Eight

A familiar vehicle pulled in, and all discussion of the two men was forgotten. Lyle watched the white truck bounce over the coral toward them. "They found us. I'm afraid we have some explaining to do." She grinned at Angela. "You'll explain to the guys why we're at the wrong dive site, won't you?"

Rick and Steve parked and climbed out of the truck damp from the ocean. Their wetsuits were unzipped and pulled down to their hips, the sleaves hung to their knees. As Rick walked toward them, Lyle hated herself for admiring his muscular stomach and strong arms. She looked down at the coral glad her hat hid her face. She took a deep breath and puckered her lips to exhale. As she forcefully blew air out, she caught Michael watching her. He shook his head, trying to understand the enigma he had just witnessed.

"So, are we the butt of some joke? Did you dodge us on purpose?" Rick asked, then turned to the three new divers. "Looks like you've picked up some strays." He put his hand out to Diego. "I'm Rick MacLean. This is Steve Williams."

They shook hands all around as Natalie introduced her group.

Steve's face lit up. "My wife and daughters are huge fans of yours. It's nice to meet you."

Michael put on a pleasant smile. "Thank you, that's nice to hear. I can always use more fans." He turned to Rick. "I hope you don't mind us borrowing your friends. They were kind enough to help us out of a jam."

Lyle bit her lip. This was the second time today she was seeing the polite side of Michael and she wasn't buying it.

"I've been diving with Angela for years," said Rick. "She really knows her stuff. She makes a great dive companion."

"Where to next? We have enough air for one more dive." Victoria asked Natalie's group, "You guys in?"

Michael stood with one hand at his forehead, blocking the sun from his eyes. "We're in. We'll follow you."

Steve looked down the coast. "We were just at Aquarius. I could've sworn someone said something about diving Aquarius first."

Lyle fished the truck keys out of her wetsuit. "Let's finish with Margate Bay. It's just down the road."

Rick gave Lyle a bear hug. "Okay, but I want my dive buddy back." He easily swept her up in his arms and carried her with little effort a few steps to the truck. He gently placed her on her feet and smiled at her. "Still light as a feather. See you at Margate Bay."

Lyle wished Rick would stop being so attentive to her. It had been a rough breakup, and his kindness made it difficult for her to get over him. With his occasional touch and subtle flirting, she was wary that he could be looking for an easy, familiar, Caribbean booty call. That would break her heart, again.

Michael watched as Rick deposited Lyle at the truck. He noticed she didn't wear a ring and thought she seemed a little put out at being carried like that. She wasn't falling for Rick's poor attempt at flirting.

He began to reassess his first impressions of Lyle Cooper. A clumsy woman stumbling over the dock chasing a sunhat. A geeky diver who carried a save-a-dive kit that looked like a child's play toy. Maybe he had read her wrong. He couldn't stop thinking of those gem-colored eyes. He had teased her to the point of irritating her, enough that she wanted nothing to do with him.

"Okay Lyle, truth or dare?" This time it was Angela asking from the back seat. They had finished the second dive and were heading back to the resort for some surface time, new air cylinders, and lunch.

Lyle turned down the radio. "Are we really doing this?" she asked Angela in the rearview mirror. "Didn't we play this game in the second grade?"

"Yes, we're really doing this, and yes, we played this game in the second grade."

"Damn, truth, I guess." She gripped the steering wheel and waited for the question.

"Of all the guys you've dated, who would you say was the best in bed?" Angela grinned. "You know, the guy who really got you going. The one you'd start dreaming about on Monday morning, even if your next date wasn't until Friday night."

"It has to be a living person," Victoria added, giggling at her own joke.

"And please don't let your answer be Rick," said Angela. "If it is, I won't be able to get that image out of my head. I'll never be able to look him in the eye again. It'll ruin my entire vacation."

Lyle grinned but said nothing. Her expression soon turned contemplative as she watched the road in front of her.

Victoria slapped her knee. "Oh my God, it is Rick."

She hadn't said a word, but Lyle couldn't keep her feelings from showing on her face. "He's just really…" She tried to think of the right words. "Generous in bed."

Angela put her hand over her eyes. "Please stop. My eyes are burning."

"You asked." Lyle added, "You know, generous. Ladies first. Always. Angela, I hate to have to break this news to you. The guys you're dating, in their twenties, they don't have a clue. Guys in their twenties are all about the orgasm. Their orgasm. But you'll learn that as these boys grow up, they begin to figure it out. If they have the patience to make their lady friend happy, the sex is so much better."

Victoria chimed in. "It's like they don't read the book until they turn thirty-five."

"Rick has read the book and passed the test," Lyle said quietly. "All I'll say is that the women he's dating, well, they're very lucky to have him." She gazed at the ocean passing by and felt something twisting in her heart.

Rick made love to her as though she were made of porcelain. He moved his hands over her with the softest touch. Each of his movements was gentle and yet deliberate, and when he finally took her, it was tender and lasted for what seemed like forever. At first, she thought he was being so careful because it was their first time together. She soon discovered that every time with Rick would be wonderfully slow and sweet.

Victoria had heard something in Lyle's voice. "You're still in love with him." She thought out loud: "You haven't dated since you and Rick broke up. The two of you have more weekend plans than any noncouple I know. My God, Lyle, why haven't you told us?"

"Because I keep waiting to get over him. I wake up in the morning and think, maybe today's the day I'll fall out of love with Rick. Maybe today's the day it gets easier for me to be near him. But in the meantime, at least we're friends. I get to see him and spend time with him." She turned to Victoria. "If I say anything, I may lose that. I work very hard to hide my feelings for him. I totally expect you two to keep my secret."

Victoria looked out her window. "Well, shit."

Angela softened her tone. "I'll keep your secret, Lyle. And thank you for this afternoon. For saving me from that creep."

Nine

Lyle studied herself in the bathroom mirror. Despite using sunscreen and shielding herself from the sun yesterday, her skin was bronzed and her cheeks were rosy, bringing out the difference in her eye color. Her turquoise bathing suit enhanced them too. It was a V-neck and cut low in the back and high at the thighs, a style she found both attractive and practical.

She was scheduled to go diving on the *Mi Dushi*, the resort's boat. She didn't have to be on the dock until mid-morning, so she skipped the pre-dawn dive and breakfast with her friends and enjoyed sleeping in past sunrise.

She gathered her hair into a high ponytail. Over her bathing suit, she put on a pair of white nylon shorts and a turquoise sleeveless top. Her heavier gear had been organized and stowed in her locker the night before. She only had to grab her small bag and slip her feet into a pair of sturdy boat shoes before heading down to the dock.

Lyle arrived fifteen minutes prior to departure time. Her friends were long gone, having ambitious plans of their own for their day of diving. She emptied her locker of gear and walked to the boat.

She was glad to see some familiar faces. "Permission to come aboard, Captain Maartin?" She wondered if the captain would remember her from the previous years.

The captain was in his late fifties, though his leatherlike skin showed the effects of constant sun and wind exposure. The deep lines around his eyes were accented by his smile. His hair hung loose to his chin, grazing his short, gray beard. He was dressed in the resort's uniform: tan board shorts and a sky-blue golf shirt with *Bon Adventure* and its logo embroidered over the breast. Captain Maartin's eyes were soft and kind. They held a mischievous twinkle. His Dutch accent had faded over the years. He greeted Lyle in his native language, "Goedemorgen, Lyle. Welcome onboard *Mi Dushi*."

"Good morning, Captain."

He took her heavier gear and placed it on the deck floor, then offered her a hand up. The boat rocked gently with the waves, and she easily timed her step to board.

"Thank you, Captain Maartin." She picked up her heavy gear and searched for a place to put it all—the boat was filling up with divers, and space was at a premium. She spotted another familiar face moving toward her, smiling.

"Hi, Francesca." said Lyle. "Where'd you like me?"

Francesca worked with Captain Maartin as the dive leader, assisting guests with gear, answering questions, and ensuring an enjoyable, safe dive. Her English was excellent. Lyle found it endearing when she sprinkled it with her native Italian.

"Buongiorno, welcome. You'd be smart to get under cover and stay out of the sun. It's going to be a hot one today." At five foot ten, she could easily see over the people already onboard. Many were beginning to assemble their gear in the shady part of the boat. She looked fantastic in her golden string bikini. Lyle wondered how she got away without wearing the board shorts and embroidered golf shirt. She took Lyle's BC and fins. "Vieni con me. Come with me."

Lyle followed her along the crowded row of benches. Enthusiastic chatter filled the air. She was careful not to step on the other diver's fins and snorkels strewn on the deck. Dozens of air cylinders lined both sides of the boat. It's standard practice among divers that you were allowed a two-foot space to stow and change into and out of your equipment. It was a practiced skill to keep from bumping and falling into other divers. The quarters were expectedly tight, and the occasional jarring easily forgiven.

The boat swayed with a wave. Everyone held onto the rails to steady themselves until it passed, and the boat leveled out.

Francesca found an available spot and placed Lyle's BC on the seat.

"Grazie. Thanks for your help." Lyle repositioned the rest of her gear in her tiny space and slid her fins under the bench out of the way. She stood up and noticed a familiar figure hunched on the bench next to her. His ball cap was pulled down to his eyes as he studied his dive computer, trying to be inconspicuous. "Michael Miller?"

Michael glanced up from his computer with a resigned look. Once he realized who it was, a brilliant smile crossed his face. His bright hazel eyes glowed against his tanned complexion. His naturally highlighted hair was still damp from his morning shower. She could smell his coconut shampoo.

"Damn, I thought you were a fan. I was hoping I wouldn't have to spend the morning signing autographs and being utterly polite. I didn't know you guys were diving on the boat today."

"Actually, it's just me. Not everyone is crazy about being on a boat. Angela and Steve get seasick if there's any surf at all. Victoria and Rick don't like the crowds. They're back in the trucks today. Are you by yourself?" Lyle searched for his sister, hoping she wouldn't get stuck with him. She was looking forward to a peaceful day of diving. Just her and the creatures in the sea.

"I think Natalie and Diego had a late night. I knocked on their door, but no one answered."

She looked more closely at him. "Nice T-shirt. Are you a member?"

He glanced down at his shirt. *Greenpeace* was written in bold script across his chest and under that, in fine print, *For a Green and Peaceful World*. "No, I'm not a member. I think someone left this at my place. I guess wearing it makes me a hypocrite."

Lyle turned her attention to her gear. "Yes, among other things."

Michael stood. "So, you're telling me *you're* a member of Greenpeace?"

"Yes, as a matter of fact I am."

He smirked.

"I don't see what's so funny about that," she snapped. "Some of us actually have some integrity." She couldn't believe he was making fun of her again. She yanked her mask and snorkel from her dive bag.

"There's nothing funny about that. Absolutely nothing. And how can you say I have no integrity when you don't even know me?"

"Let's just call it a hunch." She scanned the boat for an available spot to move to. He was still smiling. "You can laugh at me all you want. I'm moving over there." She nodded at a vacant spot at the back of the boat. She would be in full sun, but it was preferred over being laughed at all day by Michael Miller.

"No, don't move. I'm not laughing at you, really. I'm just smiling because you surprise me. Please stay here."

The boat swayed. Lyle lost her balance and fell into Michael's side. He caught her by her waist and steadied her. Once balanced, she took a step away. "I still need to gain my sea legs."

"You have two different colored eyes. One's blue and the other green. I noticed that yesterday. I'm guessing you already knew that. About your eyes. Or am I the first one to notice?"

She glanced at the available spot at the back of the boat, only to see a middle-aged man place his gear there. She resigned to the fact she was stuck with annoying Michael Miller.

Francesca called for everyone's attention. "Per favore! Please take a seat while we pull away from the dock."

Lyle and Michael sat next to each other on the bench. The boat bounced and rocked as the crew detached the lines and threw them to the staff on the dock.

"This makes us diving buddies, right?" He looked hopefully at her. "I really wanted to dive with you yesterday, but your boyfriend claimed you."

She was stuck with him for the duration of the boat trip. She could remain annoyed with him and have a miserable time, or she could put her feelings aside and enjoy the day ahead of her. She decided to make a fresh start. He seemed to be trying to do the same.

She opened her dive bag and found her sunscreen. "I thought I was playing matchmaker by putting you and Angela together. You're around the same age. I'm sure you'll find you have a lot in common if you get to know each other." She rubbed sunscreen on her face. "Did you two not get along?" She handed the tube to Michael.

"Oh, don't get me wrong. I think Angela's great." Michael squirted the thick cream in his palm and rubbed it over his neck and face. "As a matter of fact, the whole day was great. I'm happy we met you and your friends. It's just that, well, who has pink fins? And a mask and snorkel to match? Those scream to be noticed. I'm not looking for attention on this trip."

Lyle grinned at the thought of the fins.

"Your boyfriend didn't want to come this morning?"

"Rick and I don't date anymore. We're just friends now."

"Good. I think he's a bit of an ass." Mimicking Rick's words, he said, "'What did you do? Pick up some strays?' How condescending can he be?"

The boat cleared the dock and picked up speed. Francesca stood at the stern and shouted over the noise of the motor and crashing waves, "Benvenuto! Welcome on board, *Mi Dushi!*"

Michael furrowed his brows. "*Mi Dushi?*"

"It's a Papiamento term, a form of endearment. It roughly translates to 'my sweetheart.'"

Francesca addressed the divers. "You're now welcome to move around the boat. Our destination today is the bello, beautiful, little island of Klein Bonaire." She raised her arm and motioned toward the island straight ahead. "Klein Bonaire is one of the Antilles National Parks. Its six hundred acres have been left untouched, indisturbato." Her hair blew about her face. She tried to trap it behind her ear. "The reefs surrounding Klein Bonaire are some of the most admired in the entire Caribbean. They're pristine, and since the island is uninhabited"—she spread her arms wide and smiled—"they're only accessible by boat."

Lyle and Michael moved from the covered area and stood at the side rail. She held on with both her hands and squinted into the sunny day. The slight spray of salt water cooled her face, and she couldn't suppress a smile as the boat skipped and jumped over the waves. She leaned over the rail and peered out toward the front of the boat to see the little island at the horizon. Despite her unwanted dive partner, the anticipation of the day ahead had her feeling exhilarated.

Several people crowded along the sides of the boat and they soon left the resort behind them. Michael stood behind Lyle. He could easily see over her head. The boat, moving like a pebble skipping water, threw him off balance. He reached around her and held onto the rail in front of her.

After a while, she heard a commotion behind her, and Michael walked away. She saw that he had been spotted by some fans who requested a picture and an autograph. They giggled and batted their eyes at him while readying their phones.

Michael stood with his arm around the shoulder of a pretty girl. Her equally attractive friend laughed as she tried to steady the camera on the bouncing boat. He removed his hat, and his hair blew about his head. He assumed a seductive grin and tilted his head close to the girl's face, then dropped his arm, slipped it around her small waist and looked toward the camera.

Watching him, Lyle couldn't help but notice his Hollywood good looks. But it was more than that. He could turn the charm on and off like a light switch. He was the Hollywood total package. His face was chiseled and had strong lines, both over his cheekbones and in the line of his jaw. His bright hazel eyes sparkled from his tanned face. She realized what Hollywood had already known. A face that attractive would sell movie tickets and magazines. He was completely at ease in front of the camera.

The three spoke briefly while Michael signed something. When he pointed toward Lyle, the girls looked her way and nodded. He returned to stand with her but was interrupted two more times for pictures and autographs.

"Hazard of the job?" Lyle asked as Michael returned once again.

"Benefit of the job," he answered sincerely.

As the boat sped ahead, it fell into a smooth rhythm. It skipped over the waves and sent surf skyward. They cackled as a rogue wave crashed against the boat and covered them in seawater.

Soon the sounds of the engines quieted and the boat slowed. Captain Maartin yelled from the deck above, "Ten minutes!"

The excitement was palatable. People returned to the benches to put on their dive gear. Michael hadn't moved.

"That's the traditional ten-minute warning," Lyle explained. "That means we have ten minutes to gear up and should be at the entry point by then." She realized this was Michael's first-time diving from a boat and thought she should give him a quick lesson.

"Captain Maartin's in charge—not only of the boat and crew, but of the divers. He decides on the location and tells us how long we can dive before he expects us back onboard. He also has the authority to stop a diver from entering the water if he feels they're unfit to safely complete a dive."

She watched the two young women put on their gear. "You know, I bet those girls wouldn't mind adding a third to their group. I'd planned to dive with the crew anyway."

"Yes, I'm sure those girls would love to dive with me." He took a moment to look over his shoulder at the young women. "I could have either one of them when we get back to the resort. Or both, if I was so inclined." He winked down at her. "But that's not what this vacation is about for me. You don't need to fix me up."

She blushed at the obvious statement.

"I'm sorry we got off on the wrong foot," he said. "I know why you tried to dump me off on Angela"—he glanced over his shoulder again—"or anyone else you think might have me. Let me start over. Please give me a chance to redeem myself."

Wearing their heavy equipment, they shuffled forward and fell in line with the other divers. The queue moved toward the back of the boat where they would make their entry into the water.

"Did you turn your air on?" Lyle asked.

Michael found his BC inflation button, pushed it, and nothing happened. He gave her a mournful look. "I know, I know, Diver 101."

"Don't worry about it. As your dive buddy, it's my job to ask." She turned the knob at the top of his tank. He, in turn, checked her tank and found the air on. The divers were all lined up, waiting for the okay to enter the water.

Captain Maartin yelled another traditional call: "Dive, dive, dive!"

A human stampede ensued as pairs of divers hit the water and gave the "okay" signal back to the boat. They then quickly swam out of the way for the next two divers to enter.

As the line moved along toward the entry platform, Lyle offered Michael a challenge. "Today, we're looking for a juvenile yellowtail damselfish. The first one to find one wins." She tilted her head, encouraging him to accept the challenge.

They hobbled forward as divers jumped into the water. "I may have a better chance at finding one if I knew exactly what I was looking for."

"Okay, Michael. Fish identification lesson one. It's just a baby, so maybe six inches long. The body is a deep dark velvet blue, almost black. It's speckled with tiny blue scales that shine like sapphires, and its tail is a brilliant yellow." They crept forward as he listened. "I swear it looks like it swallowed a light bulb. The sapphires look like they're lit up from inside. It's quick. It'll dash in and out of the coral like a little mouse."

"You said the first to find one wins. Wins what?"

"A dollar."

Michael grinned. "You're on."

They stood side by side on the entry platform and filled their BCs with air. Together they jumped off the back of the boat into the clear ocean water. They easily floated on the surface as they prepared to descend. Lyle fiddled with her mask, making sure there was no water trapped inside. "We'll descend here and swim to the reef. Let's do this with no set plan. We'll just see what we see. Any questions, movie boy?"

Michael adjusted his mask. "No, no questions. Just don't lose me down there. Remember, I'm a stray." They put their regulators in their mouths. Before she could, he made a fist and pointed his thumb down. As they began to descend, she caught his eye in his mask. He winked at her.

They descended twenty-five feet to the sandy bottom, where the boat had safely anchored without harming the reef.

She motioned that they should swim to the reef. They intensified their kicks and swam weightlessly over the sand until they reached the open ocean. They slowed and turned back to follow the reef more closely.

Ocean life was abundant: fish, coral, and crustaceans were everywhere. Brightly colored coral served as the perfect backdrop for the brilliant tropical fish that lived among it. An entire marine ecosystem was on display right in front of them.

They came upon a parrotfish. Lyle pointed to her ear, signaling Michael to listen. They could hear the rainbow-colored fish biting into the coral, enjoying its meal.

They continued their search, and Lyle saw the elusive queen angelfish a few feet ahead. She put her arm out to stop Michael's forward movement and pointed out the shy fish. Turquoise, blue, and yellow scales glowed like a neon sign in the vast ocean. The queen proudly displayed the crown on top of its head. Once the fish spotted the curious divers, it quickly disappeared into its coral castle.

They swam unhurried as they advanced along the reef. Hidden inside a cluster of coral, she showed him the rare high-hat fish. With its black-and-white-striped body and tall dorsal fin, it was formally dressed and ready to attend any black-tie affair.

The dive was relaxing and peaceful. The only sound, their exhaled bubbles. The sun's rays had sliced through the surface and were illuminating the coral and fish.

They both saw it at the same time. There was no missing the looming shadow that moved over them, temporarily blocking out the sunlight. They immediately stopped and hovered in an upright position under the dark silhouette. Michael squeezed Lyle's arm to get her attention. She looked at him as he extended his arm over his head. He looked up and pointed at a white-spotted eagle ray, moving gracefully through the water, flying as if it had wings, its intimidating six-foot-long swordlike tail trailed rigidly behind. Its snout was flat like a duck's bill, but the eyes were big and wide, like a human's. Flat pectoral fins moved easily up and down in long, slow waves. It appeared alien; it could have been from an ocean on another planet. The elegant animal glided in front of them and then descended to the sandy bottom, disappearing into the deep.

They looked at each other with disbelief. The encounter was so unexpected. Michael clapped his hands and Lyle took a breath and removed her mouthpiece. She put on a huge grin to show him how delighted she was by the show, then returned the regulator to her mouth.

Lyle sank low and swam close to the bottom, on a mission to find what she knew was living among the reefs on Klein Bonaire. Seeking out a particular type of coral, she then searched near the base, knowing her treasure was most often found there.

Just as she thought she wouldn't find one, she spotted the seahorse swaying in the current with its tail wrapped around the coral. Later she would have to explain to Michael how rare the sighting was.

They next encountered a giant barrel sponge, purple in color and shaped like an old aluminum trash can. They couldn't resist peeking inside and floated weightlessly through the water until they hovered over the large sponge. She gave an "oh well" gesture to him when they discovered it was empty.

A giant brain coral, looking surprisingly like the human organ, begged them to stop and think a minute. Michael held the pose of Auguste Rodin's *The Thinker* while floating past it. Lyle laughed and gave him a round of applause. It was the first time she'd seen it done in full scuba gear. Her smile caused water to leak into her mask. She took a moment to expel it. She couldn't remember a time she had laughed underwater—she hadn't had this much fun diving in a long time. She had to admit, Michael had turned out to be a nice addition to her day.

Soon it was time to turn around and head back. They were getting close to the boat when she felt a tug on her fin that pulled her to a sudden stop. She turned to see Michael behind her, waving to "come here." She pointed at the hull of the boat straight ahead.

He shook his head, he wasn't ready to leave yet. He grabbed her ankle with his left hand and then her knee with his right as he pulled her toward him. He got a hold of her BC and turned her easily in the water then took her by the hand and led her back down the reef. He then pointed to what he so desperately wanted her to see.

A tiny fish darted in and out of the coral. It was blue at its dorsal fin and had shiny spots on its side. She looked at Michael, who had removed his mouthpiece and was smiling broadly. She wished she hadn't shown him that trick.

She examined the little fish. The area at its pectoral fin was yellow, but it was not the fish they were looking for. She shook her head at Michael, who stuck his tongue out at her before replacing his mouthpiece.

On their way back to shallow water where the boat waited, Lyle spotted something below them. Sticking up just an inch from the sand were several tiny tubelike structures. At the top of the tube was what could best be described as a spotted feather duster. She deliberately moved her index finger close to the creature and wagged her finger back and forth as if giving it a stern scolding. The feathery peacock worm instantly disappeared into the sand, making a faint popping sound as it vanished. Soon they were annoying the worms until they were all hidden from sight.

Francesca and Captain Maartin helped Lyle, Michael, and the other divers as they climbed the ladders back onto the boat. From their crowded spot on the bench, they began the toilsome task of removing their equipment.

Michael unsnapped his BC. "Awesome dive, Lyle. Thank you."

"I had a lot of fun. You're not so bad to dive with after all."

"Thanks. Given the chance, I knew I'd change your mind about me."

Ten

They were scheduled to take an hour surface interval before the next dive. Spending time at sea level after a dive was a typical safety measure. It gave their bodies time to recover from the excess nitrogen they had accumulated while under pressure.

Sitting next to Michael, Lyle struggled to remove her boots. They were soaked and heavy, and she had to fight to get them to let go of her feet. With a loud snap, her foot flew forward, and she broke free of the neoprene. He laughed at her antics, and she tossed her boot at him. The turquoise strap of her suit slid down her arm, and she quickly put it back in place. She then took a subtle glance at her chest and adjusted the V-neck to be sure everything was in place.

"For a minute there, I wasn't sure which one of you was going to win, you or your bootie." His wetsuit already off, he stood next to her in blue swim trunks. He raised his arms over his head and stood on his toes, enjoying a full-body stretch. She got an eyeful of tanned, cut abs, well-defined obliques, and muscular arms. A thin line of dark hair trailed from his navel into his swim trunks. He dropped his arms, and she quickly looked away.

"Would you like to spend some time on the sundeck?" he asked.

"That sounds great. Go ahead, I'll grab some water and meet you up there."

Michael walked to the back of the boat where a ladder led topside. Lyle dug into a cooler filled with bottled water and ice. She grabbed two bottles and ascended the ladder.

She stopped briefly to talk with Captain Maartin. "Captain, are you responsible for this beautiful day?"

"I can control a lot of things, Lyle," he said, smiling, "and the sunshine is one of them."

She laughed at his remark and headed to the bow to find Michael sitting on the white fiberglass hull, looking out over the water. His partially dried hair blew about his face. She sat next to him on the slippery surface and handed him his water. He leaned into her shoulder and held up his bottle. She tapped her bottle to his and said, "To the white-spotted eagle ray."

He countered, "To the peacock worms."

Michael asked several questions about the things they had seen on the dive. He tried to remember the details of the fish. She often had a fun fact to impart. She explained how rare a sighting of the seahorse was, and he thanked her for her determination in seeking one out.

The sundeck became crowded. After finishing their waters, they lay back in the sun. The day was warm, and the slight breeze smelled fresh and salty. The low rumble of the boat's motor and the voices of the other divers coaxed them into closing their eyes.

Michael broke the silence. "So, the juvenile yellowtail damselfish remains a mystery. What was the fish I found?"

Lyle raised her hand to block the sun and turned to look at him. He was just inches away, so she spoke quietly. "You were close. That was a cocoa damselfish. I may end up owing you a dollar after all." She closed her eyes again and welcomed the warmth of the sun on her face.

He took advantage of the fact that her eyes were closed, and he watched her chest rise and fall with her steady breathing, her nipples straining under the turquoise fabric of her suit. Tiny drops of water ran down her face and neck and pooled at her clavicles. Her stomach was soft, and her arms and legs were sculpted by long, firm muscles. Under her eyes were tiny lines that gave away her age.

He wanted to know her better and started with the basics. "Where's your family, Lyle? Do you all live close to one another?"

The question caught Lyle off guard, and she fought to sound casual. "I don't have much family. My mother lives in New York. We don't talk unless she can't pay her rent, or she needs spending money." She looked at him again. "I'm sorry, I shouldn't have told you that."

"No, don't be sorry. I want to know. Doesn't your dad help her out?"

"I've never met my father. My mother never told me who he was." She easily told him her private hell, "She wasn't much of a mother. Mostly it was me taking care of her or trying to stay out of her way while she slept or sobered up."

"She's an alcoholic?"

"She used a lot of drugs. She sold herself to support her habits. Damned mother of the year. She brought her work home with her. Men would come to our trailer with me at home. I was so young. I hear she's stopped using. I don't really care at this point. It's water under the bridge."

"I'm sorry to hear this."

"Victoria, Rick, and I went to New York to get her set up on government assistance. You know, to take some of the burden off of me. Once I was there, I chickened out. I couldn't see her. Rick and Victoria took care of everything for me. They keep in touch with her better than I do. They said she jumps from job to job. I'm sure she tells them I'm exaggerating and that she was a loving mother. She uses my work number when she needs to reach me."

"Tell me about you and Rick."

"Michael, you're being nosy. You don't want to hear about him."

"I'm curious, and you seem to be in the sharing mood."

"Victoria introduced us. She was working with him on a fund-raising project. We really hit it off. He broke my heart when he ended it."

"Why'd he end it?"

"I don't know for sure." Her heart twisted. "I guess I'm just not the one for him."

"I knew he was an ass. Please don't tell me he texted you. Breaking up by text message would totally suck, and it does kind of sound like his style." She giggled, grateful he was trying to lighten the mood. "Do you still love him?" He added quickly, "I only asked because he acts like he's in love with you."

"What you're seeing may be Rick hoping to get lucky. That definitely isn't going to happen." The words sounded right but a tiny thought told her she might enjoy an evening with Rick more than she should. "During our trip here last year, we were still a couple. I imagine he's having a little stroll down memory lane being back on Bonaire. Can I trust you with a secret?" Michael nodded. "I do still love him. I'm a good actor, like you. I spend a lot of time acting like I don't love him. He's the guy every guy wants to be friends with. He's the guy every girl wants to date."

"Sometimes, guys think there are women they can have whenever they want," Michael said. "I keep some girls interested in me by flirting with them just in case I ever want them. I'm not proud of it, but I think maybe that's what Rick's doing with you. Keeping you close, giving you the impression that maybe he still wants you. That way, you'll be there in case no one better comes along."

"Ouch, Michael." She turned over to lie on her stomach and rested her head on her arm. She didn't want to talk about Rick anymore. She closed her eyes and surrendered to drowsiness.

Michael sat up and pushed his hair back out of his eyes. Once again, this woman surprised him in a way he never thought possible. He stared at her as she lay with her eyes closed. He touched his finger to the base of her neck and moved it down her back to the edge of her bathing suit, studying the image there.

He asked in a whisper, "Did it hurt?"

She answered sleepily, "It was my friend Dottie's idea."

Eleven

Lyle's school bus dropped her off several blocks away from where she lived. She would rather walk the extra distance home than have the kids in her first-grade class know she lived in the old trailer park hidden behind the tall pine trees.

She heard voices coming from her mother's bedroom. Her mother hadn't been home in two days, and Lyle craved her company. She pushed open the bedroom door and saw her mother sitting on the bed. She held a cigarette between her thin fingers and had a glass in the other hand. The lacy slip she wore draped over her bones, taking no more shape than had it been hanging in the closet. She could hear the ice in her glass clinking together as her hand shook steadily. Her mother's eyes were half closed, she didn't see Lyle enter the room.

A man Lyle didn't know was standing naked by the bed, fumbling with his wallet. His hairy body was pale. She thought his stomach looked like a beach ball and his thin legs like two toothpicks with dark curly hairs covering them.

The man saw her at the door and started toward her. "Come here, sweetheart. We can make this more interesting."

She didn't understand the meaning of his words, but she knew she didn't want him to catch her. She saw her mother's face fill with fear and her drink fall to the ground as she jumped out of her bed.

"Run, Lyle! Run and hide!"

The man reached Lyle as she ran toward the front door. He grabbed for her arm but only brushed it with his fingertips. Lyle flew away from him, darted outside, and ran down the steps of the trailer.

"Hey, hey, come back here! You get back here, you little bitch!" the naked man yelled at her from the doorway.

Dirt kicked up from her heels as she dashed around the back of the trailer. She spotted the jagged opening in the foundation where some of the cement blocks had broken away. She dropped to her stomach, crawled through, and wrapped her arms around her bent knees. She looked down at her school uniform and ineffectively swiped at the dirt on the front.

Lyle worried the man would find her. She sat completely still. After several minutes, she figured the man had given up the chase. She wondered how long she would have to hide under the trailer until it was safe to go back inside. She watched several spiders working their webs nearby. She wasn't afraid of spiders; they were small and couldn't move very fast.

There was a rustling in the fallen leaves outside the crumpling hole. She squeezed her legs in tighter and tried to make herself as tiny as possible. She stared at the hole as the sound moved closer. A black wet nose appeared and sniffed the air. The curious dog easily fit in the hiding space and sniffed her face. He licked her nose until Lyle let out a giggle and scratched the dog behind his ears.

"What're you doing in there?" A girl about Lyle's age climbed into her secret hiding space. She pushed the dog out of the way and made a place to sit. "What're you doing in here? Are you hiding from someone?" The girl had a full, round face and bright eyes. Her long red hair was fixed in braids with bright bows tied at the ends. She wore a blue plaid shirt that was too big for her and jeans that were worn at the hem.

"I'm hiding from my mama's boyfriend. He tried to grab me. Is this your dog?"

"This shaggy thing? No. He's not mine. Sometimes he follows me around." She scratched the dog's head. "How long do you have to hide in here?"

"I don't know. I guess until he leaves." Lyle looked out through the hole in the blocks. "I hope he leaves before it gets dark."

"I can hide with you if you want. My name's Dorothy, but everyone calls me Dottie," she said, smiling. "Do you want to be friends?"

"Okay. I'm Lyle. Only my mama calls me Crocodile." The girls giggled at the nickname.

The little black dog snuggled between the girls as they ran their hands over his soft coat. Lyle immediately liked her new friend. It was nice to have a friend with her in her safe place under the trailer.

"Thanks for hiding with me, Dottie."

Lyle was far away in her memories when a cool mist of ocean water brought her back. She sat up and ran her hands over her face, hoping to forget her childhood. She tried to explain it to Michael. "The tattoo was my friend's idea. You see, I carry…" She tripped over her words. "I carry a burden with me. Nightmares from my childhood. Only they aren't nightmares. They haunt me during the day too. The weight of them can be intolerable."

She looked sheepishly up at him. She expected him to interrupt her with a question or give her a bewildered look, but he waited silently, his expression calm. It gave her the confidence to continue.

"My friend Dottie thinks if I can carry my nightmares on my back, out of sight, I won't have to think about them anymore. I can carry my burden, and at the same time, forget I have them with me. I know it sounds crazy."

"No, not crazy. People have all sorts of reasons for the things they do."

Michael knew he would never understand her logic, but he recognized that this woman was searching for peace in her life.

Twelve

The night air was comfortable as the friends walked to dinner at a nearby restaurant. A clam shell path let them to the entrance. Captain Jack's was an open-air restaurant perched on a steep ledge above the ocean, and a magnificent view of the sun setting over the water welcomed them. Hurricane lamps sat on each table. The candles just began to glow in the dimming light of the sky. Tiki torches surrounded the dining area. Soft, white fabric, intertwined through a wooden pergola above them, fluttered in the breeze, providing a sweet tranquility to the atmosphere.

The hostess was an older woman. "Table for eight?" She led them to a large table in the center of the dining area.

As the rest took their seats, Angela said, "I'll be just a minute. I need to powder my nose."

Rick held the chair out for Lyle as she took her seat.

"You'll have to tell us how the *Mi Dushi* trip was," said Victoria.

Steve glanced at Michael. "I can't believe you ran into our new friend." He was still starstruck over meeting his daughter's crush and tried to sound nonchalant. "I'm not much for the boat myself. It gets so crowded. Given the choice, I'll dive from the shore every time."

"I hate that we overslept and missed the boat," Diego said, sipping his beer. "We're going to see if we can reschedule for another day."

"If I hadn't run into Lyle, I would've missed you two," said Michael. "Turned out, we made pretty good dive buddies."

A waitress took their drink orders and returned with a tray full of colorful cocktails. Natalie was enjoying a rum drink garnished with fresh pineapple. "We spent most of the day in Kralendijk," she said.

"The capital is really something to see. Lots of shops and art galleries. We had lunch at a cute café." She took a bite of the pineapple. "Then we took a tuk-tuk tour and saw a huge flock of flamingos."

"The proper term is flamboyance," Diego said. "We learned that from our tour guide, Ancel. It's a flamboyance of flamingos, not a flock."

"Yes, that's right. There were thousands of them," Natalie said. "Pink feathers and black-tipped beaks. The colors were extraordinary. Like a picture on a postcard."

Victoria spotted Angela near the bar. "I think our friend has been distracted."

Angela was talking to a young man who leaned back casually against the bar. Lyle watched as he flashed a grin at Angela, clearly trying to win her over. But what caught her attention was the man standing at the far end of the dance floor. The blond-haired man they had run into at the dive site stood scanning the crowd.

She nudged Victoria. "Looks like our friend is here." She raised her chin in his general direction. "What kind of conditioner do you think he uses? His hair looks great."

"Great hair or not, I hope he keeps his distance tonight. I imagine you landing him on his ass was enough to keep him away from us for good."

Lyle kept a watchful eye on Angela. Soon she lost interest in the young man and began searching the dining area for her friends.

Angela was wearing a slinky blue sundress. The fabric was covered in large tropical flowers, with a plunged neckline that left no doubt her chest was getting as tanned as the rest of her. She wore high-heeled sandals and full makeup. Lyle looked down at her own jean skirt and blouse and felt underdressed.

The waitress returned to their table. "Have you decided what you'd like?"

Once their dinners were ordered, they fell into easy conversation.

Rick took Lyle's hand and gave it a little squeeze. "We missed having you with us today. I hope you'll join us tomorrow. We're going to dive the northern reefs."

"Sounds great." She didn't know what to make of all the attention he was showing her on this vacation. "The boat was fun today. We went out to Keepsake."

"Oh, Keepsake. It's a pretty one. Remember the eel we saw there last year?" Rick said, looking at his friends. "Green moray. I swear the thing was six feet long and this big around." He indicated with his hands the width of the eel and turned his attention back to Lyle. "I really missed you today. Remember last year when we—"

Dinner was served, and the talk at the table grew louder. Diego, Natalie, and Michael seamlessly blended into the well-established circle of friends.

Lyle watched as Angela captured all of Michael's attention. They seemed to be hitting it off. Angela told an animated story about her boss. Michael smiled and laughed in all the right places. Angela dropped her eyes to his mouth as they spoke. She seductively ran her thumb over her glossy lower lip and leaned slightly forward, ensuring her choice of neckline didn't go unnoticed. Lyle rolled her eyes and looked away. But she wouldn't let a twinge of jealousy worry her.

As they finished dinner, Lyle scanned the restaurant and saw that the blond-haired man had made his way onto the dance floor. He held a drink in his hand and swayed lazily with the upbeat music. Other dancers gave him a wide berth.

The waitress cleared the table and conversation slowed. It had been a long day of diving and sightseeing and the group was getting tired. They settled into a quiet lull as they finished their drinks and dessert.

"Please, iguana. Don't come over here." Angela spoke to no one in particular. They all followed her gaze to see a large, curious iguana weaving its way around the tables. At over five feet long from snout to tail, the lizard's size was intimidating. It walked confidently, swinging its body left and right, dragging its long tail behind it. The tall spikes on its dorsal spine stood like a long row of fence posts. It stopped, lifted its head, and appeared to be sniffing the air. It looked from table to table, scanning the area. Lyle imagined she was looking at a dinosaur that had escaped the confines of time.

"Is it coming over here?" Angela moved her chair back, ready to make a run for it.

"It's hard to tell," Rick answered with an amused tone. "He's looking at that table over there with the two kids."

A young boy could hardly sit still as he tried to get a better view of the iguana. His older sister dangled a dill pickle tempting the animal. She swung it back and forth, hoping it would come and take the bait. The iguana continued on, eyeing the pickle but deciding against the offer.

Lyle got an eyeful of the teeth and claws and was glad she could admire the magnificent creature from afar. She waited until the iguana was well out of sight then stood and put her hand on Rick's shoulder, letting him know she was leaving the table. She spotted the hostess near the entrance and walked over. "Excuse me, where's the ladies' room?"

She pointed beyond the dance floor. "Follow the path. It'll take you around back. The ladies' room is on the left." Lyle thanked her and started in the direction she had indicated.

"Hey, wait a second." The man with the blond hair was walking toward her. "I know you!" His stride was unsteady, and his eyes were glazed over. He came to a stop directly in front of her. "You and your friends were diving near us the other day." Lyle was hopeful the man had forgotten being shoved to the ground. He was drunk then and drunk again tonight. "What's wrong with your friend? She thinks she's too pretty for me?"

"I don't know what you're talking about. You must be thinking of someone else."

She tried to pass him, but the man grabbed her elbow. "Forget your friend. Why don't you dance with me?" He looked at her quizzically. "Damn, bitch. What the hell's wrong with your eyes?" He was puzzled. "They don't match up," he slurred. "Come on and dance with me."

"I don't want to dance with you," she said loudly, over the music.

"Oh, come on. Just one song." He put his hand on her hip and pulled her to him. "Or we could go back to my room and get busy. What d'ya say?"

She gave the man the full force of her palm across his face. Her hand immediately stung. Stunned, the man let go of her and put his hand on his cheek.

"You bitch!" he yelled but the music from the dance floor drowned out the commotion.

Her heart raced as she quickly put some space between herself and the drunken man and rushed to the ladies' room. It was a single room but empty, so she went right in. After she used the facility, she washed her hands and took a moment to splash some cold water on her face. She pulled the door open.

"I found you!"

She jumped back as the man barged into the small space. Anger and revenge emanated from his bloodshot eyes. The side of his face was beet red. "You should've danced with me."

She stepped backward and held her hands in front of her. She looked up at the man and kept herself composed. He was easily a foot taller than she. "I'm sorry about the slap. I only did it because you were scaring me. Let's go back to the dance floor, you and me. That sounds like fun."

"Now you change your mind. That's good, 'cause I think I really like you." The man stumbled toward her and put his hands on her shoulders to steady himself. He leaned on her, forcing her back against the sink.

She could feel the rim of the sink digging into her lower back. He pressed his belt buckle into her stomach and moved his thigh between her legs, pinning her against the hard porcelain.

She pushed on the man's chest, but he only leaned on her with more of his weight. The air turned heavy. Lyle was suffocating. Her flight-or-fight response kicked in and her body hummed with adrenaline. She squeezed her eyes shut and cringed as she summoned up the courage and dug her thumbs into his soft, moist eyes.

"What the hell!" The man snapped his head to the side and lifted his chin out of her reach. He grabbed her hands, rendering her helpless.

Lyle didn't have to think—she shot her knee upward aiming in between the man's legs. The effect was only minimal. Being trapped in the confined space, she was unable to get the full force she'd hoped for. But her effort and quick action got the man's attention. He hopped back a few inches still holding her hands. He raised his leg to protect himself from the second blow.

"Come on, honey, don't act like this. I thought you liked me."

She twisted and turned, fighting to free her hands. The man leaned on her again, his crushing weight trapping her in place. Her attempts to get free were futile. She could feel his erection pushing on her hip, and her panic threatened to render her helpless.

"Don't you like me? I sure do like you." The man sniffed her hair.

She fought to keep her senses sharp and willed herself not to give in to the fear. Her only chance to get away from this man was to get help. She took a deep breath and screamed, "Help me! Please help me! My God, is anyone out there?"

The door crashed open. Arms wrapped around the man's neck, and he was wrenched backward, thrown out the door, and pitched down to the ground. Michael moved like a madman as he threw himself on the blond man. He landed fist after fist on the drunken man's face and alternated punches to the man's ribs. The man weakly lifted his hands to his face, feebly trying to block the assault.

Lyle stood frozen and watched as Michael beat the man. She wondered why everything was moving in slow motion. She wanted to beat the man herself and clenched her hands into fists. She inwardly cheered him on with every blow. She wondered how much longer he would have to beat the man until he was dead.

A cool breeze came off the ocean and brought her out of her shock. She forced herself to blink and relaxed her fists. "Michael, stop," she said quietly.

Michael inhaled loudly and exhaled forcefully with each punch he landed.

"Michael, stop," she said a little louder.

Still, his fists raised and landed. He was in a rhythm and wasn't stopping. The man held his arms in front of his face uselessly, trying to block the next blow. She put her hand on his shoulder, staying clear of his flying fists. "Michael, stop. You'll kill him."

He sat back on the man, his exhausted arms collapsing to his sides. He fought to catch his breath and wiped at his forehead. "He deserves to be killed."

She extended her hand to him. "Michael, you've done enough."

He took her hand and moved off the beaten man. She looked down at his bloodied face. "We know him. He was at dive site the other day. He put his hands on Angela. He's staying at our resort."

"What room is he in?"

Lyle thought the question odd. "I don't know his room. I've only seen him at breakfast." The blond man moaned and turned onto his side.

"We should get out of here." He put his arm around her waist, and they started down the path toward the restaurant.

"I couldn't get away. There was nowhere to run."

They were well out of sight of the man when Lyle left the path and walked into the shadows. Her stomach gave over to the spasms. She vomited under a palm tree, unable to keep her dinner down. When there was nothing left to expel, she used the tail of her blouse to wipe her mouth and her sleeve for the tears in her eyes.

"Everything's going to be okay. You're safe now." Michael raked his hand through his hair. He glanced down the path where they had left the beaten man in a heap on the ground.

"Are you okay, M-Michael?"

"Me? Are you kidding me? That fucker attacked you. Are you hurt?"

Her voice shook. "I'm o-okay. He d-didn't hurt me." She absent-mindedly straightened her skirt and ran her trembling hands down her blouse. She looked back down the path. "I think… I think he may be really hurt. What if he hasn't gotten up? What…what should we d-do?"

"I hope he dies there, the son of a bitch." He appraised Lyle. The woman who was always so in control was falling apart in front of him. She looked like a child. A small, scared child. He held her cheek and spoke in a soft voice. "I won't let anything happen to you. I'm here. You're safe." He wrapped his arm around her and kissed the top of her head.

They were well hidden in the darkness of the palm trees when the drunken man staggered past them toward the restaurant. Lyle slid behind Michael and peered around his side. He reached behind his back and put his hand on her hip, holding her securely behind him. She didn't breathe as she watched the man from the safety of Michael's protective stance.

When he was well out of sight, she came out from her hiding place. "Do you think he knows who you are?" Thoughts of tabloid headlines and lawsuits flew through Lyle's mind. *Michael Miller, potential Academy award nominee, beats drunken man on remote island of Bonaire.*

"I'm sure we'll find out soon enough. That's not for you to worry about. Let's head back and report him to the restaurant staff. They'll call the police for us. Your friends are going to wonder where we are. I'm sure Victoria and Angela will take good care of you."

"I'd rather not involve the police."

"We need to report this."

"But what if he's really hurt? What if this gets you in trouble? If not with the police, with the tabloids. They could have a field day with this."

"Shit, Lyle," he said, his voice growing louder. "He's not going to get away with this because you're afraid of what it might do to my reputation in the tabloids."

"Please, Michael, can we do this my way? Please, no police." She held her hands together, imploring him to agree. "I'm not hurt. There's not a scratch on me."

He put his arms around her and held her to his chest. As they stood there together, quietly resting in each other's arms, the tension began to fade. He spoke into her ear. "You're going to be okay. Don't be afraid. I'm with you. You're safe now."

She put her palms on his chest and stepped back. "I'm going to be okay because you showed up in time. How did you know I needed help?"

"I didn't know. I saw you leave the table and wondered what was taking you so long. I went to find you and heard you screaming." He looked at her worried face and decided to acquiesce, for her. "Okay, we'll do it your way. Not because I want to, but because a police investigation in a foreign country could really take the fun out of this vacation." He grinned and winked at Lyle, who seemed to be contented.

"Thank you, Michael. For everything."

He looked over his shoulder. "I should've killed him."

Thirteen

They returned to the dining area and stopped near the hostess stand. Lyle ran a hand over her disheveled hair and looked at her shirt. The damp areas where she wiped her mouth and dried her eyes were showing. "I need a minute to get myself together."

"Okay. I'll go tell them you're on your way." Michael hesitated. "Are you sure you're okay? Do you want me to stay with you?"

"No. I'll be just a minute. I need to calm down and catch my breath. You go on." He reluctantly left her and went back to the table.

She stood out of the way and tucked her blouse into her skirt, hiding the moist stain. She ran a hand over her head several times to try to smooth her hair. With little effect, she then pulled the elastic out of her hair and reworked her ponytail.

A surprised voice rang out from behind her: "Lyle? Is that you?"

Lyle's expression brightened. "Dottie! You're here!" The two hugged each other tightly. "I knew you were on Bonaire. I forgot to ask you where you're staying. I'm so glad I ran into you."

"I'm here with a group from the university," said Dottie. "We're staying on the south end. We're sponsoring a research trial in the mangroves. We're studying how stormwater runoff is affecting the vegetation." She stood back and held Lyle at arm's length. She scrutinized what she was seeing. "You look awful. What's going on?"

Lyle looked fondly at her longtime friend. It seemed she hadn't changed in years. Dottie still wore her long hair in two braids as she always did as a child. Her jeans were frayed at the hem, no doubt a result of conducting field research.

"I'm fine. Just a little shook up over some guy. I'm glad to see you though." She gave Dottie another hug, unwilling to let go.

"Are you going to tell me what's going on? I don't get hugged like this unless there's something up." She rubbed Lyle's back and gently released herself from the strong embrace.

"I don't want to burden you with this."

Lyle looked at her beautiful friend. They grew up together in the same trailer park. As children, Dottie was everything Lyle lacked. She was brave and confident and always had the right answers. Dottie was more than just a friend. She was her confidant, her advisor and secret keeper. She reluctantly explained to Dottie the encounter in the ladies' room.

"I'm so sorry. Are you hurt? Do you need to see a doctor?"

"No, Dottie. I'll be fine. He scared the shit out of me, but he didn't get the chance to hurt me."

"Honey, after what we survived as children, I'm surprised anything can get you shook up. Are you sure you're okay? Is there anything I can do?"

"Really, I'll be fine. I'm so glad I ran into you tonight. I'm here with my friends." She gestured toward the table. "Why don't you come over and say hi?"

Dottie looked over at Lyle's friends. "No offense Lyle, but they're not exactly my type." She glanced down at her worn jeans and grinned. "I'm your poor and socially challenged friend. They're the rich, popular athletes. Never a good mix."

"That's nonsense. They're nice people. I've talked so much about you, I know they'd love to meet you. Just stay for one drink, please?"

Dottie glanced toward the parking area and gave a quick wave to her friends waiting there. "Thanks, Crocodile, but not tonight. I'm sorry, but I need to go." Lyle's face drained of color. Dottie placed her hands on her shoulders. "Remember how strong you are, Lyle. Don't let that guy get to you. Why sweat the small stuff when you've already survived the big stuff? Bear this burden out of sight, remember? Don't give it any thought at all."

She didn't want to see her friend go. "How long are you on Bonaire? Maybe we can get together."

"We should be here a few more days. We have to gather enough quality samples to complete our research back home. Where're you staying? If I get some free time, I'll stop by."

"I'm at Bon Adventure, just down the road. Building one, room 2A. Come by anytime. It's been way too long since we've had a chance to talk."

"Be strong, Lyle. Don't let some guy get the better of you. You're tougher than that. I know. I've seen it."

As she watched her friend walk away, something inside her crumbled.

Once Dottie was out of sight, Lyle headed back to the table. Her friends were getting ready to leave. As she approached, she heard Rick say, "There she is."

She caught Michael's eye and nodded slightly. She looked for the blond man but didn't see him anywhere. There didn't seem to be any commotion at all. No police officers, no staggering drunk beaten to a pulp. The restaurant was peaceful. The guests continued their evening, unaware of the incident that occurred in the shadows.

Rick checked the time. "Damn, we've been sitting here over two hours. If we're predawn diving tomorrow, we need to get some sleep." He raised his arm to request the bill.

"It's already taken care of," said Michael. "Tonight's on me."

Everyone thanked Michael for dinner and gathered their things.

Victoria stood to leave. "What a fantastic night. We'll have a nice walk back." She asked Lyle, "Are you okay? Your face is flushed."

Lyle patted her cheeks. "I think it's the rum."

"What took you so long in the ladies' room? I was about to come look for you."

"I can't believe it. I ran into Dottie. She's doing some research for the university here."

Having overheard part of their conversation, Rick chimed in. "Dottie's here? On Bonaire? Why would she be here?"

"She's doing some work for the university, research in the mangroves. She said they're studying stormwater runoff. Not all of us are on vacation, Rick."

"I wish you'd invited her to join us."

Lyle looked at Victoria's smart outfit and expensive shoes. She saw Angela getting ready to leave in her sundress and heels and thought of Dottie's worn jeans. As much as it pained her to admit it, perhaps Dottie was right. "I did invite her. I asked her to come over and have a drink, but she had some friends waiting for her and was still in her work clothes."

Rick whispered, "That Dottie. She's always popping up somewhere."

Michael and Angela led the way out of the restaurant and to the sidewalk that would take them back to the resort. Lyle watched as Angela walked with her hand on Michael's shoulder, continuing the conversation they started over dinner. She said a silent prayer, thanking God for sending her a hero.

It was a short walk and soon they saw the lights of Bon Adventure. The reception desk operated twenty-four hours a day. The man working there offered a greeting to the group as they walked by. They waved back at the man and stopped in the light of the desk to say their goodbyes.

Rick checked the time. "Okay, it's just after ten. Everyone interested in predawn diving, be in the water in full gear at five." He looked at the new divers and added, "We can all bring our extra lights if you guys don't have any. It's a very unique experience. You're all welcome to join us."

Diego gave Natalie a little hug. "We're in," he said.

Natalie looked surprised but didn't protest.

"We already slept in today and missed the boat dive. I don't want to make a habit of it," said Diego.

Angela asked Michael, "How about it? Up for an early start tomorrow?"

Michael hid his red, sore fists in his pockets. "I can't let you old folks show me up, can I? I'll be there." He looked at Rick. "Next thing I know, you'll be eating dinner at four thirty to get the senior discount." Lyle noticed Michael's tone was only half joking.

"Good night, Michael," said Lyle, fighting to sound casual. "Thanks again for dinn—everything."

Once everyone started toward their rooms, Angela asked Michael, "Would you walk with me back to my truck? I need to grab my mask and snorkel out of the back seat."

Michael was ready to call it a day and wanted to get some ice on his hands, but he didn't see he had much of a choice. Angela had been turning on the charm all through dinner. "Sure, I'll walk with you. You never know what kind of creep you may run into around here."

Lyle watched them walk away. She suddenly felt alone and vulnerable. The thought of the evening's harrowing events sent chills up her arms. She ran up the stairs, seeking the comfort and safety of her room, her head buzzing from the combination of rum and adrenaline. Her blouse was disheveled and still damp at the tail. She quickly removed the vomit-covered top and tossed it into the closet. She stepped out of her skirt and put on a white cotton nightie.

She had just finished brushing her teeth when there was a knock on her door. With all the attention Rick had been showing her, she wasn't surprised to find him standing there. He held up a bottle of wine and leaned against the door frame. "Remember when we shared a room and I didn't have to knock?" He swung the wine bottle temptingly back and forth. "Care for a nightcap?"

She unconsciously crossed her arms over her chest. "Rick, it's late, and I've had a long…" She paused and thought for a moment, unsure of what it was she wanted. "I don't know about this. I've been through so—"

Rick saw her resolve failing. "Humor me." He kissed her on the lips. She closed her eyes and kissed him back. She didn't want to be alone tonight. She welcomed his comforting, familiar kiss and the protection his arms provided.

Fourteen

The divers met at the dock as planned, just before five the next morning. They were getting used to the early hour and the darkness; things seemed to go more smoothly. Lyle pulled her equipment from her locker and began putting it together on a bench next to Victoria. She was pleased to see Diego and Natalie walking down the stairs toward them.

Memories of the previous night's events wouldn't leave her. She hoped to spend some time with Michael today. He was becoming a true friend.

Diego's voice was still thick with sleep. "Don't get me wrong. I'm glad we met all of you, but my next vacation is going to involve sleeping in at least until the sun comes up." He held his regulator out in front of him, letting the hoses fall freely. He tried to sort out which hose went where. "I'm going to need a nap this afternoon."

Natalie reached over and flipped the top valve around for him, allowing the hoses to fall in a more familiar pattern. He gave it a second look. "Okay, thanks. I can do it from here."

Rick's deep voice carried in the darkness. "Diego, buddy, this isn't a vacation. It's a dive trip. You can sleep when you're dead."

Lyle smiled at the familiar saying. She had heard Rick make that declaration several times now. Anyone claiming the two weeks on Bonaire was supposed to be a vacation was always corrected by Rick. No one could argue that he didn't walk the talk.

Rick caught Lyle smiling at him. He winked back at her as he assembled his gear. She was relieved that everything appeared to be back to normal between them. It was as though last night had never happened.

Once everyone had their gear on, they gathered all their underwater lights. In true diver fashion, Lyle brought several extras she had accumulated over the years. Together, they had plenty of lights for the new divers.

Lyle attached bright red and green tank markers near the valves of each of their tanks. The group looked like a Christmas show with red, green, and white lights hanging on their equipment and shining from their hands.

She hoped up to the last minute that Michael would be joining them, but he hadn't arrived and it was time to go.

In complete darkness at forty feet below, the group swam north up the reef and came upon a sunken fishing vessel. The lifeless boat cast long shadows as beams of light from the divers trailed over it. There was something unnerving about seeing the motionless boat sitting precariously on the steep reef in complete silence. Salt water had eaten away at the wooden structure over the years. Large holes in the hull were filled with blackness. The divers couldn't resist having a look inside. A yellow-tailed eel passed over the sand and disappeared under the structure. The boat, long ago a capable vessel, now served as an artificial reef, and several fish claimed it as their home.

As Lyle shone her light into a hole, her imagination took off with her. What if the poor souls of this boat were still living onboard? She knew she was being silly, but still, she quickly turned and continued down the reef, putting distance between herself and the wreck.

Charlie suddenly appeared, swimming along with them, catching fish stunned by their lights. She couldn't see the reactions of the new divers in the dark. She was sure she would have some explaining to do about the tarpon once they surfaced.

Thirty minutes after they first descended, Rick signaled for them to turn around. The sun was starting to rise, and faint light could be seen at the surface. While swimming back toward the resort, the number and types of fish changed. With the protection of the first sign of daylight, the fish that stayed hidden from predators all night began to emerge.

After following the reef back toward their starting point, the divers found an underwater marker that told them they were back at the resort. They checked their compasses and headed east, following the gentle slope upward and surfaced at the dock, the exact spot where they had begun their dive.

After taking off their gear and covering up with shorts and tees, they walked up the stairs to the breakfast buffet. Lyle glanced around the patio, thinking maybe Michael would join them but was again disappointed. She got a plate and started through the buffet line.

They found a large round table near the coffee station and planned the rest of the day while they ate eggs, pancakes, and fresh fruit.

Natalie and Diego asked several questions regarding the morning dive. Natalie had been spooked by Charlie and was sure it was the biggest fish she had ever seen. Diego felt the dive was well worth the early start time and admitted, while swimming around the creepy sunken boat, the theme song to *Jaws* had played in his head.

They planned to dive the reefs north of the resort today. Lyle warned Diego and Natalie the days of easily walking in and out of the surf were over. The entrances were more difficult and could pose a challenge. They were always an interesting addition to the experience. She wished Michael was with them. She was sure he would love the more advanced dive sites.

Lyle resumed her position in the driver's seat, Victoria rode shotgun, and Angela lounged in the back. She followed Rick's truck and glanced in the rearview mirror to see that Diego and Natalie were behind her. It was going to be another picture-perfect day on Bonaire. They drove with the windows down, and the radio turned low. The sun was already bright in the cloudless sky, and a warm breeze was coming in off the water.

As she drove past the donkey sanctuary, she noticed they had a few cars parked out front already. Herds of donkeys grazed in the fields beyond the road.

Angela had some news she could hardly wait to share. She had been waiting for the privacy of the truck to bring up the juicy subject. She had a devilish look on her face. "What would you say if one of us got lucky last night with the man of her dreams?"

Lyle glanced at Angela and was surprised to feel anger toward her friend. She had pulled out all the stops last night. She had flirted and batted her eyes at Michael and put her curvaceous figure on full display. Any warm-blooded man would easily be captured by her flawless, seductive moves.

Victoria had little patience for this game. "Angela, what the hell are you talking about? Who are you talking about?"

"Did you and Michael spend the night together?" Lyle asked, with a forced lightness in her voice.

"Me? Not me! I wish. No, I'm talking about you. You and Rick spent the night together. I know he's your best sex ever, so I'm not judging you. We're on vacation in the Caribbean. You deserve a little fun."

"I don't know what you're talking about," she said to Angela in the rearview mirror.

"We saw you! After I got my things out of the truck, Michael walked me back to my room. We saw Rick knock on your door with a bottle of wine." She went on with details she knew her friend couldn't deny. "You answered your door in your little summer nightie. You kissed Rick and let him in. Don't try to tell me nothing happened."

Silence filled the truck. Angela wasn't getting the reaction she wanted. She crossed her arms over her chest, and "Humphed" annoyed with her friends.

Victoria glanced at Lyle but said nothing. She would wait to see how this played out.

The sun was coming in the truck at a low angle, blinding Lyle as she drove. She squinted at the road ahead and irritably yanked the sun visor down. Her anger toward Angela quickly turned to shame in herself; Michael had seen them.

"Where's Michael today anyway?" Lyle asked. She couldn't go any longer without knowing why he hadn't joined them. She hated the thought of him seeing her with Rick—after her claim of not being interested in an island one-night stand. She was now the hypocrite she once accused Michael of being.

"Natalie said he went to the pool bar last night and drank until they closed the place," said Angela. "Natalie said he was, quote-un-quote, 'unresponsive' this morning."

Diving was Lyle's favorite thing, but the morning couldn't end soon enough for her. She wanted to get back to Bon Adventure, find Michael, and explain.

They had loaded the trucks with three tanks per diver and would complete all three dives before returning to town for lunch. Lyle re-signed to the fact that she had at least six hours of diving ahead of her. She tried to put Michael out of her mind—diving was dangerous enough without being distracted by unrelated thoughts. She fought to stay in the present and enjoy the time with her friends. But she headed to the water without all of her equipment.

"Lyle don't forget your mask," Rick said.

"Thanks. I don't know where my head is today."

Each dive location was more fascinating than the last. The difficult entrances made for a lot of laughs. Diego and Natalie rose to the chal-lenge and mentioned how sorry they were Michael was missing out.

When Lyle spotted the funny-looking scrawled cowfish, she caught herself looking for Michael. Its triangular-shaped body was flat across the bottom. Its eyebrows made a permanent scowl on its face while its mouth seemed to be blowing a kiss. Its bright stripes and dots would serve just as well being filled with cotton and sitting on a child's bed rather than swimming here in the Caribbean. She wished Michael had been there to see the whimsical fish.

Fifteen

It was well after two o'clock when they completed their final dive and returned to the resort. Rick and Steve were going to get a late lunch. Victoria and Angela planned to shower and head into town to do some shopping. Diego and Natalie would relax in the sun by the water and enjoy some downtime. Diego fully planned to get in the nap he had been looking forward to since the very first dive. Everyone invited Lyle to join them.

"Thanks, but I feel like I need a run."

"Are you sure?" Rick questioned, "It's still hot out here. Maybe you should wait for this heat to pass."

"I have a few things to do first." She looked up at the beaming sun. "The temperature should give way soon enough. I'll just run up to the donkey sanctuary and back. That shouldn't take too long."

She didn't know where Michael's room was, and she was sure the front desk wouldn't give out that information. She took off for the pool bar to see if she could spot him there.

Several employees were slicing lemons and limes and stocking the bar. Two couples sat together and had sandwiches and sodas at a table overlooking the water, but Michael wasn't at the pool bar.

Perhaps he joined Diego and Natalie. They were going to relax in the sun by the shore. She walked toward the chaise lounges near the water. She scanned the area well but didn't see him anywhere.

She was becoming uncomfortable in her damp suit. The fabric was drying and chafing her legs. She decided she would go back to her room and change into running clothes. She hoped a run would help burn off her frustration and take her mind off Michael.

She followed the tree-covered path through the courtyard around the back of her building. Laying in the cool shade of the coral bean trees, she saw a familiar figure. "Hi, girl." She knelt and scratched Calypso behind her ear. The dalmatian playfully rolled onto her back, legs flailing in the air, encouraging Lyle to scratch her tummy. "You've got the life, Calypso."

Lyle heard parrots in the canopy of trees. She stood and squinted to see them. With their bright lime-green feathers and shy golden faces, they were hard to miss against the dark green foliage. Called Lora by the natives, the Amazon parrot was celebrating a comeback—thanks to local conservation efforts, their numbers were climbing.

"There you are!"

She turned and saw Michael coming toward her. Calypso jumped onto her feet and trotted out of the courtyard.

Michael was wearing jeans and a sweatshirt. Lyle thought the attire was an odd choice, considering the temperature. His clothes looked like he had slept in them. His knuckles were swollen and still bloody from the fight the night before. His wild hair and bloodshot eyes told her he had a late night and had just gotten out of bed.

"Here I am. Where've you been? You missed the entire day's dives." She added softly, "I've been looking all over the resort for you." Something inside her told her to continue to her room. She took a tentative step backward.

Michael's head was buzzing with a hangover, and the bright sun was burning his eyes. He was too warm in his heavy clothes and he hadn't put any shoes on. His feet stung from the stones and hot pavement. But none of it could distract him from the memory of seeing Lyle kiss Rick the night before. He grit his teeth.

He came to an abrupt stop in front of her. His usually bright eyes were dark, and beads of sweat had formed across his forehead. Lyle could feel the tension rolling off him.

"After everything you told me on the boat? You have a one-nighter with Rick? Where was your Rick while you were being attacked in the bathroom last night? I'll tell you where. Enjoying his dinner with his friends, not a fucking care in the world."

"Wait, let me explain."

"I thought you'd be different, but you're just like all the rest."

Lyle could hear the disappointment in his voice.

"Who'd you think you were kidding?" he continued. "What was all that talk on the boat? A big lie? Were you putting on a show for me? The poor wounded girlfriend who got dumped?"

"No, Michael, I…" But she couldn't complete her thought. He took another step toward her and stood close enough for her to smell the day-old liquor on his breath.

"You and your booty call." His voice rose: "You must've been thrilled when the love of your life appeared at your door. You just couldn't turn him down, could you?" He paused. "He's taking advantage of you! Can't you see that? He knows you still love him, and he's using you for an easy fuck! Why'd you let him do that?"

She held up her palms. "Let me explain, I—"

"He's been leading you on all this time, and the sickening part is you know that! You stand around waiting for him to take you back. Why do you let him treat you like this? You deserve so much more." He yelled over his shoulder as he walked on: "I was beginning to think you were strong, but you're weak!" He'd exhausted his argument. "You deserve so much more."

"Michael it's not what you   "

But he was leaving.

"Wait a second, you son of a bitch! You don't even know what you're talking about." She was shaking with frustration. "You don't know what you saw. You're wrong."

He stopped with his back to her.

"I was upset and afraid and alone. I didn't want to be alone. We had some wine and talked. Then I asked him to leave. We didn't do anything." Tears pooled in her eyes. "We had a glass of wine. That's all." He turned and looked at her. "You're accusing me of something I didn't do!"

She marched toward him and kicked him in the shin. She began to storm off but gave it a second thought. Out of frustration, she turned back around and kicked him again. More tears threatened, so she lowered her head and jogged off.

She ran up the steps to her room. She tried to slam the door, but it was too heavy and only closed gently behind her. She took a long, shuttering breath and willed the tears to stop then got herself a drink of cool water from the bathroom sink.

"I can't believe that jerk. What a complete idiot." She paced the floor and finished her water. "That dumb son of a bitch!" With an emphasis on her last word, she hurled the empty glass at the wall, and it shattered, sending shards to the floor. The loud noise brought her out of her tantrum. She ran out of things to call him. "He's such a total... shithead."

She changed into a sports top and matching running shorts. She laced up her sneakers and put her room key in the hidden pocket inside her top. She headed toward the door but then remembered her phone and grabbed it off the nightstand. Looking at herself in the mirror—eyes red, face redder—she whispered, "Fuck me," then bolted out the door.

As she trotted down the steps, she put her earbuds in and started her music. Satisfied when the band Queen began to play, she turned the volume up and clipped the phone to the waistband of her shorts.

She waved at the young woman working at the reception desk but was unable to force a smile. As she walked toward the road, she stretched her legs, taking long strides, and lifted her arms over her head. She clasped her hands together and turned left and right, then bent at the waist to each side. She was full of the pent-up energy her encounter with Michael had created. She could hardly wait to hit the pavement.

She ran north along the two-lane road in front of Bon Adventure. Soon after she got started, she was forced to maneuver around a small herd of donkeys vying for space in the shade of the short brush that grew along the sidewalk. They pinned their ears back and stuck their noses out at her. She gave them a wide berth as she passed, but with the mood she was in, she thought she could take on the entire grumpy herd.

"You damned asses," she growled.

She fell into an easy rhythm but couldn't get Michael out of her thoughts. She spoke aloud to herself as she ran: "Forget you, Michael Miller. My relationship with Rick is none of your business."

The road curved along the water, offering her a picture-postcard view of the ocean. The blue sky, bright sun, and easy surf were a nice distraction from her angry thoughts. As she headed farther north, the road returned inland. The view of the water was blocked by low trees and a scattering of homes. She was on autopilot as her legs pumped and propelled her over the pavement. She passed a small market, but other than that, the north end of the island was sparse.

As she regarded the barren terrain, she remembered the look on Michael's face as he accused her of sleeping with Rick. Her run was moderately distracting, but her anger wasn't ebbing. "I am so done with him. He's making this vacation seem a lot like work."

With her breathing more labored, she settled into a pattern of inhaling and exhaling with every third step. Tall cactus stood along the side of the road. A warm breeze blew across and with it the desert like heat that warmed her limbs and dried out her mouth. She felt sweat running down her neck and back.

The run was not accomplishing what she had hoped it would. She couldn't lose herself in the music like she usually did, and thoughts of Michael persisted. One in particular nagged at her: why was she so upset over what Michael Miller thought of her?

Her shoulders relaxed as some of the tension left her.

The dry pavement released a tiny cloud of dust with each of her pounding steps. She felt the familiar tightening of her leg muscles as she continued north. She forced her legs to stay strong as more sweat ran down her face and between her breasts. The entrance to the donkey sanctuary, where she planned to turn around, was just ahead. She was so lost in her anger, she barely noticed the park as she ran past.

The road once again turned toward the water, but she couldn't enjoy the view. The sun was sitting lower in the sky, and the rays were burning into her eyes. She had to squint and hold her head at a downward angle to see where she was going. The sun warmed her arms and legs, and she became concerned that she didn't take the time to put any sunscreen on.

She had to admit that watching Angela and Michael at dinner the night before had left her feeling uneasy. And Angela's teasing in the truck this morning about she and Rick had Lyle really upset. She remembered Rick's visit the night before.

Rick's kiss was warm and familiar.

The assault she suffered at the restaurant had her on edge, and his arms were strong and protective.

"Do you want me, Lyle? Let me in." He walked past her, holding up a bottle of wine and two long-stemmed wine glasses. "Care for a nightcap?"

She shut the door and watched as he poured the wine and offered her a glass. When she didn't take it, he put it down on the dresser and pulled her to him. He lifted her chin and began to kiss her.

She tried to become lost in the gentle touch of his kiss, to block out the horrific events of the evening, and to relax in his arms. She tried not to think of Michael Miller, but his words ran through her thoughts.

Maybe that's what Rick is doing with me—keeping me close, giving me the impression that he still wants me. That way, I'll be here in case no one better comes along.

She pressed her hands against his chest and stepped away. He tilted his head. "I'm sorry. Have I done or said something wrong?"

She opened her dresser and removed a T-shirt and shorts from the drawer. "I'm afraid you're here because this island, and this resort, it all brings back memories for us." She pulled the shirt over her head, covering up her thin nightie. "You broke my heart. I need to do a better job at protecting it from being broken again." She put on the shorts and gestured toward the seating area by the sliding glass doors. He sat in the club chair as she brought the glasses of wine and handed one to him. She sat with one leg folded under her on the love seat.

"Lyle, I'm beginning to realize that letting you go was a huge mistake on my part." He hesitated. "I was hoping that being back on Bonaire would spur our old feelings for each other."

Lyle had been waiting to hear these words for some time now. But something was different. She suddenly felt in control and had only the faintest desire to give in to his proposal. "Rick, we could have one amazing night together, but in the light of the morning, we may decide it was a bad idea. I'd hate to ruin what we have together now."

"You may be right. Am I that transparent?"

She grinned. "I can see right through you. What if we keep up the being-friends thing at least for the duration of this vacation?" He began to interrupt. "Sorry. This is not a vacation. It's a dive trip."

"You know me so well."

"Well enough to know that if we're going to get back together, we can wait until we get back to Raleigh. Absent the influences of magical Bonaire."

Lyle jumped as a car sped passed her. She had her music on so loud she hadn't heard its approach. The tires sprayed her sweaty legs with gravel and dust, sticking to her with little trouble. With each stride her body warmed. She felt like a furnace, her body producing so much heat.

More thoughts of Michael troubled her. He was in his twenties, much too young for a relationship. It didn't matter how she felt about him—they were at different stages in their lives. A relationship with someone so much younger was completely out of the question.

The thought was depressing, and as she realized the truth of it, her anger started to ebb. Her drive was fading, and her pace slowed. Heat radiated from her face. With a slight panic, she realized she was in the middle of nowhere and had forgotten to bring water.

Sixteen

The sun beat down on Lyle. The realization that she was several miles from anywhere without any water and the real possibility of suffering heatstroke frightened her. Her leg muscles burned. She knew if she stopped running, the burn would only worsen, and her body would overheat quickly.

The best thing she could do would be to turn around and slow her pace on her way back to the resort, allowing her body temperature to gradually lower until she could find some water.

Her throat was dry, and her body was soaked with sweat. She ran her tongue around her teeth, trying to free her dry lips. The air was thick with heat and weighed on her like a wet blanket. The thought of a cool glass of water haunted her as her thirst became intolerable.

Out of the corner of her eye, she saw some movement. She had gained a partner. Whoever it was, was moving along just behind her, keeping her pace. She wondered if they had any water they'd be willing to share. She glanced over her shoulder and saw it wasn't a runner at all but a person on a bicycle.

Michael swerved in front of her, cut her off, and forced her to a sudden stop. She gasped and abruptly halted. He placed his bare feet on the rocky ground and straddled the bike, effectively blocking her from going any farther. Her head was on fire. She bent over and placed her hands on her knees. She dropped her head down low, trying to fight off dizziness, and struggled to catch her breath. She swayed but refused to let the heat overcome her. She took her earbuds out and held them in her hand as they continued to pound out loud music.

"Holy shit, Lyle. What're you thinking?" He put the bike down and knelt to look at her face.

"Leave me alone," she panted, "you dumb son of a bitch."

The run hadn't diminished her anger as much as she hoped it would. Her words were angry, but her delivery was pitiful. Sweat dripped from the tip of her nose and made a wet spot on the ground. She couldn't catch her breath and continued heaving. The gravel at her shoes went out of focus. She felt lightheaded and knew she was close to passing out.

"Do you have any water on you?" she managed. "I need some water."

"No, no water." He put a hand on her back. "My God, you're burning up. What're you doing out this far with no water?" His previous anger had faded. He watched her face turn from red to white.

"I'm enjoying a run. What do you think?" She spat the words at him and tried to still her swaying body. She was beginning to catch her breath.

"Get on the bike. I'll ride you back to the resort."

She lifted her head to look at the bike. It was red with a rusted Bon Adventure resort license plate hanging under the seat.

"I passed a small market down the road. We can stop there for some water." When she didn't move, he raised his voice. "You can stand out here and suffer heatstroke, or you can suck it up and ride back with me."

She didn't see that she had a choice. She felt weak, and the heat continued to radiate off her. She thought it strange when she felt a chill run through her. She stood gradually, evaluating her head as she rose.

His voice was firm. "Now. Get on the bike now."

She moved gingerly as she situated herself on the seat. Michael climbed on the pedals and turned the bike around. The bike swayed side to side. She hated that she had to put a hand on his back to steady herself. He turned the bike south and pedaled easily down the street.

The breeze gradually cooled Lyle. She took several deep breaths to keep from feeling faint again. She noticed Michael was still wearing his jeans and sweatshirt and wondered how hot he was getting, and how his bare feet felt against the metal pedals. Then she reminded herself she didn't care.

As they glided down the road, the full distance of her run became clear to her. She kept expecting the little market to appear at any moment. She didn't remember running by the miles of landscape they passed.

Several miles later, Michael slowed the bike. She peered over his shoulder and saw the market. They climbed off the bike and leaned it against the side wall. He offered her his hand. "Come on. At least get out of the sun."

She walked past him, ignoring his hand, and pulled the door to the store open. She was hit by a blast of cold air.

He walked past her. "Wait here." He roamed up and down the few isles and gathered up some items. She watched him pay the clerk, who placed the items in a small brown paper bag. He took a water out of the bag, twisted off the top, and handed it to her.

Lyle greedily tilted the bottle to her mouth. She stopped for air twice as she drank the entire thing. She looked longingly at the bag.

"Not so fast. Let that soak in first." He took the empty bottle from her and placed it on the counter. He caught the clerk's attention and yelled "Thanks" as they headed back out into the sun.

They continued riding south on the main road. After several minutes, she started feeling more like herself. Michael slowed down and turned into a parking area that clearly wasn't Bon Adventure. The bike crunched and bounced through the gravel lot. He rode to the end of the lot and down a path that ran alongside an outbuilding. As they emerged from the side of the little building, the ocean appeared in front of them and soon they were stuck in the deep white sand. He steadied the bike and helped Lyle climb off. He lifted the bike and leaned it against a small tree.

"Where are we?" Lyle was too tired to be mean. She felt a wave of calm as she gazed out at the water. The low sun cast an orange glow. The beach was quiet except for the mesmerizing sound of the waves hitting the sand.

"I love the coral beaches here, but I asked at the reception desk if there was any actual sand on this island. She told me about this place."

Their feet sunk in the deep sand as they made their way closer to the water. He was glad to see her color had improved as well as her demeanor. He sat down and patted the sand, inviting her to join him.

They watched in silence as a teenage boy, several yards up the beach, cast his line into the surf again and again.

He handed her a second bottle of water and a banana. She twisted the top off the water and took a long drink. She handed the bottle back to him, and he finished it off. Lyle peeled the banana, broke the top half off, and handed it to Michael. They sat quietly for a long time, both mentally and physically exhausted, both aware that the storm was over.

She broke the silence. "How'd you find me?"

"I ran into Diego and Natalie. They told me you'd gone on a run to the donkey sanctuary. By the way, you passed the donkey sanctuary by several miles. You know you could've called one of your friends. Someone would've come to get you."

"We have a strict no phone and no internet policy. We allow Steve to call his wife and kids. Victoria checks in with her husband every few days, but that's it. Otherwise, we're all"—she made air quotes—"unplugged."

"You haven't called your friends back home to tell them you're diving with Michael Miller? I am a bit famous, you know."

Lyle giggle. "No. Like I said, no phones, no internet."

They sat in silence and finished the banana.

Michael pulled another bottle of water from the bag. He removed the top and handed it to her. "Drink this slowly."

She was getting cold in her damp running clothes. The late-afternoon sun did little to warm her. She took her shoes and socks off and buried her feet deep in the warm sand, hoping to chase away her chill.

"Thanks for the rescue. Not only today but last night too. I don't think I thanked you last night." She paused. "I didn't think that run through very well today. Sometimes I just have to run, get away."

She watched Michael, who was picking up sand in his hands and letting it funnel through his fingers. She felt more relaxed than she had all day. Knowing he was upset with her had shaken her. Sitting here with him, back on speaking terms, was a relief. She looked at the dark shadow along his chin and wondered about the day he'd had.

"I can see why you come back here year after year. It's a magical island, practically undisturbed." He watched Lyle wiggle her toes in the sand.

"I love it here," said Lyle. "I love this island and the people. I love the reefs and the wildlife. It's what I look forward to every year. Once the airline ticket is bought, the resort reservations made, it just seems easier to hop out of bed each morning."

"I may not be doing much hopping anytime soon." Michael rubbed his shin. "I haven't been kicked like that since I played soccer in the sixth grade."

"If you're waiting for an apology, it's going to be a long wait."

"I'm pretty sure it's me who owes you an apology. I'm sorry I accused you of—well…" He shook his head. "I'm sorry about everything."

She pulled her knees up to her chest and wrapped her arms around them. "Since we're being so generous with the apologies, I'm sorry about your shin. And the yelling. And the names I called you, both to your face and behind your back."

"I haven't been yelled at like that in quite a while." He grinned and gave Lyle a sideways glance. "That's quite a temper you have. I'm sorry to say it's the second time I've been privy to it."

She remembered the glass she threw across her room and thought it best not to mention it.

"You really haven't called anyone to tell them you met me?" Was she really so unimpressed by his stardom?

"I've been honest with you all along—I want you to know that—even when you ask the nosy questions. Maybe it's easier to be honest because I know I'll never see you again once we leave Bonaire."

"Have you really?" He squinted his eyes. "You've been honest with me about everything?"

Lyle looked out over the water. "Michael, last night—"

"No, please don't. It's none of my business. You don't have to explain anything to me. If you say nothing happened, then that's it. Nothing happened. Let's not have any secrets." He put his arm around her shoulder. "Will you promise to always tell me the truth?"

"I think I can do that." Lyle's heart lightened. The tough stuff was behind them.

Michael motioned back and forth, pointing at Lyle and then himself. "We don't have to put a label on this. We have a lot of fun when we're together. It would be a shame if we stopped that now. I think we have a real connection, and I'd hate to lose that. Can we pick it back up where we were? I mean before I became such an ass?"

"I think we can do that. How about we take today and bury it deep, like my feet in this sand?" She leaned close to him and wrapped her arms around his arm, trying to get warm.

He rubbed his hand briskly up and down her back. "Are you cold?"

"I got a chill sitting here in these damp clothes."

"You should really take that wet top off." He stood and lifted his sweatshirt off over his head.

Lyle's eyes followed the light trail of hair that disappeared into the waistband of his jeans. She blinked and took the sweatshirt offered to her. "Be a gentleman and look away."

Michael obliged her request. She unzipped her damp top and pushed it off over her shoulders. She let it fall into the sand behind her and quickly pulled his sweatshirt on over her head. His body heat had warmed the soft cotton, and she immediately felt warm.

"I'm afraid I slept in that last night." He sat and again rubbed his hand over Lyle's back, helping to warm her. He gestured toward her phone. "What're you listening to?"

"I was running to some Queen." She put her right earbud in her ear and handed him the other one. "Left ear." He took the earbud and slid it in place. "I think I can slow things down a bit."

Lyle scrolled through her playlist and chose more relaxing music.

They laid back in the sand. It was still warm from the heat of the day. She gave in to the temptation and closed her eyes. He found her hand and held it between them.

He turned onto his side and rested on his elbow. He placed his finger on Lyle's lower lip and waited for her to protest, but she never did. He watched her mouth as he trailed it back and forth.

She asked, "Are you flirting with me? I'm forty-two. You shouldn't be flirting with me." He was so close she could feel his breath on her skin. She stole a glimpse of his lips and a warm feeling filled her. She wondered how it would feel to kiss those lips. She abandoned her good sense and hoped she would find out.

Michael ran his fingers down her neck to the collar of the sweat-shirt. He looked into her eyes. "I like forty-two. It's perfect. It's right in between forty-one and forty-three." It felt like a feather moving up her neck and under her jaw. His finger continued behind her ear, making small circles on her skin as it traveled over her. He traced over her cheek and down again to find her lips.

Lyle could see the mischief in his bright hazel eyes. She watched as he ran his teeth over his lip. He leaned toward her, making his intention clear. She lifted her chin and closed her eyes.

"Are you Michael Miller?"

They both jumped at the question. They hadn't noticed the young woman standing just a few feet away. The magical moment vanished.

"I thought that was you. Can I get a picture with you?" She had thick brunette hair and large green eyes. "I'm a huge fan of yours. I saw you in *Summertime Love* like five times. I liked it better than the John Magnum movie. Can I have a picture?" she asked again. "My friends will never believe this."

Michael hopped up and put on a pleasant smile. "Of course. I love huge fans, and a pretty one at that." He winked at Lyle and then asked, "What's your name?"

"I'm Emma." She flashed a brilliant smile.

He stood next to Emma as she held out her readied phone. They both looked down expectantly at Lyle.

"Oh! Sorry. I'll get the picture." She stood and swiped at the sand that stuck to the back of her. Michael's sweatshirt hung on her like a sack, falling almost to her knees. She pushed the sleeves up her arms, freeing her hands, and took the phone from Emma.

Lyle watched as the professional actor once again came out. Michael placed his arm around Emma, ensuring that his hand could be seen on her waist, and tilted his head toward hers. He knew the picture his fans wanted. He didn't smile but held a seductive grin and waited for Lyle to snap a picture. As she took several different shots, she couldn't help but think they made an attractive couple.

Emma took her phone from Lyle. "Thanks so much." She looked at Michael. "Are you and your mother staying at this resort?" She gestured to the scattering of buildings several hundred yards down the beach.

Michael glanced at Lyle, who smiled down at the sand. "Actually, she's not my mother." He grinned. "She's my grandmother." He raised his eyebrows at Lyle, daring her to protest. "We're staying at a resort on the other side of the island. I'm afraid my grandmother and I are leaving tomorrow."

Lyle smiled and rolled her eyes. She was happy they were back to teasing each other, back to normal.

Michael noticed they were starting to attract attention from other beachgoers. He knew all too well where this could go. With instant messaging, Facetime, and instant everything else, he knew he had to beat a quick retreat or be committed to autographs and photographs for an endless amount of time. "I better get my grandmother back to the home. Have a great vacation, Emma." He took Lyle's hand and hurried her along.

He lifted the bike out of the sand and carried it to the parking area.

"You're going to make your grandmother ride on the wobbly bike again?"

"You don't like my bike?"

She climbed onto the seat and looked back at Emma, who was watching them leave. "I don't know, Michael, that was quite a pretty girl."

He climbed on the bike and looked back at the beaming young woman. "That? That's a dime a dozen."

Lyle wasn't sure she liked the way he said that.

He began peddling toward the main road as Lyle held onto his sides. "And stop trying to get rid of me."

Seventeen

The rain that had come through overnight was moving out of the area. The humidity was noticeably higher, but the weather only slightly interrupted the day's schedule. With the predawn dive completed, the group finished a leisurely breakfast while waiting for the rain to pass.

Angela had attracted the attention of two divers who were also waiting for the weather to clear. The men were in their twenties and had a hard time keeping their eyes off her as she smiled and flirted in her not-so-subtle way.

They looked familiar to Lyle, having seen them at breakfast and around the resort for the past few days. The two men were also from the states and were visiting Bonaire for their first time.

They pulled their chairs up to the table and laughed along with the group as each one tried to one-up the other's dive story. Lyle recognized the one who introduced himself as Cameron. He had joked with them from the patio above after they had completed their very first early-morning dive. He had an attractive smile and an easygoing personality that weren't lost on Angela.

Lyle scanned the people eating breakfast on the patio. She knew she had seen the blond-haired man eating here. She searched for him in the crowd but was relieved when he was nowhere to be seen, and she quietly said a prayer of thanks.

The gray clouds were breaking up, and the sky held the promise of a sunny day. The group finished laughing at Victoria's outrageous story.

"So, the moral of your story is?" Michael asked.

"Don't dive with Vienna sausages in your wetsuit," she said, deadpan.

The table all chuckled, and Natalie clapped her hands. Rick shook his head. He had heard Victoria's Vienna sausage story before.

Cameron turned to Angela. "We're going to go. It looks like it's clearing. Maybe we'll see you around the resort later."

Angela tilted her head and flashed Cameron a brilliant smile. "I'd like that. See you later."

"Let's organize our day while we're all here," said Rick. "It would be nice to dive the north end of the island again today. Michael missed out yesterday." He looked at Michael. "I think you'll really like diving up north. The reefs fall off sharply, almost like a wall, instead of the gradual slopes you're used to seeing."

"As much as I hate to miss the fun morning ahead of all of you," said Diego, "Natalie and I are booked on the *Mi Dushi*. We overslept the other day, but they have room for us today."

Diego stood up and Natalie did the same. She then bent down to whisper in Lyle's ear: "Rumor has it that Michael Miller is on Bonaire diving with his personal manager."

Lyle asked quietly, "Who would've started that rumor?"

"Me. My brother is hoping to spend more time with you. It'll go a long way in explaining who you are if people start to notice."

Rick continued, "Wait one second, Natalie. Before you and Diego go—Mookie's playing tonight at the pool bar." There was a rumbling of recognition. "Let's meet there at seven for dinner."

Angela took the opportunity to explain who Mookie was to the first-timers. "He's kind of a legend around here. His band plays the steel drums, congas, acoustic guitar. He knows how to get the crowd moving, so wear your dancing shoes."

As they moved toward the exit, Rick put his arm across Michael's shoulder. "Why don't you ride with us? There's no sense in you driving your own truck."

Michael faked a smile and move out from under Rick's arm. "That'd be great. I'll grab my gear and meet you at the pickup area."

The group disbanded and went to gather their gear. Rick and Lyle drove their trucks down the bumpy gravel road to the grassy area where their friends were waiting.

Michael carried his gear to Lyle's truck and started putting it in the back. Victoria put her hand on his arm. "Sorry, mister, no can do. We split the trucks, girls and guys." She nodded toward Rick's truck, indicating Michael should put his gear in there.

Angela placed her bright pink fins into the bed of the girls' truck. "She means divas and downers." She grinned and fist-bumped Victoria.

Michael held his gear in his arms. "Maybe the logistics should've been explained to me before I agreed to this arrangement," he said to Lyle. He placed his gear begrudgingly in the back of Rick's truck.

"You'll be happier in the guy's truck. We just talk about recipes and dieting and current events."

The girl's truck was beginning to show the wear and tear it suffered while lugging around three divers: muddy stones and clumps of dirt on the floor mats and a salty residue on the seats where salt water had pooled and dried. Empty water bottles and snack wrappers littered the back seat. The exterior was caked in dirt, salt, and sand.

"Besides, Rick and Steve keep their truck a lot cleaner than we do."

Lyle followed Rick out of the parking lot and turned left up the main road. The rain had stopped. They drove with the windows down and the radio off.

Angela was clearly pondering something and finally asked, "Did I not look totally hot in that dress I wore the other night?"

The question took Lyle and Victoria by surprise. They remained silent.

"The one I wore at dinner the other night, at Captain Jack's, the sundress with the big flowers? Do you two not even notice my wardrobe?"

"Totally hot. Was there ever any question?" Lyle looked at Angela in the rearview mirror.

"Well, I didn't exactly get the attention I was hoping for." She cupped her breasts in her hands. "These mamas are brown as berries and practically spilled out over the top of that dress. I had it going on. Hair, makeup—I was flawless."

Victoria turned in her seat. "Exactly what kind of attention were you hoping for?"

"I gave Michael Miller every chance to make a move. Any move. If the man had sneezed, I would've said yes. Have you seen his ass in that wetsuit? No one looks good in neoprene." She crossed her arms. "Damn it. I just wanted to be able to say I slept with Michael Miller on a Caribbean island. I don't need a relationship. Just one night would do. Is that too much to ask?" Her voice grew louder. "Can't just this one thing work out for me? One night?" Her eyes narrowed. "I know a lot of people who'd be really jealous of me."

As they traveled north, the road's elevation increased. The ocean to the left was falling lower as the trucks made the easy ascent.

Angela leaned forward and rested her arms on the back of the front seat. "Do you think I should move on? I mean, there are some very hot guys here. I may be spending my best dress energy on a dead end." She looked from Lyle to Victoria. "How about those guys at breakfast this morning? That Cameron is good-looking in that rugged, sunbaked way. I'm afraid Mr. Miller and I could, unfortunately, be stuck in friend mode. I eat breakfast with him every morning and we aren't even sleeping together!"

Listening to Angela gush over Michael gave Lyle an uneasy feeling. And she knew exactly why: she was falling for him too.

"Lyle, truth or dare?" asked Angela.

Lyle didn't even think. "Dare." She was not getting pressured into giving her secrets away again. Admitting her feelings for Rick to her friends was bad enough. What if they coaxed her thoughts about Michael out of her?

"Damn, I wasn't expecting that. Let me think a minute." Angela glanced out the side window to the ocean below the cliff. "Okay, I've got it. I get to dress you for tonight's dinner." Lyle tried to protest, but Angela spoke over her. "Clothes, hair, makeup, and you won't complain. You'll enjoy it. And if you don't, you'll pretend you do. You know, to spare my feelings. I may allow you to wear your own shoes, since our sizes are different, but that's it."

"Do I have to?" Lyle whined. "Is it too late to change my answer to truth?"

"For Christ's sake. You didn't even bring any makeup with you. Let me do this. It'll be fun, for me." Angela smiled and relaxed back into the seat. They were coming up on the dive site.

Eighteen

They left the two trucks by the side of the road marked for parking. They crossed the two-lane road and walked through a narrow row of trees. The group emerged together on top of a cliff that overlooked the ocean. The sky was unusually cloudy, and white caps jumped over the water's surface. The wind was noticeably stronger. They were up so high Klein Bonaire, the island they dove from the boat, was easily visible. Looking to the right, they could see the northernmost point of the island. A large ship was docked there, unloading cargo.

Michael stood next to Lyle and took in the panoramic view. "Wow, this is amazing. Where are we?"

"Welcome to One Thousand Steps!" She raised her voice to be heard over the gusting winds. "Remember when we told you diving the northern end of the island was a little more difficult?" She nodded toward the shore below. "See that beach down there?"

Michael leaned forward and gazed at the white coral beach. "What's that?"

"That, my friend, is the dive site."

The friends laughed at her delivery. She walked with him a few feet to the right. A yellow rock with *1,000 Steps* painted on it sat before a steep limestone stairway running down the face of the cliff. Looking down, they could only see the first six or seven steps. It then turned sharply to the right and fell out of view.

"This is 1,000 Steps, one of the more famous locations on the island."

"We have to walk down there? With all our gear on?"

Victoria patted Michael on the back. "It's not the going down that's going to hurt."

With each diver carrying over thirty pounds of gear, the descent was slow and steady. They held the low limestone wall with one hand, their masks and fins in the other.

Lyle walked one step in front of Michael and spoke over her shoulder, "We've counted the steps. There are actually sixty-seven." She paused to catch her breath. "It'll only feel like a thousand when we have to climb back up."

The group enjoyed a long dive in the warm blue water. They didn't pair up but rather dove as a group, each watching out for the others. Michael stayed close to Lyle, an action that didn't go unnoticed by Victoria. Lyle missed diving with Michael the day before and felt positively blissful that they were back on friendly terms.

She fell into her habit of pointing out the unusual sea life to him. He was catching on and found some incredible things himself. They had formed their own rudimentary kind of sign language to communicate underwater. She made signs with her hands and fingers for the different fish or crustaceans they saw. If he wanted to show her something he found, he grabbed her fin and stopped her from swimming forward. She got used to him stopping her this way and would eagerly turn back to see what it was he had discovered. They may as well have been diving alone. They swam together over the reef, lost with each other in their own undersea universe.

Once they all had completed the dive, they removed their masks and floated in the shallow water. After a thorough review of the dive, Rick turned to the shore. "We can stay here all day talking, but those stairs aren't going anywhere."

Soaking wet, they began climbing the steps, one behind the other. Their calves and thighs burned under the weight of their equipment.

"Whatever you do," Steve huffed, "don't stop. And keep your regulator in your mouth. The extra oxygen will help."

They struggled up the stairs and their breathing became labored. Heavy air cylinders shifted on their backs and threatened to unbalance them. Once they reached the top, the group stopped and took a moment to catch their breath.

Lyle was winded. "What'd you think?"

"I think it would be better to access this area by boat."

They drove a short distance and pulled to the side of the road. Lyle noticed the name of the dive site painted on the yellow rock marking the entrance. "Oh, I love this place!" She paused. "Michael isn't ever going to dive with us again after today."

"I think he'll dive with us again," Victoria said. "It's going to take more than this to run him off."

They parked a safe distance from the cliff and walked toward the ledge jutting out over the water. Underwater volcanic activity had created this section of the island long ago. The ledge was speckled with small holes that ran through the stone all the way down to the ocean, where the sound of the crashing waves could be heard coming from underfoot.

Michael looked up and down the cliff face. "Where are the stairs?"

Five divers eyed one another with grins spread across their faces.

"Come on guys, where are the stairs?"

Rick looked at Victoria. "Why don't you tell him? He likes you."

Victoria put her arm around Michael's waist and walked with him to the edge of the cliff. Looking straight down into the blue waves breaking against the rock wall below, she told him, "We jump in."

After completing the dive there at Oil Slick Leap, they all drove north to Karpata, where the road had narrowed to a one-way lane. The site was in a remote part of the island, keeping the number of divers who visited to a minimum. It was eerily quiet as they geared up, with only the shrill sound of the wind circling them. Sun baked the earth and clouds of dust swept over the dry ground.

Michael noticed an abandoned structure just yards from where they parked the trucks. The wooden building had given way to the burning sun and strong winds years ago. Only bits of its original paint remained. An iguana scuttled past them and disappeared into the protection of the old shed.

"What's that?" asked Michael.

"It used to be a snack shack. They sold sodas and hotdogs. It was open for a few years, but I don't think they got enough traffic up here to sustain the business."

Accessing the shoreline at Karpata required the divers to descend a steep concrete stairway and navigate a rocky beach. The ocean was noticeably rougher than it had been earlier in the day. A torrent of white caps now cut the surface, and the wind was whistling ominously. This location lacked the natural protection created by the slope of the island's shoreline. The strong wind whipped around the tip of the island and stirred the sea.

Once in the water, they fought against punishing waves as they swam out fifty yards to the buoy marking the reef. Even with their fins to aid them, their leg muscles began to burn. When they finally reached the marker, they held on to it and took several minutes to catch their breath.

Waves lifted and dropped the divers as they tried to manage their equipment and keep from drifting away. Salt water pelted them as the ocean grew more erratic. They put extra air into their BCs to help them float higher in the rough water.

Rick yelled over the wind: "It'll be a good idea to buddy up this time. We'll all need someone looking out for us."

The wind howled, and Lyle looked to the sky. Thick clouds were rolling in. "The weather's turning. I'm our strongest swimmer, so I'll dive with Michael. If he gets into any trouble, he'll be safe with me."

"Michael, stay close to Lyle," Rick said. "This reef falls down sharply. It looks like a wall of coral, not a gentle slope like you're used to seeing. It gets deep fast and you won't be able to see the bottom. Be mindful of the current. This far north, it can be brutal. And be sure to keep an eye on your depth."

The clouds opened up and rain began to bombard them. They struggled to keep hold of the buoy. "I think we'll have an easier time if we get off the surface," said Lyle. "Let's get out of this storm, shall we?"

The group put their masks in place. Each took a deep breath from their mouthpieces and sank into the water. When they descended below twenty feet, a wall of coral appeared before them. But the brightly colored fish and coral they expected to see were muted from the lack of sunlight. Under the cloudy sky, the reef was milky gray. They only saw darkness beyond their fins.

At fifty feet Lyle motioned for Michael to level off. With no visual of the ocean floor, maintaining their depth would be a challenge. They would have to rely on their computers to tell them how deep they were throughout the dive.

Michael was excited to see a huge lobster sitting in the wall of coral. Its hard shell was purple, and it flared its antennae at him as he approached. He looked at Lyle and pointed at the angry crustacean. But when he turned back, the lobster was gone. Only it hadn't moved; Michael had.

He watched the coral wall speed past him and inhaled sharply, his heart racing. The current was dragging him down the reef. He spotted the lobster and tried to swim back to it. But as hard as he kicked and dug in with his arms, he couldn't move in the right direction and he continued to be swept away. He kicked his legs and pumped his fins, battling the powerful water, but the flow was too strong. The ocean tossed him like a puppet. He was being pushed backward, the unbearable force driving him deeper and farther out.

Lyle too was caught in the current and was being dragged along the reef. She saw Michael below her kicking like mad, arms circling like windmills, and fighting not to be taken into the deep. He was panicking, one of the most dangerous things for a diver to do. She had to get to him fast.

Lyle knew not to let fear control her. She asked herself the age-old question divers used to calm themselves: *Do I have air?* As long as she could answer yes, she had the time and the skill to get herself to safety. A clear head and slow, steady breaths were her only way out.

Michael was terrified and sinking into the murky water. He knew Lyle would want him to check his wrist computer. It was all he could do to stop flailing his arms and hold his wrist still enough to read it.

He saw that he was at eighty feet— not an unreasonable depth but far beyond where he had started. His air was already alarmingly low—he was sure he was going to run out and drown. There was nothing he could do.

Then he spotted Lyle above him being tossed about.

Her reflexes told her to fight, but against all natural instinct, she relaxed and let the water take her. It was the only way she had of catching up to him. She tumbled head over heels through the water. With one hand she held a death grip on her mouthpiece, tight against her lips. She didn't want to chance her air supply being ripped away. She saw Michael several feet below her, fighting the current, and she was certain he would lose.

Michael knew his situation was dire. He checked his depth: eighty-five feet. He searched for Lyle but saw nothing. No reef, no Lyle, no ocean floor. Just gray water in every direction. He was being taken out to sea. The ocean had captured him and was about to show him its true strength.

Lyle watched Michael as the current quickly drove her toward him. She saw him searching for her then caught the panic in his eyes when he found her. She made a "calm down" motion with her hands.

He nodded at her and tried to control his panic. He knew his air was dangerously low but couldn't stop himself from breathing erratically. His heartbeat thundered in his ears, and his blood pulsed into his temples. The only thing he could do was wait for Lyle to save him. A feeling of calm washed over him—he believed that she would.

There was no avoiding crashing into Michael. When Lyle collided with him, she clamped onto his BC with both fists and Michael grabbed hers as well. She looked into his eyes and blinked slowly, letting him know he was going to be okay. She pointed her index finger skyward and calmly nodded at him. She then found the air inflation button on his BC. She pushed the control causing several short blasts of air to flow into his vest.

With her fists still clenched onto him, she calmly kicked her feet. With the aid of the extra air in his BC and Lyle guiding them upward with her fins, they eventually overcame the current and began to rise. If she let them ascend too fast, they might shoot to the surface like a bullet and get the bends. Surely then to end up in the island's decompression chamber. She watched the depth on her computer steadily decrease as they gradually rose through the churning water.

They broke the surface and fully inflated their BCs. They floated under the dark sky as the rain hammered them.

"You're okay," Lyle said. "Take some deep breaths, I got you."

"Fuck. I had no control." He was panting. "I thought I was going to die. I couldn't swim, the current was tossing me like a rag doll," he huffed. "Thank you."

"I owed you one. Catch your breath. You're safe now."

The storm had taken them hundreds of yards away from the shoreline. Lyle searched the gloomy horizon for any sign of her friends. She shouted over the pounding rain: "I don't see anyone else. Let's head to shore. We've got a long swim ahead of us."

They made slow progress, but as they got closer to the beach, they could see Victoria and Angela standing there, looking for their friends. Lyle gave Victoria the okay sign as they approached. Victoria waved back to her and then continued scouting the horizon. Lyle had a miserable feeling that Rick and Steve were missing.

The waves crashed against their backs as they stumbled out of the water. Once onshore, Michael fell to his knees and gasped for air. "I'm worn out," he panted. "I need to sit." He unclasped his BC and slid his arms out of it, breathing heavily.

"Any sign of Rick and Steve?" Lyle asked, as she removed her gear.

Victoria held her arm over her forehead, trying to keep the rain out of her eyes as she scanned the water. "No. I don't see them."

Lyle dropped down beside Michael. "How did you two get back so quickly?" she asked Angela.

"We ended the dive soon after we descended. We felt the current pick up and got out of the water fast." She continued to look for the guys.

They all heard it at the same time: coral crunching underfoot as someone approached them from the left.

"There you are, thank God," said Victoria. "I've been searching the water for you."

Rick and Steve staggered toward them still wearing all their equipment and carrying their fins.

"The current took us south. We got out as soon as we could," Rick gasped. "That was a long hike back." He and Steve sat with Lyle and Michael and fought to catch their wind.

"Is everyone okay?" asked Rick.

"We're okay, just worn out." Lyle asked Michael, "Are you okay? I know that was frightening for you. I'm sorry, we shouldn't have brought you here. Diving this far north can be tough."

Michael let out a heavy sigh. "It's not anyone's fault that the weather turned so quickly. You can't predict the current."

Angela sat down next to Michael. "Now you have a story to tell," she said. "No one wants to hear about the pretty fish and sunshine. If you can tell a story with "I was being pulled out to sea, my life flashed in front of me,' then you've got something people want to hear."

They were too tired to laugh, so they watched the sky. The rains eased and patches of blue could be seen between the clouds.

"I don't believe it," said Michael. "The clouds are clearing out." The rain stopped and the sun started to shine. "I guess it's all in the…" They all looked at Michael and waited. "Timing."

Once they had recovered, they agreed they'd had enough diving and should head back into town. They stopped at a fast-food restaurant and took their lunches to go. They ate chicken sandwiches and french fries while they drove over rain-soaked roads back to the resort.

Angela spoke with her mouth full. "After that disastrous afternoon, we deserve a special night. I need to stop at a liquor store. We're having happy hour tonight in my room. The boys are not invited."

Nineteen

The girls planned to meet in Angela's room for a glass of wine. They would later join the guys at the pool bar for dinner and Mookie's band. Angela reminded Lyle about her dare choice from earlier in the day and suggested she come over naked since she needed a blank slate to work with. Lyle's room was next to Angela's, so she knocked on her door wearing nothing but panties under her bathrobe.

"Come in. We've already opened the wine." Angela held up her glass as Lyle walked in.

Victoria sat in her own bathrobe on a chair by the open balcony doors, with her feet up on the coffee table and a glass in her hand. "It does feel good to get rid of the salt and sand. I swear I had sand stuck in crevices I didn't know I had."

Angela's room was decorated in the same bright Caribbean blue as Lyle's room. She had noticeably more personal items around the room, making it feel more lived in. An array of lotions, sunscreen and make-up covered the dresser. The closet doors were open displaying a clothes rod jammed packed with outfits. The shelf above held several sunhats that Lyle had never seen Angela wear. Lyle was careful not to trip over several pairs of shoes as she walked through the room. The mirror over the dresser had several photos, receipts, and a new post-card tucked in the frame. Although filled with good intentions, she would bet money on the fact that the postcard would never be mailed.

Victoria poured her a glass of wine. "Let happy hour begin!" The three held up their glasses.

Angela looked puzzled. "What are we toasting to?"

"How about to new possibilities?" said Lyle.

The girls clinked glasses. Lyle took two giant steps and bounced onto the bed. She sat back on the pillows and patted the mattress next to her, inviting Victoria and Angela to join her. They cuddled in close so they could all fit comfortably.

"We had some spectacular dives today," gushed Lyle. "I mean, before the storm blew in, we were having a great day. I think Michael really liked jumping in off the cliff at Oil Slick. It's such a rush."

Victoria looked innocently at Lyle. "Why do you think that is? Why was today such a great day?"

"No specific reason. I just think it was a nice day. Granted, we all could've done without the harsh weather, but it did clear out as quickly as it came in."

Angela rolled her eyes. "Oh, please go on and say it. You and Michael have something going on. We're not blind. Even underwater we can see you two flirting."

"You're crazy. He's just a kid."

Victoria finished her wine and placed the empty glass on the nightstand. "Kid or no kid, you're crazy about him. From the looks of it, he's falling for you too."

Angela got the wine bottle and refilled Victoria's glass. "He isn't a kid. You guys are just old. He's in his twenties. I'd be all over that if he'd have me. But I'm happy for you, Lyle. Maybe this'll be just the thing you need to move beyond Rick."

"That's just it—Michael takes my mind off Rick. We have a lot of laughs when we're together, and the flirting's just fun." Victoria raised her eyebrows. "Victoria, I'm not stupid. He's way too young for me. We're just having fun, that's all. When Rick came to my room the other night, after our dinner at Captain Jack's, he was looking good. It used to be so romantic. He was always such a gentleman. And the sex was—"

"We know, it was generous," said Angela.

"Very generous." Lyle smiled. "The weird part is I didn't want him to stay. It was easy for me to tell him to leave. I didn't think I'd ever get to this place. I think Michael has shown me that something more may be out there for me. I can finally see the possibility of being free of loving Rick."

Victoria held up her glass. "To new possibilities."

The three friends touched glasses and sipped their wine.

Angela hopped up off the bed. "Lyle, I have some makeup to put on you."

Angela had brought a plethora of beauty products that now covered the bathroom counter. The cords from her hairdryer and flat iron fell to the floor. Lyle put the lid down on the toilet and had a seat. Victoria sat on the side of the tub, awaiting her turn.

Angela picked up a little bottle and applied a thick cream under Lyle's eyes. "We'll start with some moisturizer. Close your eyes. You don't need any cover-up, your tan looks great." She took a soft brush, dipped into the compact of blush, and put a little glow in Lyle's cheeks. "I haven't tried this mascara yet. It's midnight black, just open halfway." Lyle peered down her nose as Angela applied the mascara. "Look up a little." She followed her directions without complaint. "Let me put a little color on your eyelids. I have the perfect one to match your dress."

"I don't get to wear my own clothes?"

Victoria laughed. "What're you going to wear, your Bob's Crab Shack T-shirt?"

Lyle lightly nudged Victoria with her foot. When Angela was satisfied with the eye shadow, she brushed Lyle's hair and painstakingly flat-ironed it. She tried several different styles but, in the end, decided to leave it down.

"If you two can behave for a minute, I'll get the dress." Angela had a huge smile on her face when she returned with a dress on a hanger laid out across her arm. "You get to wear this! I've got another one for myself tonight. Now I know what you're going to say, this dress is too nice for a casual evening, but I insist you wear it."

Lyle's eyes grew wide, and her voice went up an octave. "Not your bandage dress. You should wear that one. I don't have the right figure for it." She was thinking her chest would be overexposed and her figure too much on display. She had seen it on Angela before—it was basically a body condom. "You should wear that one," she said again. "It looks great on you."

"Are you kidding? With your runner's body? It'll look spectacular. It won't completely cover your tattoo. Lyle, I love you, but you really should've consulted me before getting that." She slid the dress off the hanger. "I know Dottie helped you with the design, but most people get a butterfly on their shoulder for the first tattoo. I swear, Lyle, we could put you in a sideshow with a tattoo like that. We could charge a quarter to anyone who wanted a peek at the entire thing." She asked Victoria, "Would you pay a quarter?"

Victoria nodded and took another sip of her wine.

Dottie's idea for Lyle's tattoo was a spine tattooed down her spine. The design was somewhere between reality and fantasy. Somewhere between bones and fantastical metal pipes. Each bone was unique. They were made to look old and worn from the abuse they had endured. Some had holes rusted right through them, and others were bent and dented. Dottie was certain the new spine would have the strength to hold all of Lyle's burdens. All her troubles could be put away. Neatly tucked within her new, stronger backbone.

Lyle mumbled to herself, "I never had it completed."

Angela wasn't sure she heard her correctly. "What do you mean? It's not done?"

"The guy who did it wants to add gremlins. He left spaces to add some in later. He thought they could represent people in my life."

Angela motioned for Lyle to stand. She took her bathrobe and tossed it to the floor. Angela ran her finger down the tattoo. "You never let him finish it?"

"It hurt so much. I never went back."

Angela eased the dress over Lyle's head, being careful not to smudge her makeup. "I imagine tattooing over your spine would hurt. There's no fat or muscle to cushion against the bones."

She turned Lyle to face the mirror and ran the zipper up her side. The dress fit like a glove. It was an eye-catching chocolate brown with a capped sleeve. The horizontal drapes of shimmering fabric hugged Lyle's figure. Her breasts were just a tease at the top of the bodice. Her tan glowed, and her eyes stood out like jewels. Angela had worked her hair pin-straight. It now fell to her eyes and tumbled down to her bare shoulders and over her back. Angela put her hands on Lyle's hips. "He's going to want to be all over this."

Lyle wondered which "he" that was.

With Lyle dressed, Angela sent her back to her room to fetch her sandals. "Don't come back here in flip flops."

Back in Angela's room, Lyle now had her turn sitting on the side of the tub. She refilled wine glasses and complimented Victoria as Angela gave her a new look. Victoria didn't argue, and the two watched as Angela worked the same pattern on her. Makeup, hair, and clothes. Victoria was nicely surprised by her new look. She wore a blue-and-white striped halter-top sundress. The outfit looked great with her strawberry-blond hair. Angela placed a large red zinnia behind Victoria's ear. She smiled and clapped her hands. "I'm so glad I found that flower growing in a pot near the reception desk. It looks perfect on you."

When Angela had completed her own hair and makeup, she stood in her panties and held up two dresses. Unable to decide between them, she waited for input from her friends.

"Honestly, Angela, it's just Mookie at the pool bar." Victoria said. She and Lyle broke out in giggles.

Angela whined. "I know, I know, but this is our girl time. No salt water, no blistering sun. No gravel, no sweat or heavy equipment to lug around. No stinking truck."

"You're right, you're right." Lyle controlled her laughter. "This *is* our girl time. I'm glad we're doing this. Hold the dresses up one at a time. Let us look at them again."

They all agreed on the pale green dress that ended midthigh and had a princess neckline.

The three girls stood in front of the bathroom mirror with their arms around each other. Victoria said what they were all thinking: "We look like Charlie's Angels."

The three burst out laughing.

Twenty

They followed the tree-covered path to the pool bar. At the entrance, they saw Mookie testing his guitar, strumming a soft melody. He wore a multicolored flowered shirt and cutoff jeans. The band's equipment was set up under the thatched hut that also contained the dance floor. Just beyond the dining area, the sunset put on a magnificent show. Vibrant yellows and oranges streaked across the sky, and where the sky touched the ocean, a glowing red seemed to burst free and spill across the water.

Victoria spotted their friends at a table near the water. Lyle started to follow her when Angela grabbed her arm and stopped her. "Don't look now, but our growing circle of friends just got even bigger."

Lyle studied the table full of friends. Steve and Michael were deep in conversation. Rick was speaking to a woman sitting next to him. Lyle could just make out short blond hair and a red sundress. Rick had brought a date. She stared at the woman at the table as she felt a lump form in her throat. She swallowed hard. Rick had knocked on her door just two nights ago. He kissed her, and she kissed him back. They talked about getting back together. Rick touched his date's shoulder with his finger and Lyle fought the urge to run.

Angela fished a compact out of her handbag and checked her makeup. "You ready?"

She walked away, but Lyle stood still, dreading the energy it would take to smile and laugh with Rick's date. By the end of the night, her face would hurt. Frozen, and unable to decide what to do, she looked over her shoulder at the path that would lead her back to the safety of her room. She recalled what she told her friends just this afternoon: that she might be getting over Rick. But seeing him with the pretty blonde threatened her resolve.

Lyle watched as Victoria and Angela approached the table and Michael stood up from his chair. He then scanned the area, and she knew he was looking for her. If she were going to leave, it would have to be now. She took a tentative step backward as her friends greeted each other. She took a second step back.

Michael said something to Victoria, who turned to look for her friend. They saw Lyle at the same time. She took another step backward, hoping to fade into the shadows.

Michael, wearing jeans with holes in both knees and a faded blue T-shirt, caught Lyle's eye and headed toward her. He took both of her hands in his and leaned down to kiss her cheek, then spoke quietly into her ear. "I could skip dinner. You look absolutely delicious. I hope you plan to stay. Will you dance with me?" He led her to the dance floor. He buried her small hand in his and held it close to his chest and placed his other hand on the small of her back.

"You look delicious too," said Lyle, blushing.

They moved over the dance floor and became lost in the sweet melody. They closed their eyes and for the first time, experienced the closeness of the other, unaware they were the only two dancing.

When the song ended, Michael motioned for her to walk ahead of him to their table. He watched her soft hair swing gently across her shoulders and over her tattoo. The rich brown dress hugged every curve of her body. He blew air out his pursed lips as he watched her hips sway with each step.

Rick stood and greeted Lyle with a kiss on her cheek. She couldn't help but notice his gaze fell to her dress. She silently thanked Angela, glad that her breasts were peeking out. "Lyle, this is Jeanette. She's joining us for dinner."

"It's nice to meet you, Jeanette. We're glad you could join us."

Michael held a chair for Lyle. He watched as she ran her hands down her hips and over her rear end, tucking her dress under her as she sat. He picked up a menu but had a hard time taking his eyes off Lyle. She absentmindedly combed her fingers through her hair, drawing his attention to her bare shoulders.

Lyle joined the conversation at the table, but Michael remained aloof. He noticed the rise and fall of her chest with each breath she took. He admired her tanned thigh half hidden under the white tablecloth. Something stirred within him, and he shifted his attention away from her. He decided a drink might be a good distraction. He excused himself and went to the bar.

He was gone long enough for Lyle to wonder where he was. She spotted him near the bar, signing an autograph and talking to a group of fans. He soon returned carrying two draft beers. He placed a glass in front of her and took a long drink from his own. He leaned into Lyle and spoke near her ear. "I'm sorry it took me so long. I'm afraid I attracted some attention at the bar."

She looked down at his lips and then back into his eyes. "You've attracted some attention right here as well."

He was encouraged by Lyle's forwardness and a mischievous grin crossed his face. He placed his hand on her thigh and squeezed it. "This attention I welcome."

Dinner was served, and soon the plates were being passed back and forth as everyone wanted a taste of what the other had ordered. The friends were used to sharing dinners, a nice way to have a sampling of the menu selections. Jeannette looked confused as she waved a tiny goodbye to her grilled salmon. She perked up as Steve passed her his filet mignon.

Cameron, whom they had met at breakfast while they waited out the rain, approached the table. He stood behind Angela and put his hand on her shoulder. "Hi, Angela. I was hoping you'd save me a dance later."

Angela put down her fork and looked up over her shoulder. "I'd love to, Cameron."

The sun fully set, and tiki torches glowed around the patio as they finished their dinners. The music from under the thatched hut picked up its tempo. Mookie called to the diners to come join him. Diego and Natalie excused themselves and were some of the first to start dancing.

Angela didn't have to wait long for Cameron to return and claim her. They walked to the dance floor hand in hand and were soon lost in the crowd.

The empty dinner plates were removed from the table, and beer gave way to rum. Jeanette turned out to be a nice addition to the group. Lyle silently scolded herself for thinking the worst of her. Rick's taste in women seldom faltered.

Pounding rhythmic music filled the night air, and the crowd on the dance floor was enjoying every beat. Steve, in Bermuda shorts and a clashing Hawaiian shirt, got up to join the others dancing.

Michael stood and reached for Lyle's hand. The form-fitting dress had been teasing him all night. He desperately wanted to get his hands on her, and the dance floor was a good place to start.

As they passed Victoria, he grabbed her hand as well. She jumped to her feet and followed them to the dance floor.

The music grew louder as the night wore on. As they danced, Michael placed his hands on Lyle at every opportunity.

When they became entangled, he took advantage of her loss of balance. He pulled her close and hastily ran his hands down her hips and around to her rear end. The fabric of her dress was soft, but her body was firm and curvaceous. After a beat, he reluctantly let her go, aware of the crowd around them.

Mookie slowed the music down, and several singles left the floor. Michael took Lyle in his arms, and they swayed to the melody. He had been waiting to get her back in his arms. It was all he could do to keep his hands from wandering over her body.

He pulled her closer. "Will I ever see the rest of that tattoo?"

"I think you have to pay Angela a quarter."

He looked out over the dark ocean. "Does it…" He paused and looked back at her. "Does it go all the way down?"

"Oh yes, it goes all the way down."

"Well then, that's worth the quarter."

Angela danced with Cameron with a rare timid grin on her face as she spoke quietly to him. Lyle could see him falling under her spell. Glancing at the other young women on the floor, Lyle was sure Angela was the most beautiful among them.

As they left the dance floor, a teenaged girl approached Michael. A wide headband was failing to tame her unruly hair. She nervously pulled at the hem of her shirt. "Hi, I'm Darby. Will you dance with me?" Her face turned ruddy as she waited for a response from the handsome star.

Michael gave Lyle an apologetic look then turned toward the girl and smiled. "I'd love to."

Lyle had been studying Michael as he interacted with his fans. She thought he put on a different face as he spoke with them. His expression went artificially bright, and his voice sounded lighter. He stood a bit straighter.

As Darby stepped up onto the slightly elevated floor, her sandal caught on something. Her foot slipped right out of it and she stumbled forward, bumping into several people, but caught herself before she fell. Her face turned beet red as she tried to find her sandal.

Michael knelt and picked up the wayward shoe. Like Prince Charming finding his Cinderella, he made a show of holding the shoe as the flustered girl slipped her foot back into it. The act drew considerable attention. Some people put a hand on their heart as the crowd swooned over his act of chivalry.

Lyle shook her head. "Damn, he's good." She returned to the dinner table alone and watched Michael dance with Darby.

A split second after the song ended, a second fan approached him for a dance. Lyle got hot under the collar as she eyed the tall brunette woman with voluptuous curves moving with him over the dance floor. Taller than Michael, she smiled down at him with bedroom eyes.

Lyle would much rather he dance with clumsy Cinderella.

Lyle disregarded her own jealousy as she noticed Michael's face. He held the same pleasant smile that he had with Darby—the one he reserved for his fans. Not the genuine smile he used with his family and friends.

Lyle took a sip of beer and tapped her toe to the music. She would wait them out. Every last one of them.

Twenty-One

Victoria returned to the table and took a long drink of water. "I needed that. It's getting hot out there." She looked back at the crowded dance floor. "Poor Michael can't get away. Everyone wants to dance with him or get a picture or an autograph. Some guy wants to buy him drinks. It just keeps going and going."

Natalie had seen this happen many times. "I'm afraid the news that Michael Miller is at Bon Adventure is out." She watched as her brother posed for a photograph with a young family. The tall brunette he had been dancing with earlier waited not far away.

"I'm going in," said Victoria to the others. "Rescue and recovery—who's with me?"

She and Natalie marched back to the dance floor. In no time at all, they returned to the table with Michael between them, a little red-faced from all the commotion.

"Sorry about that," he kissed Lyle's cheek. "I couldn't get away without looking like a snob. I kept trying to excuse myself, but they were persistent."

Victoria raised her eyebrows and tapped her own cheek with her index finger. Lyle pretended not to see her. Michael took his seat and finished what was left of his beer. He then picked up his water and finished that too. He saw Lyle watching him and gave her a smile, his genuine, only-for-friends-and-family smile.

Victoria had an idea. "What do you say we make this a private party?"

They planned to move down near the water. The girls insisted they change out of their dresses and into more comfortable beachwear. Everyone agreed to meet on the beach in thirty minutes.

Lyle changed and worked her hair into a ponytail and slipped her feet into her flip-flops. She stopped at Angela's room and knocked.

Angela threw her door open. "Thank God. Come in. We need to talk. What do you think of Cameron? The guy I was dancing with." She shimmied out of her dress and dropped it on the bed then riffled through her drawer. "You know Cameron. The guy we met at breakfast. The rugged-looking one." She chose a bright orange top and white shorts from the dresser. "He's from Colorado. He's here with two friends." She hopped on one foot and then the other, working herself into her shorts. "They're staying two weeks." She pulled her top over her head, but it got stuck. She continued talking to Lyle through the fabric. "We have so much in common." She popped her head through the neck hole. "He loves to dive, and he drives a Ford. I love to dive, and I drive a Ford too! So, we already have all of that in common."

The static in her hair had created a halo. "I invited him to join us at the beach." She slid her feet into her sandals and opened the door. She looked at Lyle. "What're you waiting for?" She motioned her out the door. "Thanks for the talk. Let's go!"

The beach was dark except for the limited light still shining from the resort. The sky was filled with stars, and the moon hung low on the horizon.

The guys moved chairs and chaise lounges close to the water to escape the eyes of any Michael Miller fans. Lyle stretched out on a lounge chair and propped her feet up. Calypso jumped onto it, turned in several circles, and laid down at her feet.

Cameron moved two chairs close together for him and Angela. They sat with their shoulders touching and holding hands.

Lyle was tired from a long day of diving, drinking, and dancing. The wine and beer were doing their best to put her to sleep. She rested her head against the back of the lounge and soon gave in to the distant cadence of the waves breaking and closed her eyes.

Victoria's voice rang over the others. "I can't believe it. Look what he brought."

Lyle opened her eyes. Coming down the beach toward them were Steve with a six-pack of beer and Michael with a black guitar case.

"Please don't tell him I play," pleaded Lyle.

But even as the words came out of her mouth, she heard Steve say to Michael: "Yeah, she's getting pretty good."

Calypso lifted her head. As Michael got closer, she hopped down from the chair and trotted off. Lyle pulled her feet under her, making room for Michael to sit.

Rick nodded at the guitar case. "Michael, you play?"

"My brother's quite good," said Natalie. "He dreamed of a music career before he was sidetracked by Hollywood." She smiled at him, clearly proud of his accomplishments.

He removed the guitar from its case. "I borrowed this from Mookie." He strummed the instrument and glanced at Lyle. "I understand I'm not the only one who plays."

"I've only been playing a short time," Lyle said dismissively. "We'd love to hear *you* play."

"Oh no. You're first." He handed the guitar to Lyle. She began to strum the strings and dance her fingertips up and down the neck of the instrument. Her friends quieted as she started to sing.

"I come from a family of lowlifes. We lived underground by and by, so I left my poor family of lowlifes to see just how high I could climb." She had sung this very song months ago, the day she'd gotten her tattoo.

She continued through the verses, never hesitating or missing a beat. The music flowed effortlessly from the guitar. She encouraged them to join her at the chorus. They sang quietly, not wanting to disrupt the serene ambiance. *"I stood on the shoulders of giants, but the giants were only yay high…"*

As she sang the final verse, she slowed the tempo and softened her voice until the last note ran away with the breeze. She looked at Michael, who was grinning at her, but remembered another. The man, who over several hours of intense concentration, tattooed her new spine on her back.

She grinned back at Michael and wondered what Grey Locklear was doing this night and what he would think of her, having never returned to him. Denying him the opportunity to finish his design.

"That was beautiful. You're full of surprises," Michael said.

She handed the guitar back to him. "Your turn." She kicked off her flip flops, leaned back in the chair, and tucked her toes under Michael's leg.

He played familiar beach songs, perfect in their surroundings, and followed them with romantic love songs. She was mesmerized by his natural singing style, how smoothly his voice mixed with the chords. She especially liked the way he glanced at her while singing. He gave her a wink now, acknowledging a secret between them, although she didn't think it was a secret. They weren't just falling for each other. They had fallen.

"If we're going to dive tomorrow, we should call it a night," Michael said, after finishing his last song.

Rick stretched his arms over his head, then stood and helped Jeanette to her feet. Lyle wasn't surprised to see Cameron stealing tiny kisses from Angela. The night was heavy with romance. Diego sat up and gently shook Natalie awake. She had fallen asleep early on. Steve fought to open his eyes and get his bearings. He collected the empty bottles and placed them in the cardboard carrier. Lyle slipped her feet back into her flip flops while Michael packed away Mookie's guitar.

Rick yelled over his shoulder, "The morning predawn dive has been canceled due to hangover. Thank you all for a great day. Good night." He walked toward his building with Jeanette in tow.

As they strolled past the quiet pool bar, Lyle wondered who would be sleeping alone and who wouldn't. She was sure she would hear all about it in the morning.

Michael stopped her and put his hand on her shoulder. He touched his forehead to hers. "Will you walk with me? I should put this in my room for safekeeping. I'll get it back to Mookie tomorrow."

She recognized the indirect invitation to his room. She looked into his eyes. He was so close she could feel his breath on her lips. She forced the words out. "I should go to my room. It's been a long, exhausting day. Thanks for everything tonight. The dancing and the music, it was wonderful."

He placed his cheek on hers and nuzzled her ear with his nose. "Walk with me. Stay with me, please."

His warm breath tantalized her and melted her fragile resistance. He ran his nose down her neck and under her chin. Lyle looked up at the stars, welcoming the moist kisses he placed on her neck. She opened her eyes and struggled to say the words: "No, Michael. I'm sorry, but we shouldn't." She stepped back.

"Please Lyle," he said in frustration, "you were going to let me kiss you on the beach yesterday, before we were tragically interrupted." He grinned. "I'm calling a rain check on that kiss. Let me redeem it tonight." He took her hand. "Come with me, please."

"Yesterday would've been a mistake. We shouldn't be kissing on the beach. I mean, we shouldn't be kissing. I'm sorry."

But even as she said it, she wanted more than anything to kiss him. Too young or not, she wanted to do more than just kiss.

He held her and nuzzled her ear once again and ran his hands down her back. He gently squeezed her ass and pulled her hips to him. She could feel every inch of him pressed against her. She squeezed her thighs together, trying to quiet the need. She placed her palms on his chest, shook her head slightly, and pushed away from him. "This isn't right. You're too young for me. I mean, I'm too old for you. You're famous, and your fans…"

"No, that isn't true. Your age, my age. You know if the tables were turned, this wouldn't be an issue."

"I really should go." The cool night air took the place of his warm embrace. She called over her shoulder, "I'll see you in the morning."

He stood in the dark and watched her as she disappeared around the corner of the building. He couldn't remember the last time he'd been turned down. He made it perfectly clear that he wanted her, and still, she said no. He was a prize. Women always said yes. He never had to work this hard to win over any woman.

He thought about the chocolate-brown dress she wore at dinner, the way her hair brushed over her back, and wondered if he would ever see the rest of that tattoo. He pictured the way the dress hugged her hips, waist, and breasts. He remembered her thigh, partially hidden under the tablecloth. How her chest rose and fell with each breath, unknowingly teasing him all night until he thought of nothing else. His body responded, but he would find no release.

"Damn her. I'm Michael Miller," he said through gritted teeth. "Everyone wants me!"

He ran his hands over his head and kicked at a stone with his toe. Could he measure up to other lovers she'd had? He tortured himself wondering if Lyle would find him lacking compared to Rick.

Did Rick know secrets to pleasing women that he wasn't privy to? Maybe she blatantly turned him down because she knew he wouldn't satisfy her.

Michael watched Calypso sniffing the ground as she approached then sniffed his hand and waited for a welcome scratch behind her ear. He pulled his hand away from the dog's nose and slammed his foot on the ground. "Fuck you, Rick!" Startled, Calypso tucked in her tail and ran off toward the beach.

Twenty-Two

Lyle wasn't used to the bright sun in her room as she woke. Last night was the first time she had gone to sleep without setting her alarm. She decided to allow herself to wake at leisure. She stretched her arms above the fluffy pillow.

She found her phone on the nightstand and saw it was just after seven. She toyed with the thought of turning over and going back to sleep. Yesterday had been a hard day of diving. The sites at the north end of the island were physically more taxing, and the night hadn't ended until well after midnight.

She closed her eyes and rolled onto her side. She pulled the blanket up over her shoulders and willed sleep to overcome her again. After a few minutes, she opened her eyes and scowled at the bright light illuminating the room. She could see the trees and hear the birds just outside the balcony doors.

"Fuck me. I'm awake." She pushed off the blanket and sat up on the side of the bed. She stretched her arms over her head and twisted left and right, easing her back into the new day. She took a minute to evaluate the state of her head and was surprised to find it hangover free.

The warm shower fully woke her and gave her a needed boost. She took the extra time to shave her legs and underarms. She put on a bathing suit and covered up with shorts and a tank top then brushed her hair and slid her feet into heavy-soled boat shoes. She grabbed her room key and the truck key and headed out the door. There were no plans to meet up with her friends this morning, but she thought the breakfast buffet was a sure place to run into them.

The resort was bustling. Staff members in their blue golf shirts hosed away mud from the rain the day before and swept the walkways clear of stones and sand. Employees pushed large rolling carts from room to room, cleaning and restocking linens and towels for their guests. Divers walked toward the dock, carrying their equipment, ready to start their day. The *Mi Dushi* had already left the dock. Several smaller boats were being equipped for the day.

Lyle entered the restaurant and scanned the tables for her friends, but she didn't see anyone. She couldn't help but look to see if the blond-haired man was there. She felt relieved when she didn't see him among the throng of diners.

The scent of freshly baked croissants and mouthwatering bacon grabbed her attention. Her stomach churned and let out a demanding growl. The smell of coffee filled the air, and her outlook on the day lifted.

A voice from behind startled her. "Looks like it's just you and me this morning." Michael's hair was still wet and again smelled like his coconut shampoo. His face was darkly tanned, and his hazel eyes stood out like two sparkling emeralds.

"Hey, Michael." She gave him a bright smile. "You're up. Where's everyone else? Did I miss them?"

After his failed attempt to seduce her the night before, he was relieved at the greeting and returned her brilliant smile. "I'm afraid the wine, beer, and rum from last night took a toll on our friends." He put his hand on her back and led her to a table for two by the railing, overlooking the dock.

"The fact that we're here definitely entitles us to some major bragging rights." He raked his fingers through his hair, pushing it away from his eyes.

"Major bragging rights. I'm sure Victoria and Steve are waking up with hangovers." She grinned wickedly. "I'm not sure who Rick and Angela are waking up with." She surprised herself at the indifference she felt about Rick sleeping with Jeanette.

"How's your head this morning? Are you up for diving?" He looked around at the diners. "From the looks of it, I'm in need of a buddy."

"I feel fine. I'd love to dive with you. Even if it's only because you're desperate for a buddy." She said flatly, "Thanks for the invitation."

He winked at her as he stood. "Maybe you need more sleep. You know you're my number one choice."

He walked to the coffee bar and Lyle watched as he filled two mugs and returned to the table. She added cream and sugar and took a sip. "Mmm, so good."

They finished their coffees and went through the buffet line. Lyle filled her plate with eggs, bacon, two pancakes with hot maple syrup, and a fresh baked croissant. Michael's plate was covered in scrambled eggs, bacon, and six pieces of sourdough toast. They enjoyed their enormous breakfasts without much conversation.

She took their coffee mugs to refill them. While she waited for the urn to be free, she saw a familiar young lady approach Michael at the table: one of his dance partners from the night before. She remembered how she stood taller than he. A crop top showed off her tanned stomach and shining navel ring. Michael stood, raised his eyebrows, and put on a pleasant smile as he spoke to the gorgeous girl.

She refilled the coffees and then, stalling, she filled two glasses with pomegranate juice. She returned to the table, awkwardly balancing the beverages just as the young lady was about to leave.

She looked down at her. "Are you Michael's manager?"

Lyle beamed. "Yes. Manager. Yes, I am."

"I saw you two dancing last night. I thought you were probably his manager. A few of us are going to dive the salt pier this morning and we were wondering if Michael would like to join us."

Michael took the two juice glasses from Lyle and gave her a knowing look. "I told her I wasn't sure what was on the schedule for today. I thought I had an interview with the local press."

She put the mugs on the table and looked from Michael to the stunning girl. "Yes, that's right. He has an interview today."

The young woman wasn't going to be dismissed quite so easily. "We thought he might want to meet some new people, you know, hang out with people his own age." She turned to Michael. "We're doing two dives at the salt pier and then driving up to Rancon. There's a little

distillery there where you can try some of the locally made liquors."
Silence fell over the three of them. Lyle looked at him and raised her
eyebrows. The girl's plan sounded fun. Maybe he would want to go.

"Thanks for the invitation, but I'll be busy most of the day."

Although slightly wounded, she put on a dazzling smile. "Maybe
I'll see you tonight at the pool bar. I'll save you a dance." She ignored
Lyle but gave Michael a flirty wave. "Bye".

Lyle leaned back and patted her full stomach. "You know, Michael,
if you want to…"

"No." He fought to keep his voice low. "Don't even say it, Lyle."
He gave her a hard look and clenched his fist. "I swear, if you tell me
I can go with her and her friends, I'm going to explode right here."

"Actually, I was going to say you'd better not even think about it.
You've committed to diving with me today, and if you back out now
I'll never forgive you."

"That's more like it. I hate when you try to get rid of me." He
turned his attention back to his breakfast but only pushed the eggs
around his plate. His demeanor had changed. He was quiet and
seemed in deep thought.

A server came and took Lyle's empty plate. He looked at Michael's
half-eaten breakfast. "Mr. Miller, are you done with your breakfast? If
it wasn't satisfactory, I'd be glad to bring you something else. Perhaps
our kitchen could prepare an omelet for you?"

"No, thank you. I'm finished." The server took his plate, and he
gazed out over the ocean.

Lyle was tired of waiting. "Are you upset about something that
girl said?"

"No. It's just that people are starting to realize I'm here. I've had a
great time the last few days. You and your friends have treated Diego,
my sister, and me like we've known each other for ages."

He glanced at the table where the girl was sitting. She was eyeing
him and dishing with her companions. "Sometimes things get com-
plicated." He looked at Lyle, not wanting to continue but needing to
explain. "My face ends up on the cover of magazines that shouldn't be
in print. They say things that shouldn't be said, lies. Sometimes they

get the story right, even though it's no one's business. My life is on the front page. I just need to be careful."

"It would only take the *impression* of something going on to cause trouble for me. A picture on a dance floor. An overheard conversation. Stories could be made, leading questions asked, over innocent things." He paused. "I was totally blown away when I was asked to play John Magnum. And now we might be up for some big awards. It was just released, but it's making a ton of money and getting kick-ass reviews. All eyes are on me. There's some talk of an Academy award. Best actor. I can't screw this up."

Was Michael ending it between them? Lyle felt a wave of worry then realized how meaningless that was; there wasn't anything to end. "Fans can be fickle," she said. "If they're suspicious that you're dating me, an older woman, they could turn on you. I'd never forgive myself if I did anything to hurt your career." She remembered last night, dancing so closely, the innocent kisses on the cheek. "I'd totally understand if you—"

"No! Please don't say it. We're not changing anything!" He glanced at the other diners and quieted his voice. "I just think it would be a better idea if we spent our time together out of the spotlight. I loved dancing with you last night, and you know I want to spend more time with you. We just need to be more mindful of who's around."

"Maybe the rumor Natalie started about me being your manager will sustain for a while. That should keep any gossip to a minimum." Lyle heard the hope in her voice.

He touched the back of her hand with his finger. "Let's go get lost sixty feet below. No one will find us there, and I still have a juvenile yellowtail damselfish to find."

As they walked through the crowded restaurant, Lyle couldn't stop herself from scanning the room.

"Are you okay? You look a little pale."

"I'm sure I saw that man here at breakfast earlier this week. I just wonder why I haven't seen him again."

"I won't let him near you again. You're safe with me. He's probably holed up in his room, considering what I did to his face."

Twenty-Three

They drove down the island to another popular site. Angel City was a double reef—two individual reefs ran perpendicular north and south along the island's coast. The vast topography created a location where divers could spend an entire morning and never see the same area twice.

After completing the long routine of putting on gear, Michael checked Lyle's air to be sure it was on and working properly. She did the same for him. The sun glistened off the surface of the water, and a tranquil breeze came in over the coral beach. They entered the warm ocean water and leisurely swam out to the buoy marking the reef below them.

Lyle held her mouthpiece up out of the water. "We'll descend and check the current, then you're in charge. I'll follow along with you."

"I'm in charge? You're passing the torch?"

She splashed water at him, and he lunged for her. He grabbed her and held her in a death grip. He wrapped his legs around her and wouldn't let go. She fought back, trying to dunk him under the water, and he did his best to soak her.

"You're drowning me!" She laughed and splashed more water at him. He captured her arms in a bear hug, trying to keep her from splashing him more. They both floated easily above the water; with their BCs filled with air, it would be impossible to sink. "We're not going anywhere attached together like this!"

He let go with his legs but held her close with his arms wrapped around her. His face was inches from hers. "Put on your mask and try to keep up." He pointed his thumb toward the water, and they vanished together below the surface.

As they sank, they watched their depth displayed on their computers. At ten feet below the surface, they released air from their BCs to aid in their descent. At twenty feet, Lyle caught Michael watching her and gestured for him to watch his computer. As they approached the thirty-foot mark, the top of the reef could be seen below them. At forty feet, she glanced at Michael, who was again looking at her. They exchanged a shy smile, each having been caught watching the other. At fifty feet, they hovered above the colorful reef teeming with different schools of fish.

Angel City was properly named. An abundance of brightly colored angelfish swam over the reef. Michael pointed to a French angelfish that seemed to spend as much time putting on its makeup as Angela. Its lips were painted white, and the eyeshadow an attractive yellow. Its dark body, highlighted by scales rimmed with gold, was bigger than a dinner plate and about the same shape. It showed some curiosity, swimming cautiously along with the divers, but eventually lost interest and disappeared into the coral.

They floated weightlessly through the clear, silent water. They spotted several rock beauties swimming among the different species of coral. The contrast of their glowing neon yellow scales on their heads and tails and the velvety black scales that covered the rest of their bodies made them real standouts to divers.

Lyle was swimming just behind Michael when he suddenly pulled up and turned to look for her. She could see by his eyes he had spotted something he was excited about. He backed away from the reef until he was floating upright in front of her then extended his arm and pointed to a spot in the coral. She hovered behind his tank to better see his point of view.

There, in the coral, head held high and small eyes looking right at them, was a green moray eel. It held its mouth open, displaying a long row of sharp teeth. Its bright green body was eye-catching. It looked soft and as inviting as a velvet blanket. She had seen several species of moray eels, as they were abundant in the reefs of Bonaire, varying in both color and size. Their inimitable beauty, combined with their eerie appearance and undue reputation of being aggressive, made them one of her favorite finds. Being sedentary creatures, they were easy to study, unlike the small fish that darted in and out of the coral.

The eel didn't like being exposed to such large creatures—the divers—and swam down the reef. Its single dorsal fin ran the entire length of its body and moved like a lime green ribbon in a gymnastic dance. Soon it was out of sight.

The dive continued at a relaxing pace, both divers spotting unique fish and coral. After forty-five minutes, their computers told them it was time to turn back. Michael used his compass to find their entry point, and they swam to shore. Lyle carried her fins in one hand and mask and snorkel in the other as they walked out of the water.

She stopped and looked back at the ocean. She marveled at the wonders they had just seen hidden under the surface. "I believe that when I die and go to heaven, I'll be here, diving at Angel City."

Michael was surprised by the sentimental statement. "I thought heaven was in the clouds. How can you be so sure there will be an ocean?"

Lyle looked out over the wide expanse of water. "If it's truly heaven, there will be an ocean there."

They stayed at Angel City and dove both the inner and outer reef. The farther reef was covered with a multitude of corals. Golden elkhorn mixed with purple sea fans and fuzzy pillar coral created an undersea forest. Michael watched the purple horn coral, taller than he was, as it shifted gently with the current as he floated by. The massive but delicate elephant ear appeared to be made of fine lace.

They moved weightlessly over and through a land of shapes and colors that only an accomplished artist could have produced. They swam between huge formations of coral in a kaleidoscopic scene not witnessed anywhere else on Earth. But all of it was real, there under the waves and beyond the surf. All hidden from human eyes.

Eventually, it was time to leave, and they swam toward the shore, the digital displays on their computers moving gradually from fifty to forty to thirty feet. They hovered when they reached fifteen feet. As a safety precaution, they waited there for three minutes to allow their bodies to burn off accumulated nitrogen.

They emerged from the ocean, salt water running down their faces and pouring off them like a river to the coral at their feet. They had depleted their air cylinders.

"How about a swim?" asked Lyle. "I mean a real swim. Just suits. No magical equipment."

The ocean water felt wonderful against their skin. Without all the heavy gear, they moved easily through the water. They raced each other out to the floating reef marker and back until Michael conceded Lyle was the faster swimmer. When other divers arrived at Angel City, they kept a safe distance from them, either by staying in the truck or swimming in the shallow waters.

They were getting hungry. Not wanting their time together to end, they stopped at an ice cream shop in town and ordered chocolate cones. They sat at a small table outside the parlor.

"What would you think of going out on the *Mi Dushi* again tomorrow?" said Michael.

"Great idea."

With no other tasks to delay them, they pulled the truck into Bon Adventure. They stopped at the registration desk and added their names to the list of guests to set sail on the *Mi Dushi* the next morning.

"Will you have dinner with me tonight?" said Michael.

"Sure. I'll meet you at the pool bar."

"No, not the pool bar. I have an idea how we can have an evening together out of sight of unwanted guests." Just as he finished his thought, two girls approached him. He stood as their mother posed them and took picture after picture. He was uber-polite and struck what Lyle was beginning to recognize as his standard pose. The mother seemed just as excited to be in his company.

"Excuse me," said Lyle to the mother. "Would you like me to get a picture of you with Michael?" It bothered her a little that the mom looked to be about the same age as she. The woman handed over her phone and stood with Michael.

The three left but had attracted the attention of another group of fans, and the process started all over again.

When the third group was satisfied with their pictures, Michael was able to make a polite exit. He walked with Lyle back toward the rooms. "I'll pick you up at seven. What room are you in?"

"Building one, room 2A. See you at seven."

He called after her, "Plan on very casual. Shorts and a T-shirt."

"I like this idea better and better."

The ice cream they had didn't make up for the lunch they missed. Lyle walked to the dive shop to get a snack to tide her over until dinner. Chocolate bars were on special, two for the price of one, so she bought four. She left the dive shop and headed around the back of her building. A hammock lay empty in the shade between two trees.

She tossed her candy bars onto the white netting. She picked up a long rope that was secured to a tree several feet away from the hammock then took off her shoes and sat down. She tied the end of the soft rope loosely around her ankle and laid back, feeling the lump of candy bars between her shoulders. She hung her ankle lazily over the side of the hammock and pulled the rope, rocking the hammock back and forth.

She found a candy bar and tore it open. She slid the wrapper down and took a mouthful of the delicious chocolate. She chewed slowly, letting it melt into a soft puddle in her mouth. She swirled her tongue around it and swallowed. "Mmm, chocolate."

The lora in the trees sang a sweet song, and Lyle closed her eyes.

Twenty-Four

At seven sharp, there was a knock at Lyle's door. She pulled it open, and there stood Michael, with his hair still damp and dancing around his head in no particular style. His bright hazel eyes were only outmatched by her own. He had on a pair of well-worn jeans and a short-sleeved shirt. She liked the way he had left several buttons undone. He held a pizza box high at his head as a waiter would and gripped a six-pack of Dive O'Clock, a local beer, in his other hand.

She held the door open wide then cleared off the coffee table and gestured for him to put the pizza down there.

"Nice room. I'm staying in a place that looks remarkably similar." He smiled at his own bad joke.

"Michael, thank you. This is great. A quiet night in is just what I need. A nice ending to a fantastic day." She slid the patio doors open, and a cool breeze filled the room. "What if we sit out here? It overlooks the courtyard, so there's minimal foot traffic." She tried to be more conscious of his exposure to the public since his comments at breakfast that morning. "Or would you be more comfortable inside?"

He grabbed two beers and nodded toward the balcony. "Let's sit outside. Lord knows we could use some fresh air. And I'm glad to hear you think today was so nice."

They sat in deep wicker chairs. He opened both beers and handed one to her. The courtyard was surrounded by three other buildings. The trees were tall and full of greenery, any view was obscured. She balanced a slice of pizza in her hand and managed a large bite. The hot cheese and warm crust melted in her mouth. The beer had just the right amount of hops and she closed her eyes as she swallowed it down. They each ate two pieces of pizza in relative silence.

"Nice job finding that moray," she said. "I was hoping we'd see one this vacation."

"Did you see it threatening me? It kept opening and closing its mouth. At least I had the good sense to move away."

She tried to hide her amusement. "The eel wasn't threatening you. They open and close their jaws to move water over their gills. It was just breathing."

"Oh, so those razor-sharp teeth are nothing to worry about?"

"Well, you only saw some of its teeth. The moray has two sets of jaws. The sharp teeth you saw are used to catch its prey." She put her beer between her knees. "Once the prey is caught, a second set of jaws that are deeper in the esophagus are thrown forward, helping to pull the prey down." She motioned with her fingers and hands trying to replicate what that might look like. "It's called a pharyngeal jaw."

"That's straight out of a horror movie."

"I'm not afraid of the big bad eel."

"I know," he said quietly. "You're not afraid of anything."

"I was afraid the other night." She glanced at him. "You saved me from something I can't even bear to think about."

A knock at the door interrupted the conversation. Lyle got up and went to answer it.

Standing at her door was Angela. "I saw Michael come this way with a pizza. Mind if I grab a slice?" She walked in before Lyle had a chance to respond and spotted the pizza on the coffee table.

Michael stood in the glass doorway and tried to hide his annoyance.

"Hi, Michael. Haven't seen you all day." She took a piece of pizza out of the box and sat on the love seat. "Where have you guys been?" But before they could answer her first question, she asked another. "A beer would really hit the spot. Do you have another one?"

Michael opened a bottle and handed it to her. He sat in the club chair, and Lyle perched on the arm next to him.

Lyle didn't remember inviting her in. "We spent the day at Angel City. No one showed up at breakfast, so we took off."

"Angel City is one of my favorites. You'll have to tell me what you saw." She took a bite of pizza and spoke with her mouth full. "Victoria should be on her way. I ran into her a few minutes ago. She thought pizza sounded good."

Just then, a knock at the door. Lyle opened it and wasn't surprised to see Victoria. She was leaning over the railing, yelling down to Rick and Steve, standing below. "Pick up more pizza and beer and meet us in Lyle's room. We're staying in tonight." She turned to see Lyle behind her. "You don't mind if I invite the boys, do you? They've been at the bar and should really have something to eat."

Six people had now squeezed into the room. Rick brought an extra pizza and more beer, and Steve picked up chicken wings from the pool bar. It was every man for himself, finding a place to eat, and balancing a beer and a slice of pizza at the same time.

"I can't help but notice our new friends from last night haven't joined us." Victoria looked from Rick to Angela.

Recalling Rick kissing Lyle, Michael took a shot at him. "Rick, where's Jeanette tonight? Out looking for a better fuck?" A bit of tension seeped in the room.

"It's none of your business." Rick took a long drink of his third beer, unwilling to share anything about his evening with Jeanette.

Victoria lightly nudged Angela. "And where's Cameron this evening?"

Angela became animated as she talked about her night. "I'm afraid Cameron didn't quite live up to my expectations. You know what I mean?"

"No fireworks in bed?" asked Victoria.

Lyle noticed Michael shift his weight. They all saw where this conversation was going.

"So here I am on this incredible Caribbean Island," Angela began. "This guy I'm with is just fumbling around under the sheets, clueless. He was making moves like a frogman in a blender!"

Michael shifted a second time.

"They should at least be required to read a book or something. Lyle, what you said in the truck the other day was right on. These guys in their twenties don't have a clue. Why does a man have to reach his late thirties, early forties to figure out what a woman wants in bed? I hate to think I have to date a dinosaur to find any satisfaction."

Lyle became very interested in her beer and scratched at the label. But Angela wasn't finished yet.

"I really think Lyle's book idea is good. Cameron could've used it last night. One with pictures and diagrams and little arrows pointing at the right spots."

Rick grinned at Lyle. "I think I've had women figured out for quite a while now." The beer was clearly talking. "Lyle never asked me to read a book on how to have sex."

"Rick!" Victoria exclaimed, "That's enough."

He took another drink. "All I'm saying is, I know all of Lyle's right spots, no diagram needed." He pointed his thumb at his chest. "She's a sure thing in my hands."

Michael noticeably stiffened.

"Be careful what you're saying," Victoria said with a warning in her voice. "Remember who you're talking to."

Rick took a long drink and finished his beer then stood to leave. "So, we'll meet at breakfast and load up the trucks. I heard a rumor the salt pier is back open to divers. We should take a drive down there and check it out."

Michael shot at Rick: "Lyle and I are going out on the *Mi Dushi* tomorrow. We'll get our own breakfast. And don't count on us the rest of the day either. We need a break from you, old man."

"We booked it without you guys because I know you're not crazy about diving on the boat," Lyle said.

"You disappeared on us today, and now you already have plans for tomorrow?" His dark hair stayed in place, his designer clothes were neatly pressed, his shirt tail was tucked into his belted waist, but Rick MacLean was coming undone.

Victoria jumped in. "Rick, you weren't ready to dive today until after lunch. Lyle just—"

"I know. I know. It was just easier when we didn't have so many peo-ple to organize." Rick glowered at Michael, then shifted his focus to Lyle.

"Are you Michael's private scuba instructor now? Is he paying you for your time? For Christ's sake Lyle, I know you're lonely after our breakup, but don't you see? Behind all the fame he's just a snotty-nosed kid."

Michael lunged at Rick. Lyle grabbed ahold of his shirt and pulled, only to have the fabric rip out of her hand.

Michael clenched the front of Rick's shirt with his fists. "You son of a bitch," he growled, then pushed Rick backward and rammed him against the wall, knocking over the club chair and spilling half-empty beers. "I'll show you who's a kid."

Steve jumped to his feet and swung his arms around Michael and pulled him off of Rick. He stood between the two and placed his hands on Michael's chest. "Michael, I'm an old man. I know I can't hold you here forever, buddy. You don't want to do this. Just take a breath, and let's all calm down."

Michael looked past Steve at his target. He knew a fight in these tight quarters was a bad idea, so he held his hands up in surrender and stepped back.

Lyle walked out onto the balcony, hoping to find solace alone in the night.

"Rick, why don't you walk out with me?" said Steve. "It's getting late, buddy. We could all use some rest."

Angela joined Lyle outside and gave her a hug. "He's being a total butt tonight. Just ignore him. You know he didn't mean the things he said." She gave her a pitying look and went back inside.

Victoria came out and hugged her as well. "Rick's completely out of line. For what it's worth, I've never seen him drink like this. There must be something troubling him. It's no excuse, I know. He certainly wouldn't have said those things otherwise. I know he'll feel horrible about it in the morning. Can you forgive him?"

Lyle nodded to appease her. The things Rick said were not easily forgiven, nor easily forgotten. She waited on the balcony to be sure her friends had left. She couldn't remember a time she ever wanted to be free of them.

Michael stepped outside and put his hand on her back. "Lyle—"

"Please go. It's late."

He raked his hand through his hair. "No, don't do this. I won't leave you tonight while you're upset with me."

Rick's words screamed in her head. *He's just a kid.*

"Damn it, Lyle! Look at me!" He composed himself. "We need to talk. I won't let this day end like this."

"What the hell was that? You let the comments of a drunk man push your buttons? You thought you had to attack him?"

"He was talking shit about you! He made you sound like a whore. The bastard was asking for it. I just reacted. I wasn't thinking. I'm sorry."

Lyle went back inside and gathered empty bottles and paper plates.

Michael righted the overturned chair. "Rick can say all he wants. He's so jealous. He's still in love with you, he wants you back. But remember, he left you. He blew his chance. You're free to see who you want." He added sheepishly, "Even some snotty nosed kid."

Lyle put the last of the trash in the can. "I don't know what's up with him. That was all very out of character. And please," she said looking at him, "don't feel you need to defend me. I'm tougher than that."

He placed his palms on her shoulders. "We're not done having fun yet," he said, touching her nose with his. "I want us to have more days like today. Nothing Rick says is going to change that."

He kissed her cheek and inhaled the flowery smell of her and ran his hand down her back. He dropped his voice and spoke in her ear. "I wanted to beat the shit out of him for those things he said about you."

Since dancing together they hadn't been this close. He was nice and warm, and Lyle liked the way he ran his fingers up and down her back. The closeness of his body and his warm breath near her ear tantalized her.

He whispered, "Angela's right. Knowing what women want in bed. I'm clueless. I've been with a lot of women. I must say I'm always completely satisfied." He flushed with mortification. "But the women, I don't know. I know they want to sleep with me because of who I am. But I wonder…I wonder if they talk about me the way…the way Angela was talking about Cameron."

Michael spoke the raw truth. Such uncharacteristic embarrassment in his voice that Lyle knew it was paining him to say it. Angela's rant and Rick's mean words hit home. Now Michael was questioning his sexual abilities.

"Angela was in bed last night with a complete stranger," she said, and held his face in her hands, forcing him to look at her. "When you love someone, it's different. When you completely trust who you're with, you aren't afraid to tell them what you like, what you want."

He looked at her with such expectation, she went on. "When you love someone, that love will go with you into the bedroom. It's a powerful thing. Feeling completely safe and protected is very powerful."

"Will you show me?" he asked.

"Let's start with the first kiss," she whispered.

Twenty-Five

"Fucking finally." Michael pulled her close and tightened his arms around her. He leaned toward Lyle and tilted his head. At last, he had permission to kiss her.

"No." She placed her palms on his chest and pushed him away. "It has to be slow."

He gave one quick nod and looked from her eyes to her lips. He moved toward her again. She stopped him a second time. "Slower."

Before he dared to try again, he considered his best approach. Going straight in for the kiss was getting him nowhere. *Why was he not breathing? Breath Michael, think.* Each movement became unhurried and deliberate. He touched her nose with the side of his nose then stopped. He waited for her to push him away. He slid his nose slowly to rest on her cheek and stopped there and waited yet again. He took a deep breath, inhaling the intoxicating scent of her, and closed his eyes.

He exhaled with a shutter then risked touching his lips to the corner of her mouth. He stilled, so close. Then, brushing his lips back and forth so minutely, he hardly moved them at all. He waited there, lips so close. Certainly, she heard his heart thumping.

He slid his hands under her top and ran them up and down her back. He found her parted lips but paused there, controlling himself, willing himself not to move. The feel of her soft lips, her warm breath, his hands on her skin was testing all self-control. His pulse pounded as he struggled to wait there. His body responded to the closeness of her. He fought his urge to end this game and take her then and there. He rested his forehead on hers and whispered, "You're trembling."

"Am I?"

"Do you want me to kiss you now?"

Breathless, she panted, "Yes, now."

Michael was finally granted permission to kiss the woman he had been fantasizing about both in his waking hours and in his dreams. Lyle had consumed his thoughts and starred in his daydreams for far too long now. His lips devoured hers as he pressed himself close and his dreams were realized.

Lyle held the back of Michael's head. She explored his lips and tongue. Soon they fell into a rhythm that drove faster and faster. There was nothing slow about the way Lyle kissed Michael.

She gradually ended the kiss and looked timidly up at him.

"Michael," she said reluctantly, "I don't have a young body anymore. I'm not like the women you're used to seeing. I'm forty-two, and I… I just don't know if you—"

"Shhh." He touched her lips with his finger. "How can you doubt that I want you? You must know that. Trust this, Lyle. You amaze me. You surprise me at every turn. I want you. I've wanted you since the day we first met."

"Tell me what I can do to make you happy," he said. "I want you completely satisfied." He pulled her top off over her head and tossed it to the ground. "We can draw pictures if it'll help." They both giggled.

She opened the last few buttons on his shirt and slid it off his shoulders. He kissed her chest and ran his tongue over her sensitive skin. His warm, moist kisses on her breasts excited her. She held his face in her hands, encouraging him to continue, and let out a low groan then began to undo her shorts.

He watched her as she ran the zipper down her shorts. She wiggled her hips to work them down and let them fall to the floor. She stood in white lace panties and smiled shyly up at him. He kissed her neck. His hands traveled down her back, and he groped her ass.

She found the button and zipper on his jeans and opened his pants. She dropped her hands inside and grinned when she discovered he wasn't wearing any underwear. There was no doubt he was ready for her.

"Lyle, please." He placed kisses on her neck and down to her breasts. The foreplay was driving him, fueling his arousal. He became more insistent and she completely relaxed into his aggressive assault. She swayed as he explored her body. He needed to take her. His pulse drummed and his body ached. He turned to lay her on the bed.

"No, Michael, not yet" she said, breathing heavily.

"Lyle, please, I…"

"I know you're ready, and I'm excited for our first time too, but for me, it's more of a slow burn." She slid her panties down to her ankles. She hooked them on her toes and tossed them aside.

He kissed her and knelt, brushing the soft skin of her stomach and fondling her ass, pulling her to him.

He searched her body, and she inhaled sharply as he discovered her. She threw her head back and closed her eyes. Soon she was fighting for air. She arched her back and took deep breaths, but still, she was unable to get enough air. Her breathlessness excited him, and he became unrelenting, holding her and teasing her, pushing her on. She fought for each breath as waves pulsed up and down her body. She cried out. Her body tensed and then went limp.

She dropped to her knees and held his face between her hands. She kissed him sweetly as a low thrum silently beat deep within her. She could feel his urgency and wanted to satisfy him as completely as he had pleased her.

He lifted her and placed her on the bed. He watched his hand as he ran it down her thigh, then slid his fingers behind her knee and positioned it to the side. He covered her entirely with his body.

"Slower."

"I can't." He moved relentlessly, taking Lyle fully, pulling the satisfaction from her that he had once only dreamed of.

She wrapped her legs around him. Her blood boiled as tiny sparks turned to burning flames, and she groaned as the fire consumed her once again.

His body stiffened. His arms tightened around her as he found his release. He then fell limp, collapsing on top of her.

They lay under the comforter, heads on the billowy pillows facing each other. Satisfied and snug in the bed with Michael, Lyle felt ridiculous for ever questioned the two of them together. They were quintessential friends and now perfect lovers.

"Women I date may be younger than you," he began. "That doesn't make them more attractive to me. Fake boobs that don't move, glued-on eyelashes, and hair extensions. Yes, they're stunners, but it's like having sex with a damned mannequin." They snickered. "For days I've been dreaming of touching you, fucking you," he blushed. "You finally gave me permission and all I can think is when do I get to fuck you again?" They giggled. "I've never met anyone as much an enigma as you. You're a mystery and I can't wait to discover more about you."

"Thank you, Michael. I needed to hear that. I worried about…" She let the thought trail off. "I better set the alarm. It's getting late and we have a boat to catch in the morning." She tapped on her phone screen.

"What's this?" he snatched the phone from her, "I thought you had a strict no-phone policy. Unplugged, remember?" He raised his eyebrows, sure he had caught her cheating.

"I only use it as an alarm clock and for my music. I've made no phone calls or gotten online since landing on Bonaire. Now give it back to me."

He tapped on the screen.

"Who are you calling?"

Once his phone started ringing from the pocket of his jeans on the floor, he ended the call. "Now I have your contact information as a missed call." He tapped on the screen again. "Now I'm in your contact list."

She tried to take her phone back but he rolled away from her. "Hang on, let me pick my ringtone."

When he returned the phone to her, the time flashed on the screen. "Shit, it's almost three o'clock. We've got to get some sleep." She returned it to the nightstand and climbed over him to turn off the lamp. He caught her by her hips and refused to let her go. She put up only a little fight then gave him a slow, deep kiss. "We should really get some sleep."

"I'm not tired yet."

He suckled her breast with his lips and tongue. She gasped and watched as he moved his mouth over her. She felt his body harden and marveled at the benefits of having a younger lover.

"Just relax," she growled. "I'll take care of this."

Twenty-Six

They managed three hours of sleep before the alarm went off at seven. Lyle struggled to sit up and silence it, but she was trapped under Michael and couldn't move. His leg was thrown over her, and his arm rested across her chest.

"Fuck me," she whispered. She had a headache and a slight buzzing in her ears. She hadn't had enough to drink the night before to cause a hangover; she had two beers with her pizza, but that was early in the evening. She attributed her unpleasant state to a lack of sleep.

The alarm continued to sound, but Michael didn't seem to hear it. Lyle looked at his chiseled face resting on the pillow next to hers. His hair was tossed about the pillow, his lips slightly parted. His breathing continued at a slow, even pace. She hated to wake him. She couldn't help but trace her finger over his cheek and down to the corner of his mouth. He looked so peaceful while sleeping, having left his angst back in the conscious world.

"Michael." She ran her finger over the tip of his nose. "It's seven." She traced his lower lip, back and forth. "Time to wake up."

He caught her finger between his teeth, gently biting it, then closed his lips around it. He still hadn't moved or opened his eyes. The alarm continued to sound.

"Give me my finger back." She wiggled it in his mouth.

He grinned, her finger securely between his teeth.

"A green moray has my finger."

He released her only to roll over on top of her. He nuzzled his nose in her messy hair and ran his hands over her. She closed her eyes and

144

was tempted to ignore the alarm. She thought of Captain Maartin, wondering where his divers were, and stopped Michael's advances before they went any further.

"We have a boat to catch. We need to be on the dock in forty-five minutes." She painstakingly untangled herself from him and turned off the alarm.

He followed her across the bed. He kissed her neck and ear and trailed his hand down between her legs.

She moved out of reach and sat naked at the foot of the bed. "I feel like I have a hangover." She stretched her arms over her head and twisted left then right. She looked over her shoulder at Michael, who was admiring her with his eyes only half open.

"Or we could just stay in bed all day," he said, his voice scratchy and low.

"Or we could go diving and then come back here and spend the evening together. Haven't you had enough?"

He lifted the sheet and peeked at himself. "No, I haven't had enough. Come back here."

"I'm going to shower."

Lyle studied herself in the mirror. After a long night of lovemaking, her cheeks were rosy, and her eyes sparkled. She ran her hands over her breasts, where small red marks caught her attention. Double crescent moons were imprinted on her. She leaned in closer to the mirror, remembering the feel of Michael's teeth on her and how she had enjoyed the aggressive foreplay. She looked at her glowing face. She wouldn't have changed a thing about the previous night. It had been exhilarating and he had more than satiated her.

Once showered, he went to his room for his bathing suit and new clothes. They agreed to meet at the lockers to gather their equipment, and then board the boat together.

As Lyle stepped into her bathing suit, her toes got hung up in the stretchy fabric. After a few futile hops to try to regain her balance, she fell back against the bed and slid down onto the floor. She grunted then carefully worked her feet into the suit. She covered up with a tank top and shorts then slid her feet into flip-flops and glanced at the time. If she left now, she could grab a coffee before heading to the boat.

She held her arm up across her forehead, in an attempt to block the rising sun from her eyes and walked toward the breakfast patio with one goal in mind. Early-morning activities were going on all around her, but her sole focus was on getting a cup of coffee.

She tripped in the gravel and stubbed her toe. "Damn it." She ignored the sting, repositioned her foot in the sandal, and continued on. Someone was walking next to her. Still groggy, she didn't realize they were trying to get her attention.

Rick had fallen into step with her. "Are you going to ignore me the rest of this vacation?" He stopped in front of her, blocking her path. "At least give me a chance to apologize. I feel awful about last night. Can we sit and talk for a minute?"

"Not now. I'm trying to make the boat." Lyle peered around him to the patio. "I need to grab some coffee first." She walked past him; she didn't have time for this discussion and wasn't in the forgiving mood.

"We need to talk about this. We need to talk about what happened last night," he implored. "He's young, and he's like an explosive with a very delicate tripwire. You saw what happened last night."

She stopped and turned to face him. "Are you kidding me with this? It's none of your business. After your embarrassing show last night, I really don't feel like talking to you. How could you say those things in front of our friends?" She continued on her way and yelled over her shoulder, "I can't do this right now!"

She focused on walking straight ahead. His words were jumbled in her thoughts. Had she just made the biggest mistake of her life? She slept with Michael Miller. He was totally wrong for her. A torrid affair was clearly an inappropriate thing between a woman of forty-two and a young star with a hair-trigger temper. She rubbed her eyes and decided she would have to sort all this out later. She was having trouble thinking straight and still had an entire day of diving to get through.

She glanced at the crowd on the patio and the small line at the coffee station. She didn't have time to maneuver through them and wait in line. Deflated, she passed by the patio and walked down the stairs that led to the lockers and boat dock.

"Lyle." Michael was standing a few feet from her, wearing a ball cap low on his forehead. She had ambled right past without seeing him. His equipment was stowed on the boat already. He handed her a cup. "I thought you might like some coffee before we get started. I'll get your gear and meet you at the boat." She handed him the key to her locker.

"You're a lifesaver, thank you." She took a sip. Cream and sugar, just the way she liked it. She took a long swallow and willed it to snap her out of her daze.

Waiting for Michael by the boat, she tried to stay out of the way as several people boarded. Calypso sniffed her and plopped down by her feet to be petted. Lyle didn't see the dog, and soon she gave up and trotted off.

Michael returned with his arms full of Lyle's gear, and they waited for their turn to board.

"How's the coffee?"

"Heavenly, thank you."

Captain Maartin stood on the boat deck and took the gear from Michael. He took a step back and motioned with his hand for Lyle to board first.

Two men approached and asked Michael for a photo. He graciously agreed and sparked an easy conversation with his fans. Lyle wondered idly what pose he would use when the fans were two men. She rubbed her eye and turned her attention back to Captain Maartin.

"Permission to come aboard, Captain?" She put an obligatory smile on her face.

"Goedemorgen. Welcome aboard, Lyle." He took her hand to help her board.

She tried to time her step with the rocking vessel. She placed her foot on the deck and hopped up, but her timing was off. Her foot slid out of her flip-flops, and her body propelled forward. Her coffee flew off to the side as she fell into the boat. She landed on her butt, almost taking Captain Maartin with her.

"Lyle! Flip-flops on my boat?" He looked at her feet while she sat, baffled, on the deck. She knew she had committed a major infraction. She didn't remember choosing to put on flip-flops. "Since when are they a good idea on my boat? What are you thinking?" He extended his hand and helped her to her feet. "Don't let an air cylinder fall on your foot—we're out all morning and there's no doctor onboard. And watch yourself on the hatch. I've seen that come down on people's feet." Satisfied that he had made his point, Captain Maartin glared at her and then went to help the other divers.

Michael climbed onboard. "Are you okay, baby?"

It came out of his mouth so naturally, Lyle immediately forgot about the fall. "I'm fine. Just my ass and my ego are bruised."

They put their gear down and organized their things.

"You better be careful, Michael. People could've heard you."

He looked around the boat, assessing the divers and staff. An Asian family placed their equipment on the bench across from them. He heard conversations in both German and French coming from their fellow divers.

"I love this island. It's so cosmopolitan—not everyone has heard of Michael Miller." He winked at her and asked boldly, "Is that okay with you, baby?"

As the *Mi Dushi* sailed toward Klein Bonaire, Francesca welcomed everyone and gave last-minute dive instructions. Walking around barefooted in her string bikini, she invited the divers to move about the boat during the thirty-minute ride. Several people shifted portside and starboard. They laughed as the mist soaked them and joked among themselves.

Michael leaned back against an uncomfortable row of air cylinders. "I may stay here and rest my eyes until we get there." He pulled his ball cap down low. "I'll get ready at Captain Maartin's ten-minute warning."

Lyle agreed it sounded like a good idea and rested her head back against a cylinder too. Sleep evaded her and she found herself staring straight ahead at nothing in particular. A woman sat down in her line of sight, but she simply stared at the woman's sunhat, too tired even to blink. The thimbleful of coffee she was able to drink had done little for her sleep-deprived state.

Francesca walked around the boat, answering questions and helping people with their equipment. She stopped in front of Lyle. "Are you feeling poorly?"

"Just a late night."

She nodded and continued on her way.

The *Mi Dushi* sped over the water. The other divers chatted up a storm, their excitement was palatable. But Michael dozed, and Lyle stared for the next thirty minutes.

"Ten minutes!" Captain Maartin yelled from the deck above.

They stood up to face the task of assembling gear. They fought with their wetsuits and fumbled with their equipment. Lyle couldn't remember a time when she found her gear so cumbersome. Ten minutes later, they were standing in line at the entry platform, where Captain Maartin was helping divers into the water.

Next thing they knew, Captain Maartin was checking her air valve. "No air? You forgot to turn on your air?" He turned the valve on. "What's up with you today?" He scolded her for the second time. "This is a beginner's mistake."

Her stomach churned. "Captain Maartin, please check Michael's air. I forgot to check it. I don't know if it's on or not."

Captain Maartin gnashed his teeth. "Move to the side, both of you. I can't let you two dive together. Francesca tells me you had a late night. I'll let you dive, but not with each other." He pointed to the benches behind them. "Have a seat."

Lyle capitulated to the captain's demand and sat down. Michael parked himself on the bench across from her. Captain Maartin was in charge. They had no other choice. She silently chastised herself for putting them both in danger. Michael was still a new diver. He should be able to count on his dive buddy not to fuck up so royally.

Twenty-Seven

The line of divers moved along between them, jumping in the ocean and descending two at a time. Lyle looked longingly at the clear blue water and couldn't wait to get in. It was just what she needed to wake her up.

As the queue came to an end, a family of four stopped and spoke briefly with the captain.

"Michelle," Captain Maartin said, "I have a diver here in need of someone to dive with. He's had a late night, so can you keep a close eye on him?" Michelle was in her early fifties and very athletic. Her blond hair was kept neatly under a neoprene headband.

She looked from Captain Maartin to Michael and answered in a heavy French accent. "Oh oui, yes, we'll dive with famous Michael Miller."

Michael stood to introduce himself.

Michelle's partner was her teenage daughter, Nicole. She had her mother's coloring and blushed at Michael as they shook hands. "John Magnum."

As Michael prepared to enter the water with his new dive group, he turned to Captain Maartin. "Captain, I trust you'll give the same instruction to Lyle's new partners. I wouldn't want anything to happen to her."

Captain Maartin helped Michael's group off the back of the boat and motioned toward the two remaining divers. "Let me introduce you to Michelle's husband and son, Peter and Bayard. They will keep a close eye on you."

"I'm afraid Captain Maartin feels I'm only operating on two cylinders." She wasn't sure how her slang would translate. "I'm Lyle Cooper."

Peter shook her hand. "We're glad to dive with you. I'm Peter. This is my son, Bayard." Peter's English seemed to flow easier than his wife's had.

Bayard, younger than his sister, could hardly stand still. "Allons-y!"

Captain Maartin checked their air and helped them to the entry platform.

Once in the water, the group gathered to discuss their dive plan. They agreed on a fifty-minute dive at a depth no greater than fifty feet. Peter took the lead, allowing Bayard and Lyle to follow along.

She fell easily into her routine of scanning the reef for interesting creatures and taking note of things she wasn't familiar with. She caught herself staring at a school of goatfish and realized she was falling behind. She saw Peter looking back, waiting for her to catch up. She swam quickly and was soon at their side.

The reef was alive and teeming with fish. She could hear a parrotfish pecking away at the coral, but she couldn't find where the sound was coming from. A school of butterfly fish swam by her, but she hardly noticed them.

Four large fish caught her attention. They were hovering in the water in front of her, daring her to cross their line.

The great barracuda lived up to its name. A long, narrow fish, it could move like an arrow through the water. When it opened its mouth, the teeth pointed in every direction like a broken barbed wire fence—some small and short, others long and jagged. If she was nervous about any of the ocean life, it was the great barracuda. She was told horrifying stories about them as a young child.

Lyle tried not to splash any water on the floor. Her school uniform was too big to wash easily in the bathroom sink, but they didn't have a washer or dryer in the trailer. She picked up a bar of soap and rubbed it into the heavy navy-blue fabric of her jumper, trying to wash away two weeks of spills and splashes from eating lunch in the cafeteria.

The heat in the trailer wasn't reliable, and her small hands were getting cold.

The fourth grade at Saint Mary's Elementary School had planned a trip to the zoo in Syracuse. She wanted her uniform to be clean for the special day. She was most excited to see the small aquarium. The ocean-life exhibit included sting rays, lionfish, and barracuda. The students had found pictures of barracuda showing off their menacing teeth. One classmate warned them not to fall in the barracuda tank—they'd be eaten alive.

A knock on the bathroom door startled her. "Lyle, what the hell are you doing in there? It sounds like you're flooding the place."

She didn't mind her mother's current boyfriend. He was better than some she had known. Her voice quivered from the cold. "I'm w-washing my uniform for t-tomorrow. Roy, is my mama home yet?"

"No, she ain't here. Hurry out of there. I picked up a hamburger and fries for you."

She sat on the toilet seat and used her fingernail to scrape at some stubborn apple sauce. The wet uniform had soaked the front of her pajamas, and she shivered. When she felt the uniform was as clean as she could get it, she draped it over a chair to dry and went to eat her dinner.

In the morning, another shiver ran through her as she slid the damp jumper over her head. It was the only uniform she had, and if she wanted to go to the zoo with her class—wet or not—she had to wear it.

Sister Meredith rapped her ruler on her desk to bring the fourth-grade class to order. The kids all scrambled to their desks and sat up straight with their hands folded in front of them.

"Lyle, come here, please."

Being singled out by the teacher was never a good thing. Lyle hesitated and looked around at her classmates. Twenty-four sets of eyes stared back. She walked to her teacher's desk as all eyes followed her.

"Lyle, who signed your permission slip?" She slid the paper forward so she could see the signature.

She whispered, "R-Roy."

Sister Meredith tapped her finger on the paper and asked loudly, "Who's Roy?"

"He's m-my mother's b-boyfriend. He lives with us," Lyle said, blushing.

"Well, he's not your guardian. He can't sign for you. Now I need to make plans for you to stay behind." The teacher looked at Lyle, who was visibly shaking. Her teeth were chattering, and she was having a hard time standing still. The nun softened her tone. "There's nothing to be afraid of."

"I'm not afraid. I'm cold."

Lyle dragged herself back to her desk, plopped down, and dropped her chin to her chest.

She felt an arm wrap around her shoulder. Dottie stood beside her, freckles speckling her nose, two braids over her shoulders with small red bows at the ends. Her face was filled with compassion, seldom realized by one so young. "Don't worry Crocodile. I'll stay behind with you."

Lyle jumped at the touch on her arm. She turned to see a stranger looking at her and whipped her head around, searching for Michael, only to see the vast open ocean before her. She tried to remember the last time she saw him on the dive. She spun in circles, looking for him with wild eyes. How could she have lost him? What if he had an emergency and needed her?

Peter grabbed her arm to stop her panic and get her attention. She recognized the face behind the mask and remembered where she was and who she was diving with. She scanned the water for the barracuda, but they were long gone.

He gave her the "okay" signal and waited until she replied with her own "okay." He then pointed at his computer and motioned for her to check hers. She read the numbers displayed on her screen.

She was currently at a depth of ninety-five feet, and her air was dangerously low. They had agreed to no more than fifty feet—somehow she had descended far beyond the limit.

He put his palms together and made the universal sign for "boat." He pointed over his shoulder, indicating its direction. They swam back as a group and hovered fifteen feet below the *Mi Dushi* to complete the three-minute safety stop. While waiting, Lyle took her last breath. She tried to breathe, but it was like trying to suck air out of an empty balloon. She was out of air. She grabbed Peter's arm and made a slashing movement across her throat. He immediately passed her his backup regulator. In all her years of diving, this was the first time she had ever run out of air. The most dangerous of diving mistakes.

Captain Maartin helped her out of the water and steadied her tank as she walked back to the bench. "How was the dive?"

"Wonderful," Lyle answered with a forced smile.

She calmed when she saw Michael's group coming out of the water. He sat next to her and began taking off his wetsuit.

"It wasn't as much fun without you. No peacock worms." He whispered into her ear, "I missed you." But instead of finding it romantic, she found it annoying and leaned away from him.

"I missed you too," said Lyle. "I was looking for you."

"What do you mean you were looking for me?" he asked, drying himself off with a towel.

She watched as Captain Maartin helped Peter climb back onboard. He stopped and talked quietly to the captain, looking at her as he spoke. She turned her attention back to her gear and started pulling off her boots.

"Lyle!" the captain yelled to her. He made a slashing motion with his hand. "You're done!"

"Fuck me." She snatched her boot off and threw it full force across the aisle. It hit an air cylinder and burst with a spray of water before it fell to the floor.

"What the hell happened down there?" Michael threw his towel down on the bench.

"I got distracted. I wasn't paying close enough attention." She leaned over and held her head in her hands.

"Don't be upset, we've got plenty more days to dive. Today's not our day. I don't know what happened down there, but from the captain's reaction, I'd guess it was serious." He pulled his T-shirt on. "We're done. Captain Maartin's a smart man, and we're following his orders." He started to disassemble his equipment. "We can spend the rest of the day on the sundeck."

"Fuck me." She threw her second boot with less effort. It plopped on the deck and landed in a puddle.

They grabbed beach towels and climbed the ladder to the sundeck. They spread their towels on the boat's bow and laid down side by side.

Captain Maartin took roll call to make sure no diver was left behind then started the *Mi Dushi* and drove to the next reef. The hum of the boat's engines and the warmth of the sun were too much for them. They soon fell fast asleep.

Twenty-Eight

Lyle heard people raving over their dives, and she opened her eyes. Michael saw her stirring. "Hey baby, feeling better?"

She stretched her arms and legs and looked around. "Can I get back to you on that? Where are we?"

"We're heading back to Bon Adventure. It's almost three o'clock. You slept the whole day."

She sat up. "I'm sorry. I was so tired I couldn't keep my eyes open. I actually do feel more human though."

"Don't worry about it. I woke up about thirty minutes ago." He noticed they were quickly approaching the island. "We should get our stuff together and be ready to disembark."

Once they docked and put all their things away, they headed up the stairs. They walked past the empty restaurant and by the pool bar. Realizing their rooms were in different directions, they stopped. Michael kept a safe distance from her lest any curious onlooker think there was something going on between them.

"Do you have plans for the rest of your day?" she asked.

"I thought I should spend tonight with Natalie and Diego. Their flight leaves early in the morning."

"Why are they leaving so soon?"

"We only planned to stay a week."

Her heart sank. "You're leaving tomorrow?"

"Well, I was. Two days ago, I extended my stay. By the looks of you, you're glad I did." He started toward his room. "I'll pick you up at seven."

She climbed the steps to her second-floor room and started down the short walkway—and stopped. Rick was leaning against the railing outside her door.

"Rick, what are you doing here? Why aren't you out diving?" She fished her room key out of her shorts pocket and slid it into the lock.

"I dove this morning with everyone—everyone but you. I saw the *Mi Dushi* pull into the dock and thought I'd meet you here." He followed her into the room. "I was hoping we could talk." He slid open the balcony doors. "Will you sit with me?"

"Sure, we can do that. Do you mind if I shower first? I've been out on the boat all day."

"Take all the time you need. I'll wait out here."

As she turned off the water and stepped out of the shower, she realized she hadn't brought her clothes in, so she wrapped a towel around herself and went to the dresser. She saw Rick look over his shoulder at her, but he quickly returned his gaze to the courtyard. That was the Rick she knew. He was a gentleman and a friend, and she hoped he was back to stay.

She chose her clothes knowing she would be going to dinner with Michael, Natalie, and Diego. She put on a pretty lime-green top with embroidered flowers and a pair of shorts. She brushed her hair and teeth and applied moisturizer to her too-tanned face then joined Rick on the balcony.

Her feelings for him were surprisingly neutral. Wanting to get this little talk over with, she decided she'd appease him for now and worry about him later.

He broke the silence. "I love the parrots in the trees here. When I see them, I always think someone's pet got loose." He grinned at her, hoping for a response. When he got none, he continued. "I didn't mean to make you mad this morning. I didn't realize you were in such a rush to get to the boat." She remained silent. They heard muffled voices coming from the hammock below. "Am I getting the silent treatment?"

"No, no silent treatment. I'm just thinking." Having him at a disadvantage made her bold. "You'll never know how crushed I was when you broke it off with me. You've never told me why you did it, why you ended it. I thought we were great together. I kept trying to think of what I'd done or what I'd said to make you walk away."

"At the time," he explained. "I thought it was the best thing for us. I thought we'd be better as friends."

"That's not much of an explanation."

"Seeing you here, on this island, watching Michael Miller flirt with you every day has been tough on me," said Rick. "He's infatuated with you. Instead of being shocked by it, I should've seen it coming. Can I apologize for my behavior last night? I had no business saying the things I did. It was mean and embarrassing for everyone, including myself."

She acknowledged the sincerity in his voice. This was the Rick she had fallen in love with.

"The truth is, I like Michael. He's a lot of fun to be around when he's not trying to take my head off. This doesn't mean I don't have concerns about his temper. He's hot-headed. He reacts first and thinks afterward."

"Well, soon we'll all board an airplane back to reality, and any concerns you have about him will be left behind," she said.

"I guess you're right," agreed Rick. "He's only a temporary problem."

His comment pulled at her heartstrings, and she cringed.

"Remember, when we get back to Raleigh, you and I have some things to work out. I won't apologize for my actions the other night—I'm not sorry I came to your room. I am sorry I failed to seduce you. But I do understand your concern about my intentions—this island can make someone do things they otherwise wouldn't." He stood to leave. "I'm supposed to meet Steve for a trip into town. I just wanted you to know how sorry I am. It's been bothering me all day."

They stopped at her door, and he kissed her on her forehead. "Do you know what room Michael is staying in? I owe him an apology too."

"I don't know where he's staying. I think it's one of the buildings behind the volleyball court."

She watched him walk down the stairs. He was so familiar to her, if they were ever to get back together, it would be effortless to pick up where they left off. It would be as though they were never apart at all.

She dug through her carry-on luggage and pulled out a book. She climbed into bed, opened the cover, and looked at the inscription written in green crayon. Dottie's name was fading over the years. Lyle turned to chapter one, when Dorothy was still safe and sound in Kansas. Disaster loomed on the horizon in the form of a tornado.

She finished the first chapter. Her eyes got heavy, and she gave in to sleep.

When Lyle woke again, she rolled onto her side and saw her book lying next to her. She placed it on the nightstand then got out of bed and stood in front of the mirror over her dresser. Her hair was a mess, and she had lines on her face from the pillowcase.

She glanced at the time. "Fuck me." She had twenty minutes before Michael would arrive. After a trip to the bathroom and painstakingly brushing through her hair, she reassessed herself. "Good enough."

She slid her feet into her sandals as a knock came at the door. She pulled it open to find Michael, Natalie, and Diego ready for dinner. Michael stepped inside and wrapped his arms around her waist and kissed her deeply. He touched her cheek. "I missed you. Did you have a restful afternoon?" He grinned at the messy blankets and pillows on the bed.

She blushed and looked at Natalie and Diego.

"He told us," Diego said. "Your secret is out and safe with us."

As they walked toward the parking lot, Natalie turned to Lyle. "I thought we deserved something special for our last night. There's a restaurant in town that looks perfect. They serve my favorite, chateaubriand. They have an outdoor seating area that's surrounded by greenery, and it's off the main road."

"It takes a little planning, doesn't it?" Lyle asked. "Going out with your brother and not being stopped for photographs all night?"

"Yes, but if you're smart, it becomes second nature."

At the truck, Diego got in the driver's seat. Natalie rode shotgun while Michael and Lyle climbed into the back.

Michael held Lyle's hand the entire drive. He absentmindedly ran his thumb back and forth over her palm. "Rick came by my room this afternoon."

"I thought he might. He stopped by my room earlier and said he wanted to talk to you. How did he know where to find you?"

"He ran into Natalie and me in the dive shop," said Diego. "We told him where Michael's room was."

"He apologized for last night," Michael said. "He blamed it on having too much to drink."

"And?"

"I told him I was sorry for wanting to pulverize him and that I was perfectly sober when I did." He grinned.

They ate dinner in the restaurant's garden. Lush greenery surrounded them and offered plenty of privacy. Natalie sliced into her chateaubriand and the juices dripped to her plate.

Lyle asked Natalie, "What did you mean when you said it only took a little planning to be out with your brother?"

"We've found that half the battle is keeping the public from knowing where to look for him. How do you know the president of the United States isn't sitting at that table over there?" She nodded to a group having dinner not far from them. "You don't. We don't look at everyone's face. But if you knew the president was vacationing on Bonaire, you may look at people a little closer."

"It's not as bad as she makes it sound. I put on a ballcap, pull it down low, no one recognizes me. Most of the time, it isn't a problem at all."

"Well, for good or for bad, Michael's fan base is mainly young women. They can be relentless when they smell blood."

"I don't know, Natalie," said Lyle. "Michael's been signing autographs for older men and women all week. Maybe his fan base is changing, growing."

Lyle twirled the angel hair pesto around her fork. Michael gave up on his utensils and used his fingers to eat his fried chicken.

"So, Michael, you're staying another week?" asked Diego.

Michael put his arm around the back of Lyle's chair. "I think I will. I'm enjoying myself more and more each day."

She put her hand on his leg. "I guess I have to put up with him one more week."

They finished their drinks, and the waiter brought the bill. Without looking at the total, Michael put his credit card on the table.

Lyle pulled out some cash from her pocket. "Michael, I can pay for my dinner."

He looked confused at first then simply shook his head, smiling.

She put her money away. "Thank you for dinner."

He winked at her.

Once back at the resort, the friends all said a final farewell. Lyle wished Natalie and Diego a safe flight, and each promised to keep in touch. As they walked their separate ways, she called over her shoulder one last goodbye. She had grown to like Natalie and Diego and would miss them.

Michael looked up the stairway that led to Lyle's room. "Can I come up?"

She loved that he didn't assume it. She watched as he nervously pushed his hair back out of his eyes while he awaited her answer.

"I'd hoped you would."

Twenty-Nine

They listlessly climbed the stairs to Lyle's room on the second floor. Despite her nap that afternoon, she felt worn out from the day's activities. As they stood at her door, she patted her hips and bottom, trying to find her room key.

"Let me." Michael slid his fingers into her front pockets and ran them along her skin under the fabric. "I don't think the key's in here." His hands travelled over her hips and slipped into her back pockets. He pulled her close. She grinned up at him as his fingers circled over her rear end as he hunted for the key. He was sure to search each pocket thoroughly, to move his hands all around her several times before finding it. "I knew it was here somewhere." He smiled mischievously and opened the door.

She removed her sandals. "I want you to stay with me but we can't be up all night like we were last night. I was a zombie this morning. I really don't like feeling that way. Promise me we'll get some sleep tonight."

He placed his fingertips on her jawline and held her gaze. She could feel his firm body against her stomach. Her shoulders relaxed and her body grew warm. He ran his nose and lips up her neck and breathed into her ear: "I'm not going to let you sleep, Lyle, not until I'm done with your body. After we're both spent, we'll sleep."

She closed her eyes and let him tantalize her. His lips grazed her cheeks, jawline, and under her ears. His warm breath excited her. As he knowingly tormented her, she wished she hadn't taught him quite so well. Her body started to melt, and she grew impatient. She tried to find his lips, but he pulled away.

"Oh no, baby. It has to be slow. Don't make me push you away."

With her hand behind his neck, she pulled him to her. "Please kiss me."

His self-control was fragile at best. He abandoned it when he heard the need in her voice. His lips met hers as they explored each other's body with their hands.

"Michael, take a bath with me."

"You're the boss." He removed her top.

She undid her shorts and slid them down to the floor. He helped her out of her panties and regarded her bare body. He ran his index finger down her breast and over her nipple. "You're gorgeous. Every inch of you is beautiful."

She stood stark-naked and watched as he took off his shirt. He removed his jeans and tossed them on the bed. She stole a look at him, turned and walked into the bathroom.

Michael sat in the tub and extended his hand toward her. She held it and stepped into the warm water. She sat between his outstretched legs and began to lay back on his chest, but he put his hands on her shoulders and stopped her. "I finally get to see the rest of this tattoo. I was too preoccupied last night to have a good look at it."

She hugged herself and studied the tiled wall in front of her. The water ran from the faucet and warmed the room. She waited uncomfortably while he examined her back. Angela's words came back to her. She claimed Lyle belonged in a sideshow. Of course, her friend was only joking, but still…

He touched the image etched into her back. "They really have the detail down. Whose idea was it to make the bones look like pipes? Was it Dottie?"

When he was satisfied, he wrapped his legs around her. She laid back on his chest and put her toes under the warm running water. He ran his fingers up and down her arm and put his chin on top of her head.

"To be honest, the experience of getting it done completely turned me off the thing. It's something I'd rather forget." She realized that forgetting the tattoo was on her back was exactly what she was supposed to do. It was carrying her nightmares for her. She wasn't supposed to have any thought of it at all. Why then did she still have nightmares?

Michael pushed her forward again, giving himself another clear view of the tattoo. "Well, let me tell you, it's huge and wildly dramatic. Except he's left a few areas incomplete, like he purposefully left spaces in between the bones. I've got to be honest with you, baby. It totally gets me going. I think it's really hot." He reached around her and held her breasts in his hands. He kissed the back of her neck and nibbled on her ear.

She could feel his body harden behind her as she rested her head back on his shoulder. "It's not finished. I never went back to have the guy finish it. I imagine that's the reason for the empty spaces."

"Not done? What else could he possibly add?"

"It's supposed to have gremlins. The guy said it wasn't done until he added the gremlins."

"Why haven't you finished it?"

She trembled, remembering the pain, the smell, and the burn. She picked up a bar of soap and rubbed it up and down her arms and over her stomach. "He lives in Pearl, a town on the North Carolina coast. I haven't gotten back down there."

The truth was, she had been back to the coast twice since she was tattooed. Her boss, Dr. Patel, let her stay in his beach house when he wasn't using it. While there, she stayed as far away as possible from the tattoo shop and her tattoo artist, Grey Locklear.

He took the soap from her and lathered her breasts. The bubbles grew thick as he massaged her and rolled her nipples between his fingers. He then filled his cupped hand with warm bathwater and let it drizzle over her, washing away the suds.

"I'm wondering how Dottie compelled you to get a tattoo of this size and design."

"It's a long story. I'd rather not get into it." She clumsily turned to face him, and water sloshed over the side of the tub. She ran her hands greedily over his chest and eyed his abs. She kissed him.

"Whoa, baby." He captured her hand in his and held her chin in his other. "No secrets, Lyle. We agreed on the beach we wouldn't keep secrets from each other."

She stammered. "I…I have dreams sometimes, nightmares from when I was a kid. Sometimes they hit me during the day when I'm wide awake. I was so little. I grew up with the worries of an adult."

"Tell me what you worried about, baby."

"About being left alone with no one to take care of me. My mother was gone for days at a time. I stressed out when our food supply got low—I remember being hungry many times. I worried about my mother's boyfriends. Would I be fast enough to get away from them?"

"I'm sorry. I'm sorry your life was shit as a kid. I wish I could do something to change all of it for you. I don't understand what your childhood has to do with your tattoo."

"Somehow, Dottie has wrapped the miserably wretched life I had into a neat little catchphrase. She put all my years of suffering into two words: *my burden*. She explained that it's something I have to carry with me my whole life, that my past is always right here with me. She thought, since I can never get rid of it, I should at least carry it somewhere out of sight, where I won't be forced to remember it so often." She purposefully painted Dottie as the crazy one, the one who came up with the idea. "She thought this tattoo would carry my burden for me and take away my nightmares, that it would give me a stronger backbone."

"Has it worked?"

"No, no, it hasn't worked." She turned off the tap and leaned back against his chest. The steamy room was comfortably warm. "I still have the memories. They haunt me night and day. Hours of that needle carving ink into my flesh—all that for nothing. Wouldn't you know I'd end up with a malfunctioning tattoo?"

He remembered her telling him on the *Mi Dushi* about her mother. He hadn't grasped the extent of her suffering. Certainly, such a tortured childhood would leave scars. "Thank you for telling me. No secrets. We have no secrets." He thought a moment. "I would love to meet Dottie one day."

She put her toe up to catch the drips from the faucet. "She's on Bonaire this week. She's with a research team from her university. I'm not sure where she's staying." She quietly chastised herself for not getting more information from Dottie. At the time, she was getting over the attack in the ladies' room and was only thinking of herself.

He whispered in her ear, "I'm sorry the tattoo isn't working."

When the water cooled, she climbed out of the bath and wrapped herself in a towel. "Meet me in bed?"

He came out of the bathroom with a towel around his waist. He stood and shamelessly looked at her lying naked.

Lyle was right. Her body wasn't like the younger girls he dated. Her body was the perfect combination of soft and hard. Her breasts were small but naturally full and her hips rounded. Her stomach and strong legs showed off the muscles she gained through her athletic lifestyle. Her body never failed to entice him.

She stayed still, allowing him to look at her, unashamed. She no longer worried about his opinion of her body. He made her feel sexy and attractive. He wanted her, and she him. It was clear to them that they were suited for each other, both physically and in the easy banter and friendship they developed.

He pulled the towel free from his waist, wiped his face with it, and ran it over his shoulders. She appreciated the moment he gave her to admire his lean, muscular body.

He tossed his towel to the floor and sat next to her on the cool sheets. "I'm sorry about your childhood. If I could carry your burden for you, I would. If I could make that damn tattoo do the job it was supposed to do, I would." He kissed her then found her breasts with his lips and ran his tongue over her tender skin.

She arched her back, the feel of the warm moisture on her breasts tormented her. "Michael," she moaned

He turned on the lamp and a soft glow filled the room. "Can I have another look?"

"Now?" Disappointed, she rolled onto her stomach, stretched her arms up, and rested her cheek on the pillow.

He straddled her and kissed the back of her neck. He kissed her tattoo from the base of her neck down to the small of her back. He used his lips, tongue, and hands to explore the intricate design that covered his lover. He massaged her, moving his hands over her shoulders and down her sides to her bottom.

Her body melted underneath him. She let out a low moan as warm, strong hands explored her molten body. He touched her rounded behind with his fingertips, tracing the animated bones at the end of her tattoo.

Her patience was growing thin and she was done letting him examine her tattoo. She rolled onto her back and held his face in her hands. He pushed his knees between her legs, making room for himself.

He started gently. He knew she would want him to go slowly and would chastise him for anything else. He moved tenderly, not wanting her to reject him. But soon his need demanded satisfaction and his pace intensified. His breathing became labored, and his heart pounded against his chest. The headboard beat like a drum.

"Stay with me, baby," he panted.

She could feel the tension building within her. He continued, relentlessly, until she cried out. "Michael, Michael, Michael."

His body crushed her, slamming her into the headboard. He went rigid, and he laid still. Lyle struggled to breathe under the weight of her young lover. Exhausted and satisfied, she couldn't stop the smile that grew on her lips.

Thirty

Lyle balanced a hamburger on her thigh and wedged a soda and large order of fries between her legs. They had completed three dives and the rigorous activity always fueled her appetite. The fast-food restaurant wasn't healthiest choice, but they didn't feel comfortable leaving the truck, full of expensive gear, unattended. She turned off the main road and into the entrance of Bon Adventure, the truck hopping and skipping over loose gravel. She held only a lax grip on the steering wheel, letting the truck find its own path. She continued past the parking lot and buildings and inched toward the waterfront.

"I'll drop you and the gear at the dock and go to park," she said, stuffing several fries into her mouth. She popped the clutch, and the truck leaped forward. "Damn this stick shift." Her hamburger slid across her leg, but she scooped it up in her hand, saving it from hitting the floorboard. She took a large bite and spoke with her mouthful. "A person could starve to death having to eat like this."

Victoria balled up her trash and stuffed it in the bag from the drive-thru. "We'll clean the gear. If you give me your locker key, I'll make sure your stuff gets put away."

The carton of fries between her legs squished as she reached into her shorts pocket. She handed Victoria the key. "How about something different this afternoon? Who's up for a game of badminton?"

Angela rolled her eyes. "Badminton? Really? Isn't your generation more into shuffleboard?"

Lyle ignored the remark. "I'll stop by the reception desk and pick up some rackets and birdies." She turned her attention back to her burger and managed another bite.

She drove the truck on to the grassy area and parked behind Rick and Steve. She watched in the rearview mirror as Michael parked behind her. Although he and Rick had begrudgingly made up, in order to keep the peace, Michael wanted nothing to do with Rick and decided this morning to drive his own truck.

Victoria and Angela lifted the gear out of the back.

Lyle spoke to them out her window. "I'll see you on the court in an hour." Michael walked up to her window. "Badminton in one hour, bring your best game." She winked at him and drove off.

Michael was hoping for alone time with her. Diving with her friends all morning kept the two of them at a safe distance, and the actor wanted a break from all the acting.

The resort's volleyball court doubled as the badminton court. A sand-filled pit with a net across the middle. It was hidden behind the reception desk and surrounded by the funny-looking divi-divi trees, which stood completely still but looked as if they were blowing in the ocean breeze. They didn't know their roots should be buried deep in the ground, and seemed to sit, roots and all, on top of the sand.

Lyle was the first to arrive at the court. Calypso was enjoying a roll in the cool sand and came to greet her. She scratched the dog behind her ear until Calypso had had enough and trotted off.

She sat on a bench for spectators and took her shoes off. With a racket and a shuttlecock, she stepped onto the sandy court. She held the plastic birdie between her fingers and deftly took a swing at it. Practicing, she soon had it flying high into the air.

She maneuvered herself to prepare for the next swing. Lost in her game, she hadn't noticed Michael watching her from the bench, admiring her determination to keep the object in the air.

Her ponytail danced as she lunged and sailed over the court. Sand flew from under her feet as short stops and sudden starts drove her.

He had an easy time sneaking up on her from behind. He grabbed her around her waist, pulled her off balance, and caught her in his arms. He kissed her neck. She smelled of flowery soap and shampoo, and he ached to take her to bed right then.

The birdie plopped down in the sand next to her.

"We better be careful. Eyes are everywhere," said Lyle.

"You smell so good I can't help myself."

"I know we've been together all day, but still, I feel like it's been forever."

"Fuck Rick, making you dive with him," Michael said irritably.

She looked beyond him and froze as she saw a familiar man walking toward them. Her hands balled into fists, and her rigid posture alerted Michael to her unease. He followed her line of sight and turned in the direction in which she was looking.

The blond-haired man from Captain Jack's was approaching the court. His hair flew about his still swollen and black-and-blue face. His expression was that of cool relaxation. He looked proud at having been in a fight and seemed to have no compunction about walking around with such wounds.

As he came nearer, she moved behind Michael and placed her hands at his shoulders, feeling vulnerable in her bare feet. She put her forehead on his back and closed her eyes.

"Hey, you're Michael Miller, I heard you were here. How's it going man?"

Michael didn't reply. He watched him as he continued past the court.

Out of nowhere, Calypso charged the man, stopping just behind him and nipping at his heals. Her lip curled and she bared her teeth, barking and growling, forcing the man to pick up his pace.

"Damn dog! I'll use you for fish bait!"

Once he was out of sight, Michael turned to Lyle. "He was so drunk he doesn't remember it was the famous Michael Miller who turned his face into ground beef. Damn it, Lyle. I knew we should've gone to the police. Now he's walking around here like Robinson fucking Crusoe."

Angela and Victoria arrived at the court.

"Hey, you made it!" Lyle called to them in an artificially cheerful voice.

They began removing their shoes.

"I hope we're not interrupting anything," said Victoria.

Michael whispered, "Don't worry about him. I won't let him get near you again."

Victoria shot Lyle a suspicious look. She picked up a racket and took her place on the court. She had been extra observant of Lyle and Michael all day, wondering if the flirting Lyle admitted to had advanced to something more. Were they still just having fun, as Lyle described it? Victoria began to formulate a plan to get some answers from her friend.

Angela wore a pair of low-rise shorts and a bikini top. Lyle nodded at her outfit. "Pretty daring for a sporting event, don't you think?"

Angela adjusted her top. "I need to get rid of my wetsuit tan lines. I don't plan on playing hard enough to jostle things out of place."

Michael called out, "I'll team up with Lyle. I haven't played badminton since grade school and I'm hoping she can cover for me."

After a brief review of the rules, the birdie shot into the air. It took several short-lived volleys to get the players in their game, but soon it was flying back and forth over the net. Sand flew out underfoot as the players raced to make their next shot.

Michael and Lyle ran into each other and got in each other's way as each tried to single-handedly keep the shuttlecock in the air. They ran toward it at the same time and collided as it landed on the court next to them.

Lyle fell back into the sand and looked up at him. "You're supposed to call it."

He extended his hand and pulled her onto her feet. She wiped the sand off her bottom and stood ready for the next shot. Angela served and the birdie flew toward Lyle. She took an overconfident swipe at it, and it flew straight off her racket, hit Michael in the back of the head, and fell to the ground.

Lyle exploded with laughter. Michael played it up and rubbed his hand over the back of his head. He turned to see the source of his discomfort and sprinted toward her. She saw him coming and dashed around the court dodging his reach.

Victoria and Angela watched them as they circled the court. Angela caught Victoria's eye and shrugged. Victoria responded with an eye roll as they waited to resume the game.

Victoria regarded the body language on the other side of the net. Michael and Lyle seemed very comfortable with each other. When she stumbled a little, he placed his hand on her waist to steady her. It all seemed too natural. She needed to get Lyle alone. She needed to know what was going on between her and Michael Miller.

By the second game, the heat of the sun had taken its toll on them. Victoria was out of breath. "Let's take five." She walked toward the bench.

Michael put his hands on his knees. "I'll run down to the pool bar and grab us some water."

Lyle joined Angela and Victoria at the bench. Victoria waved the tail of her shirt up and down, trying to create a breeze. "This is way more work than carrying gear all day."

Angela squinted into the sun. "I'm beat. You and Michael are a good team."

This was the opening Victoria needed. She chose her next words carefully. "Lyle, I couldn't help but notice—"

"Who's ready for a little fun?" Rick tossed a volleyball in his hands and looked fresh and ready for a game.

Steve, trailing a few feet behind him, noticed the girls looked exhausted, sweat running down their faces. "Take a little break, then we'll team up. We'll have to play three against two."

"Michael's gone for water. He'll be back in a minute," said Lyle.

"Of course he'll be right back," said Rick.

Michael returned with the water. If he was upset to see that Rick had joined them, he didn't show it. He passed the ice-cold bottles to the girls, and after a few minutes they were ready to start.

As they prepared to serve, the French family Michael and Lyle dove with arrived carrying their own volleyball. They recognized them at the same time and exchanged subtle glances.

Steve jogged over to the new arrivals and briefly spoke to Peter. He called to his friends, "Come meet our new team members."

Peter's face brightened with recognition. "Lyle Cooper, good to see you again." His English was good, and his French accent was endearing.

"It's nice to see you and your family." She smiled and made introductions.

"We had the pleasure of diving with Lyle and Michael on the *Mi Dushi*," Peter began. Lyle prayed that he would leave it at that, but he continued. "They weren't feeling well and needed dive buddies. We've known Captain Maartin for several years. He knew we'd watch over your friends."

Lyle saw Rick's eyes flick to her. She concentrated on looking straight ahead. She knew she would have some explaining to do later and began constructing her story.

Nicole, wearing matching shorts and top, walked over to Michael and asked in her thick French accent, "John Magnum, you play?" She pointed at the volleyball.

"Yes and no. Not well," he said.

Nicole looked confused.

Michael held his thumb and index finger very close to each other. "Un peu, a little."

Nicole nodded and the two strolled onto the court.

Peter stood next to Lyle in the sand. "Are you feeling better? You didn't look so good on our dive the other day."

"Yes, thank you."

Lyle smiled when she saw Michael facing her on the opposite side of the net. Nicole was on one side of him and Angela on the other. She looked to her right and saw Peter smiling at her. She looked to her left, and Rick gave her a nod. She spoke through her clenched teeth, "Fuck me."

The volleyball games were played with a lot more heart than the badminton games. There was no trash talk, and most of them turned out to be good players. Lyle had some experience in high school gym class. It came back to her as they began the game. When Rick constantly tried to back up her volleys and pick up her shots, he proved to be a genuine annoyance. She could only imagine how tired he was going to be after playing for two all afternoon.

When Lyle rotated into the server position, she shot Rick an evil look. She tossed the ball straight up, took a little hop, and smashed her fist straight into it like a pro. She glanced over the net in time to see Michael duck from the torpedo that had been sent his way. The ball hit the sand, and she yelled, "Point!" Michael looked at her in shock. She winked at him and waited for the ball to be returned to her.

"That's my girl," said Rick, stunned.

Michelle gave advice and encouragement to her family. "L'obtenir sur le net!"

After two games, Victoria called it quits. "I've got a girls' night out to plan. I'm going to need some time to spruce up." She motioned for Lyle and Angela to join her on the bench. "Tonight is officially our girls' night out. You're both invited since you fulfill the qualifications so well." They were too tired to argue. "We'll meet by the truck at seven."

"Where're we going?" asked Angela. "I need to decide on my outfit."

"Welcome to the world of karaoke, my friends," said Victoria. "You'll enjoy dinner, drinks, and suffer amateur entertainment all under one roof. It'll be a blast."

Peter and his family regrouped and were starting a new game on their own.

"Come on, Victoria, girls only, really?" Rick thought Michael would somehow end up going and he wanted to be there too. "Where're you going?"

"Sorry, no way. We need some girl time. You know, to catch up on things." Lyle and Angela sat exhausted on the bench. Victoria barked at them, "Seven o'clock at the truck," and she strode off.

"I think I'll wear that black silk dress I brought. That's not too formal for Karaoke, is it?" But Angela left before Lyle could answer her.

Michael stalled putting his shoes back on, searching for a moment alone with Lyle. "Girls only! What the hell is that all about? We haven't had any time alone all day and now I'm not going to see you tonight?" His irritation grew. "What could you possibly need to catch up on? You spend hours in your truck together every day. To hell with this. Get out of it. Tell them you're not going."

Lyle swatted at the sand on her feet. "Victoria's up to something. I know her too well."

"Last time. I mean it. I don't like being left out and left behind!" He kicked a badminton racket that was lying on the ground and stomped off toward his room.

Having been left alone, Lyle awkwardly gathered up all the badminton equipment and the volleyball. She looked around for help. Steve and Michael were off in the distance, heading toward their rooms, and Rick was talking with Peter at the far end of the court.

"Thanks for all the help, guys." She rearranged the equipment and managed to return it all to the reception desk.

A cold blast of air hit her as she entered her room. Saturated with sweat, a shiver ran through her. She adjusted the thermostat up until the air stopped blowing. She was tired but ignored the bed that was calling to her. Housekeeping had made it up and fluffed the pillows. It was hard to resist but if she laid down now, she may not wake until morning.

She peeled off her sweaty T-shirt and shorts and went into the bathroom. She didn't hear the knock on her door. Once in the shower, she didn't hear the pounding either.

Thirty-One

"Give the key to Angela. I need your undivided attention." Lyle dropped the key into Angela's palm and climbed into the back seat.

After all three doors had slammed shut, Victoria asked Lyle, "Truth or dare?"

"Dare," she replied immediately—maybe Angela would dress her up like Malibu Barbie again.

Victoria narrowed her eyes. "Let me rephrase the question. Are you going to tell me the truth now, or will I have to beat it out of you later?"

"You're playing it wrong," said Lyle. "You're supposed to ask the question first, then I get to decide truth or dare." She wondered how long she could stall.

"Welcome to the Caribbean. We play by island rules here."

Angela turned the key, but the truck refused to start. She looked at the steering wheel, hit it a few times with an open hand, and tried again. Still, the truck remained silent.

"Angela, you have to be sure the clutch is all the way to the floor or it won't start," said Lyle.

Victoria tried a different approach. "Since when do we keep secrets from each other? I thought we shared everything, especially the important things," she coaxed. "If I had a secret involving, say, a guy, I'd share that with you. Even if it was very important to keep things quiet. I would know I could trust my best friends."

Lyle had a bad feeling she and Michael had been found out. She was now trapped in the truck in front of her own Spanish Inquisition.

"It's not that simple. I don't think what I'm doing is right, and if I keep it a secret, I don't have to explain it."

The truck started and Angela moved the gear shift into Reverse. She looked over her shoulder and prepared to back out. The truck leapt one foot backward and stalled.

"I don't know how this happened. It just snuck up on me. One minute we're joking around and having fun and the next…" She looked thoughtfully out the window. "I can sit here and make excuses, but the truth is I'm not sorry about it."

Angela got the truck started again and turned to back out of the parking spot. The truck reversed with sudden starts and stops, brakes squeaking. They finally cleared the parking space only to have the truck stop and stall again.

"He really loves diving. We have fun together. He's so funny, we laugh a lot."

The truck started up, and they inched forward in sudden bursts. Lyle was thrown forward and back several times until the truck stalled yet again.

"We're only here a few more days. Then it's back to the real world. It'll be a good story to tell afterward."

Victoria raised her eyebrows. "I don't think you should write Mr. Miller off so easily. I see how he looks at you. He's been falling for you since we rescued him that very first day. I could see it then. The best part of this vacation has been watching the two of you fall in love."

Angela looked at Victoria. "Who's in love?" She glanced at Lyle in the rearview. "Oh yeah, Michael and Lyle. That is so yesterday's news. Will one of you please teach me how to drive this stick shift?"

With a little instruction and a lot of encouragement, the truck leaped and stopped most of the way into town. Angela found a parking spot safely away from other vehicles.

A simple sign out front let patrons know they had arrived at Sunshine's. Near the door was a sandwich-style chalkboard that read *Karaoke nightly*.

Small tables filled the floor. Against the back wall, a stage held the equipment and a stool for anyone brave enough to give singing a try.

Angela glanced at the limited menu. "It's a good thing we had lunch. They only serve bar food." Her face lit up. "Oh, look! They have the rum from the distillery in Rincón. We've got to have that. It's not every day you can drink rum made from a cactus."

When the drinks arrived, the girls ordered potato skins and wings.

Angela turned to Lyle. "I must admit, at first I was heartbroken when Michael ignored my advances. But if it couldn't be me, I'm glad it's you. He isn't what I expected. He blends in with us like he's one of the guys. I thought hanging out with Michael Miller would be all glamour and glitz. Instead, it's just everyday life. A bit of a disappointment if you ask me."

Lyle sipped her drink and blew a stream of air from her pursed lips. "I forgot how potent this cocktail is. Well, after this vacation, it'll all be water under the bridge. If we can keep things quiet for a few more days, we'll all fly back to our homes and leave this island and our secret behind."

"You've talked about it? I mean, the whole 'leaving it all behind' part? Because, quite frankly, Lyle, that doesn't sound like you." Victoria had watched Lyle suffer through her breakup with Rick. She knew Lyle wasn't one to take a romantic relationship lightly.

"No, we haven't talked about it. But it goes without saying. There's a real chance, if we're found out, his fan base could turn on him. When you're the ultimate bachelor and fans dream of winning your heart, having a love affair with an older woman could backfire."

"You do realize that if the tables were turned and he was older than you, all his friends would be slapping him on the back," Angela said. "Unfair, outdated double standards."

The waiter arrived with their order. The girls were pleasantly surprised at the appetizers. The potato skins were thick and drenched in cheese and bits of crispy bacon. Chopped chives were sprinkled on top with a generous helping of sour cream on the side. The buffalo wings cleared Lyle's sinuses as soon as they hit the table. The tangy smell made her mouth water. They passed small plates to each other and loaded up on napkins.

There was some commotion at a table a few feet away. A woman stood and ambled toward the stage. She teetered while holding a drink in her hand. "Get ready. This is going to be bad," said Lyle.

The girls devoured their potato skins and wings while they listened to the woman try to sing an Adele song.

"Promise me, no matter how much I drink," said Victoria, holding a chicken wing, "you won't let me get on that stage tonight. While I'm sober, I'm completely aware that I can't sing. Get a few of these cocktails in me and I think I'm Beyonce."

A deep voice rang out at their table: "Whose idea was this?" Rick watched the woman onstage. "Bad enough you're settling for bar food. Add to that the excruciating entertainment. You really should've included me in planning tonight's activity." He grabbed an empty chair from a nearby table and joined them, quite uninvited.

Victoria did nothing to hide her annoyance. "Rick, you clearly don't understand the premise of a girls' night out. What are you doing here? You don't exactly fit the criteria."

"I heard the word *karaoke* and asked the front desk where you could've gone. Lucky for me there are only two karaoke bars on Bonaire. The other one went out of business last spring." He looked at the woman onstage struggling through the last verse. "I can't imagine why."

He lifted his finger into the air. The waiter appeared immediately and soon brought him a draft beer. "So, what's the topic of conversation?"

"Tampons," Angela deadpanned, looking directly at him.

Lyle held a dripping potato skin in her fingers. "We're trying to decide which brand is most absorbent. Glad you're here. Maybe you could help us out." She took a large bite.

He picked up his beer and used the small cocktail napkin to wipe up the ring of moisture it left on the table. "Maybe you could answer a question for me. Why did Captain Maartin ground you from diving the other day?"

A chill ran down Lyle's back and she felt a thump in her chest. The potato, cheese, and sour cream went down like a lump of dry earth.

Angela and Victoria stopped eating and looked from Rick to Lyle. She searched for an easy explanation, but he didn't give her a chance to respond.

"Peter told me you and the famous Michael Miller were so strung out that morning, it appeared you were still high on something when you boarded the boat."

Lyle's throat felt tight. Tension hovered in the air.

"He said you fell getting on board, and Michael slept the entire ride to the reef. You hadn't turned your air on prior to the dive and your worthless dive buddy forgot to check it for you."

Heat billowing up her neck, her flight-or-fight impulse had her searching for the door.

"Peter told me your air was dangerously low. You had submerged to a depth well beyond—"

"Stop it, Rick! Peter doesn't know what he saw. Michael and I were fine. Peter's story was probably lost in translation." It was a half-truth, but it was the only explanation she had to offer.

"Then let's hear the story from you," said Victoria. "What really happened? Did Captain Maartin prohibit you guys from diving or not?"

"You're making something out of nothing. I was simply tired from the late night we had." Lyle added in all innocence, "Remember, we were all having pizza in my room. After the fight between Michael and Rick, Michael was really upset. We stayed up a while to talk about what happened." She had to give it to her friends: they didn't flinch or change their facial expressions at all. "The lack of sleep caught up to me. Some mistakes were made on the dive the next day." She thought of the barracuda she had seen on the dive. One of the last things she remembered.

Rick put his elbows on the table and folded his hands together. One strand of his perfectly groomed hair fell forward into his dark eyes. He spoke to Lyle as if she were a child: "I don't like it. Whatever the story, I don't like it. Diving can be dangerous, and the simple fact that Captain Maartin grounded you tells me there's more to the story than you're willing to admit."

Lyle felt like a five-year-old. She clenched her teeth and waited for him to finish.

"From now on, any trips on the *Mi Dushi* will include one of us." She began to protest, but he continued. "Michael isn't experienced enough to know the signs of a diver in distress. If he was, he wouldn't have let you dive at all that day." He sat back. "End of discussion."

Lyle tried to form a rebuttal. After coming up with nothing, she decided keeping her mouth shut would be the best way to go. She took a long drink of her rum and turned to the singer onstage. Her appetite had vanished. It was easy to sit there and be upset with Rick. It was hard to sit there and admit he was right.

Victoria touched her hand. "We don't want anything bad to happen to you. Maybe sticking with more qualified divers isn't a bad idea."

The waiter brought the bill, and Rick reached for it. "On me. Since I crashed your party." He pulled his wallet out of his pocket. "Victoria and I were talking about our next great excursion. We're thinking we should look into camping in Glacier National Park. We did a little research. We could backpack or—"

"I don't camp," Lyle snapped.

"I'm sorry I've made you mad. Believe me, that's not my intention. I really am trying to look out for you."

"I understand your concerned. It really is that I don't camp." She could hear the shortness and anger in her voice and softened her tone. "I camped with my mother as a child, and I don't camp anymore."

"Okay, then," Rick said. "You learn something new every day. She swims, she dives, she runs. She's a wizard at volleyball, but she draws the line at camping." He left cash on the table and stood to leave. "I'll see you in the morning. Good night."

Angela giggled. "I don't camp. That's priceless. I don't camp. You told him." She fished the truck key out of her purse. "Do you want me to drive? Or do you want to get back to the resort before the sun comes up?"

Thirty-Two

Lyle huddled under the Caribbean blue comforter on her bed. Rick's comments at the bar troubled her. Peter's impression that she and Michael were high was upsetting. She watched her own mother destroyed by drugs and alcohol. Yes, she enjoyed a beer or a mixed drink on occasion, but never to excess. She'd never even tried drugs. Peter's opinion shouldn't upset her, but she couldn't let it go. She wasn't like her mother.

After returning from the bar, she switched off the room's air conditioner. She put on sleep pants and a sweatshirt but still couldn't seem to get warm.

Rick's suggestion that they go camping had conjured up memories of doing so with her mother when she was very young. She pulled the blankets up to her chin, and her head sank into the downy pillow. Her eyes closed and finally she began to doze.

A knock sounded at the door. "Lyle? It's me. Lyle, it's Michael. Let me in, baby." He knocked again. "Lyle, baby. I really need to talk to you." Three more raps on the door.

The fire at the campground crackled, and the embers glowed a deep red. Moonlight shone through the trees.

Lyle leaned against her mother with a well-used marshmallow stick in her hand. Her belly was stuffed with hot dogs, chips, and soda, and she had her fill of toasted marshmallows.

She stared into the fire and listened to "Kumbaya" being sung for the umpteenth time. The soft voices were comforting, and she was now familiar with the lyrics. Several families sat around the campfire. Most of them had children who were out of school for the summer. They would spend a week or two at the campground before heading back home.

People had arrived in cars, campers, and trucks. They came and went all summer long. Lyle had an endless number of children to interact with—playing countless games of hopscotch, drawing with sidewalk chalk in the parking lot, and watching the older kids play tether ball. She played red rover with the bigger kids until she was trampled again and again, and her team had her sit to the side.

One evening, the mother of a girl she had been playing with, stood over a grill full of burgers. She had the biggest hair Lyle had ever seen. It was the first time she had ever seen orange hair. The woman wore a large red bow on the top of her head and a handkerchief around her neck. The woman looked through the trees toward Lyle and her mother's small tent. "Lyle, where's your mama? Have you had dinner yet?"

The woman handed her spatula to her husband and had him tend the grill. She disappeared into her camper and returned with a hairbrush. "Come stand by me, honey pie." The woman sat in a folding chair and situated Lyle between her knees. "Let me get the knots out of your hair."

She took the elastic out of Lyle's hair and worked the hairbrush through the tangled mess, taking her time, trying to be gentle.

"I'm sorry, honey, but you shouldn't let your hair get so knotted up. You have such pretty hair." She pulled it up onto the crown of Lyle's head and put the elastic back in place. "That's better. Now how about a hamburger?"

Eventually the summer ended and as the leaves turned brilliant shades of yellow and orange, the summer visitors returned to their homes. The wind picked up and blew the dry brown leaves in circles on the ground. Branches snapped high up in the old trees as they swayed. The frightening sounds of fall in the empty campground had Lyle listening with wide eyes from her small tent.

The few remaining staff members prepared to shut down for the off season. They told Lyle's mother that Sunday was the last open day and that she'll have to pack up and be out before the gate was locked. Her mother smiled and agreed to be gone in time.

When Sunday came, they rolled up their sleeping bags, took down their tent, and left. Lyle followed behind her mother down the side of a long country road. They stopped at a store that served breakfast and lunch and sold gasoline out front. They sat in a booth and shared a tuna melt and a soda.

When they finished eating, the waitress cleared their plate away, but they remained seated. They had nowhere else to go. Lyle's mother stared out the window and didn't say a word. Lyle saw tears in her eyes. She didn't know mothers could cry.

Once the sun began to set, she took Lyle's hand. "Come on, Crocodile, we're going home."

They walked back down the country road in the direction from which they had come. Under the name of the campground someone had hung a sign that read *Closed for the Season*. As promised, the long pole gate at the entrance was locked, blocking vehicles from entering. Lyle and her mother simply went around it.

"What if we set up near the evergreens this time?" Lyle's mother asked. "No one will see us from the road, and it has a nice view of the pond."

Fall gave way to winter, and the nights became excruciatingly cold. Still, Lyle and her mother stayed in the campground. The fires they made were large enough to warm a hot dog but did little to chase away the cold. At night, she snuggled as close as possible to her mother. She learned to place her head in the crook of her mother's neck and tried not to move the entire night. The trees stood bare of leaves and appeared black against the white sky.

She didn't know where her mother went in the evenings, but she always returned with cash and food. She sat next to the little fire that her mother had lit for her before she left. She learned to feed it dry twigs and small branches to coax the heat from it. She was always frightened that the fire would go out. Lyle knew she'd be chilled to the bone, that there would be nowhere to go to get warm.

A knock at the door made Lyle stir under her Caribbean blue comforter. She sat up and saw her mother running the zipper up the opening of their little tent.

A second knock at the door. "Lyle?"

Her mother looked at her bundled in her sleeping bag.

A third knock. "Lyle, let me in, baby."

Lyle's mother smiled at her as she climbed through the opening. "Hey, Crocodile, I'm home."

With a final knock on the door, Michael placed his forehead against the door in defeat. His voice was quiet but laden with despair. "I need to talk to you. I need to tell you something. Lyle, please wake up."

Lyle shifted under her warm blankets. "I don't camp."

Thirty-Three

It was pitch-black in the room when Lyle pushed Snooze on her phone for the third time. She knew she had missed the predawn dive. If she was going to catch up with her friends at breakfast, she needed to get up. Her disturbing dreams replayed in her head. Only they weren't dreams. Rick's idea at the bar last night to plan a camping trip out west had awoken her memories. Thoughts of the tiny tent she lived in with her mother were never far away.

She brushed her teeth and hair and got a swimsuit from her drawer. The sun was starting to rise. She knew her friends were rinsing their gear by now. She put her suit on and covered up with her Dive Bonaire T-shirt.

She spotted her friends eating breakfast at a table near the center of the patio. She grabbed a plate and went through the buffet line, but for the first time since arriving on Bonaire, nothing looked appetizing to her. She needed her strength for diving, so hungry or not she would force herself to finish the toast and measly serving of scrambled eggs on her plate.

She turned to join her friends and bumped into Michael directly behind her. His hair was dripping wet, and his clothes were soaked from the damp bathing suit underneath.

"I'll get your coffee. Go have a seat." He looked at her closely. "Everything okay? Did you sleep well?"

Lyle eyes were red, and her hair was pushed behind her ears. She lacked the neat ponytail she always wore.

"Are you okay? You look a bit pale. Do you feel well?"

"I had some crazy nightmares last night and overslept."

"Damned tattoo still isn't working? Why don't we stay behind today? I have something I need to talk to you about, and you could use some more sleep."

"I'll be fine, Michael. I'll wake up in a minute. Besides, if I fall asleep again, the nightmares may come back." She lowered her voice. "I missed you last night. I thought you were going to come by."

"I did come by." He looked around to be sure they weren't overheard. "Twice. I have something I need to tell you."

"I'm sorry. Once my head hit the pillow I didn't hear a thing. What did you need to tell me?"

"It can wait." He looked around the crowded patio. "I'm afraid it isn't something we can talk about here. Besides, you look exhausted, baby. It'll wait until later."

Lyle laughed off the comments and teasing from her friends for missing the first dive. Rick greeted her warmly, but she found it difficult to look him in the eye. If she was being honest with herself, she would admit that what he said at the bar last night was right. But she wasn't ready to be honest with herself, so she let the chip sit on her shoulder.

She forced herself to pick up her fork and dig in. The scrambled eggs and toast were about as tasty as an old leather shoe. Maybe the coffee Michael was getting her would improve her outlook. If nothing else, she would force herself to feel better and enjoy the day. The sun was shining. The clear blue sky was only surpassed in beauty by the tranquil sapphire ocean.

In the line for coffee, Michael was approached by several fans for pictures and autographs. His plate sat untouched on the table. It was time for Lyle to start acting like the manager Natalie's rumor claimed her to be. She felt a bit awkward as she marched over but found that a strong, brisk pace right to the center of the group gave her the confidence she needed.

"Michael's breakfast is going to get cold. Has everyone gotten a picture?" Fans nodded and smiled. "Michael, would you come with me? You need to finish your breakfast."

One young lady spoke up. "Michael, will you be at the pool bar later today?" Everyone went silent, awaiting his reply.

"I'll be visiting patients at the hospital today." The fans all oohed and awed. Some placed their hands on their hearts.

They rejoined their friends at the table. "I get my breakfast and I look like a hero." He picked up his fork and explained, "I always try to visit patients at the local hospitals wherever I'm working or vacationing. Natalie was hospitalized as a child, leukemia. She underwent a lot of medical treatments. It was really frightening for her. On one of her worst days, someone showed up dressed as Hermione Granger. She read stories to the kids and did some magic tricks. Natalie loved those books and just like that, her worst day turned into a day she still remembers."

"I had no idea."

"I'm no Hermione, but if I can distract people from their worries for an hour, I'm willing to try."

Michael saw his second green moray that morning and realized it was something he would never get used to. He watched the imposing animal from a distance as it moved like a ribbon over the reef.

In the shallows, the divers interrupted a green sea turtle foraging for food. Lyle placed her hand on Michael's chest, stopping his advance. It was pointless to try to follow a turtle; they may be awkward and slow-moving on land, but in the open ocean, they were graceful and quick.

While hovering at fifteen feet to complete their safety stop, Angela alerted them to an inconspicuous area in the coral, and they waited. Their patience paid off when a well-camouflaged octopus shimmered, changed colors, and jetted out of sight.

Along with the octopus, Michael saw a lot of firsts that day. A massive southern stingray hid in the sand right below him. Angela pointed him out and, startled by the size of the ray and length of its spine, Michael quickly swam away.

As they neared the shore, they ran into a shoal of squid. They kept their distance and watched the cephalopods as they shimmered and changed colors.

They completed three dives and were ready to break for lunch. Rick opened his truck door and placed one foot inside. He yelled to Lyle and Michael, who stood by their trucks: "Let's get some lunch and reload fresh tanks. We can dive at Toro this afternoon."

"I promised Michael I'd go visit the hospital in Kralendijk with him. Rick looked unimpressed. "It's for the patients, you know." Since this was a nondiving event she didn't see how he could protest.

"What are you, his personal public relations rep now?" He closed his eyes for a beat. "Have Victoria and Angela meet us at the sandwich shop near the first traffic circle."

Lyle got in the truck. "Did you guys hear that? Meet them at the sandwich shop near the first traffic circle. I'll grab some lunch with Michael and meet up with you later tonight."

They drove through the resort and Lyle parked the truck near the water. She climbed out and pulled her things out of the back.

Victoria slid into the driver's seat and adjusted the rearview mirror. "Enjoy your time with your secret man."

They washed and put their stuff away. Michael stood a safe distance from her. "Thank you for joining me. I know it's hard for you to give up an afternoon of diving. As a consolation, I'd like to strip your clothes off and ravage your body. I've been dreaming about getting my hands on your ass all morning. How about a quick roll in the sheets before we head to the hospital?" They hurried to Lyle's room with wicked grins on their faces.

Lyle put her key in the door. "At breakfast you said you had something to talk to me about and it could wait until later?"

They entered her room.

Michael was becoming uncomfortable in his swim trunks. "It can wait, but I can't."

He removed her T-shirt. "We finally have some time alone. I don't want to spoil it with my problems." He placed his hand on her cheek and moved his thumb over her soft skin. He kissed her gently, but the kiss soon started to escalate.

She parted her lips and ran her tongue over his lower lip. He tasted of salt water and sunshine. "I need a shower before we head to the hospital." Fully aware that he was watching her, she undid her shorts and let them fall to the ground. Standing in her bathing suit, she teased him with her slow progress and carefully orchestrated movements. She slid one shoulder strap down her arm and freed her hand, keeping her breast hidden. Once she had the second strap off her other arm, she gradually worked her suit downward exposing her breasts inch by inch.

Michael followed Lyle's every move.

She revealed her soft stomach and moved her hips from side to side. She gradually lowered her swimsuit. As it slid over her hips, she turned her back to him, tempting him with her round behind. The suit finally made it to the ground. She stepped out of it and tossed it on the floor.

Michael swallowed hard and shifted his weight from one foot to the other.

She ran her hand over her breast.

He watched as she caressed herself and teased him mercilessly. "Lyle, shit."

She stroked her breast and kneaded herself. She ran her hand down her stomach and made circles with her finger just below her navel. She then sauntered to the shower. "Join me?" she said over her shoulder.

"You're such a harlot."

Michael removed his shirt in one smooth motion. He grabbed her and pulled her to him, crushing his hardened body against her. She tugged at his swim shorts, and he removed them immediately. They moved, locked together in their embrace, toward the shower.

The hot water hammered Michael's back as he pressed Lyle against the tile wall. Steam filled the small space, making their skin glisten. He devoured her mouth with his and ran his hands over her hips and down her thighs. She kept up with him, returning his kisses, caressing his chest. She didn't want to go slow.

Michael lifted her and held her against the shower wall. He moaned, "Now, baby. I need you now."

She gripped his hips with her knees and allowed him to take her under the pounding stream of hot water.

Thirty-Four

Michael circled the block for a second time. "Lyle, I think this is it. It's small, but it looks like this is the hospital."

She glanced at Mookie's guitar in the back seat. "What if they don't know who you are?"

"Thanks for that, baby. I really needed to worry about that." He grinned. "Then I guess they'll have to suffer bad singing from some guy off the street."

The glass doors whooshed open as they approached. To their left was a desk with the word *Information* above it. A middle-aged woman sat there, concentrating on her computer screen. She pointed and clicked a mouse with a scowl on her face then looked up from the monitor and instant recognition lit up her face.

Michael explained why he was there. The woman quietly clapped her hands together. She picked up the phone and spread the news that Michael Miller was visiting and would be glad to meet with patients.

Soon a gentleman in a brown suit hurried down the hallway. The woman introduced him to Michael but failed to notice Lyle. He led Michael away, leaving Lyle in the reception area. She sat near the entrance and, having been forgotten, waited.

After some time, the woman returned and motioned for Lyle to follow her. There was much commotion going on in the ward. She had a feeling as to what was causing all the excitement and followed the woman toward the source of the noise.

They stopped at a double doorway and peered into a large room. Michael was sitting on a chair holding his guitar in the center of a large group of people. Three patients sat in wheelchairs. Several others wore pajamas or hospital gowns. In their scrubs, lab coats, and professional attire, it was clear that half the crowd was hospital personnel.

The crowd was laughing at a story he had just finished telling. Some clapped their hands together while others yelled out funny comments. He was in his element and had a big grin on his face. He nodded at Lyle standing in the doorway. She smiled and gave a single nod back.

A young man in a hospital gown spoke up. "Play us another song!" Michael strummed the guitar gently. He began a song and encouraged everyone to sing the chorus with him. As the song came to an end, the same young man yelled, "Michael, what's your favorite thing about Hollywood?"

"The flight to Bonaire." The crowd roared and applauded his answer.

The woman from the front desk turned to Lyle. "He's such a wonderful young man, isn't he? Gosh, his parents must be so proud."

As they drove the truck out of the hospital parking lot, the sun was past its peak and the temperature was pleasant. The resort was quiet as they pulled into the main entrance.

"I may rest for a while. I'll meet you at dinner," said Lyle.

In her room, Lyle sat on the loveseat and picked up her tattered copy of *The Wonderful Wizard of Oz*. She turned to the page she had dog-eared years ago. She read and then reread a paragraph not registering the meaning of the words. She couldn't concentrate. The woman's comment at the hospital had her thinking. *Young man. His parents must be so proud.*

Tired, she gave up on reading. The well-loved book lay completely flat on her chest. Her head sank into the pillow, and she closed her eyes.

By the time Lyle was old enough to start school, she and her mother had left Florida and moved to New York State. They lived in an old trailer outside the village of Chittenango. The trailer park was in the middle of the woods, well hidden from the main road.

Lyle loved having her own room. It was simple, with a single mattress on the floor and a closet. They lived with a man named Roy. It bothered Lyle that on very cold nights, when she climbed into her mother's bed to keep warm, he would send her back to her room. She and her mother had always slept wrapped together in the tent, but Roy would have none of it.

"Mama, how many girls can I invite?" It would soon be Lyle's eighth birthday. Her mother sat at the card table in the tiny kitchen while Lyle danced around her.

Her mother removed the cellophane from the packet of party invitations. "Well, there are eight invitations here, so how about eight?" She held a pen in her trembling hand. Her cigarette lay smoldering in an ashtray.

"May I have chocolate cake? And can we have ice cream on top?"

Lyle's mother closed her eyes and rubbed her temples. "Crocodile, please settle down, and not so loud, my head is pounding. I'll pick up a cake and some ice cream." She put the pen down on the table. "My back is really aching. Can you fill out the invitations on your own?"

On the morning of Lyle's birthday, she hopped out of bed. She was dressed and ready for the party several hours early.

She went to find her mother in her bedroom. Roy was alone in the bed and still asleep.

She shook his shoulder. "Roy, wake up. Where's my mama? Is she coming home?" It wasn't unusual for her mother to stay away for days.

"Shit, kid. What time is it?"

"It's almost nine o'clock. Is my mama coming home?"

"She must've had a busy night. I'm sure she'll be home soon. Did you make yourself some breakfast? There's cereal, and I bought milk yesterday." He sat up, and she left the room as he pulled a T-shirt over his head.

She searched the kitchen. There was no cake or ice cream to be found. She worried about what she would tell her friends. Before Lyle could ask him any more questions, Roy walked through the kitchen and out the front door.

A few minutes after noon, a knock at the door had Lyle running to answer it. Her first friend to arrive was Dottie, who lived in a trailer one block away. Dottie's jeans were worn at the knees. Her red flannel shirt was too big, and she had rolled the sleeves up to her elbows. She had tied red ribbons at the ends of her two long braids. She had ridden her bike to Lyle's house and had leaned it against a tree. She handed Lyle a gift wrapped in a brown paper bag.

"Do ya wanna watch TV?" asked Lyle.

They waited for the other girls to arrive, but none of them ever did. The girls became bored with the television and went outside to play.

Lyle watched as Dottie rode her bike in circles around her. "I don't know how to ride a bike."

"It's easy." She stopped and climbed off. "You try."

Dottie peered through her fingers as she watched Lyle struggle to keep her balance and fall several times, crashing the red bike onto the ground. She was determined to ride that bike. She gave it several tries but her bloody palms convinced her to quit.

Dottie climbed back on. "I'll let you try again tomorrow."

As she peddled away, Lyle called after her. "Sorry there wasn't any cake or ice cream. I guess my mom forgot."

"That's okay. It was still a fun party."

Lyle's mother came home just as the sun was going down. Lyle was eating cereal at the table.

"Hey, Crocodile. Did you have a good day?"

Lyle, sitting on her mattress, held the birthday gift from Dottie on her lap. She opened the paper bag and removed a copy of *The Wonderful Wizard of Oz*. She opened the book. Inside the front cover, Dottie had written in green crayon: *Happy birthday, Lyle, from your best friend, Dottie.*

Thirty-Five

Lyle woke from her brief nap but felt anything but rested. As she sat up, her book fell to the floor. She put it on the nightstand and glanced at her phone. It was approaching dinner time.

She went next door and knocked on Angela's door.

Angela pulled the door open and gave Lyle the once-over. "We thought you were going to meet up with us after you got back from the hospital."

"I fell asleep. I'm not feeling so well."

She hoped this was all the explanation she would need. She was tired and emotionally taxed, struggling to make sense of her relationship with Michael. She wanted some alone time to sort out her thoughts.

"What's wrong? Do you want me to stay with you?" Angela noticed Lyle's messy hair and rumpled clothes. "You look awful. Did you sleep in those clothes?"

"Yes, I slept in these clothes. I'm going to read a little and then go to bed early. I'll be fine. Please tell everyone I'm taking the evening to rest." She gave her a quick hug. "I'll be back in touch later. Enjoy dinner."

She was getting ready to climb into bed when there were several knocks on her door.

"Lyle, it's me, Dottie. Are you in?"

Lyle threw open the door.

Dottie smiled at her, braids still in place. "I wasn't sure if I'd find you here."

"Come in! I'm so glad you came by." Relieved, she flung her arms around her friend. She couldn't stop the tears from falling down her cheeks.

Dottie put her hands on Lyle's shoulders and held her at arm's length. "I'm glad I came by too." She took a long look at her friend. "What's wrong, Crocodile? Why're you crying?"

She took Lyle by the hand and led her to the love seat, and they sat. "I'm on my way to the airport. I know I told you I'd stop by and see you, but my week got so busy. I'm afraid today was the best I could do. After the shape I found you in at the restaurant the other night, you had me worried. Crocodile, you look upset. What's going on? Is it the same problem as before? The guy at the restaurant?"

"No, not that. I don't know what's going on, Dottie. I've made some bad choices, and now I'm paying for it." Lyle wiped at the tears on her face. "I'm afraid I've gotten myself into a real mess, and I'm not sure what to do about it. My first instinct is to run." Inspiration hit Lyle. "When's your flight leaving?"

"Run? You? I've never known you to run from your problems before." Dottie's round face and soft eyes emanated her caring spirit. "Sometimes problems are faster than you. Running or not, they catch up to you."

"Hopping on a flight and heading home sounds really good right now."

"Okay, spill it. What the heck is going on?"

"Well," she said, hesitating. "I've been seeing this guy. We only just met, here on Bonaire. I've started something I shouldn't have. I tried to resist his advances, but that only worked for so long. Now I'm having a hard time ending it." She paused and Dottie waited patiently. "He's pretty young."

"And this is a problem because?"

"He has a bit of a temper. He's fought with Rick and this other guy too." She wrung her hands. "I'm questioning myself, falling for someone completely inappropriate for me. Is there something wrong with me?"

"No, absolutely not. Did you ever think the two issues are not mutually exclusive? Perhaps he has trouble controlling his temper because he's young, maybe a little immature." Dottie held her hands. "Has he hurt you? Has he been physically abusive?"

"No!" She explained, "He can be aggressive when it comes to sex, but I've never felt threatened or afraid."

"You're going home soon. Will the relationship end once you're back in Raleigh?"

"I suppose it will." She was surprised by the sadness in her voice.

Dottie touched her face with her hand. "I love you too much to see you hurt. If this relationship has the potential of blowing up on you, then end it. End it now. You don't need any more nightmares to carry around." She glanced at her watch. "I need to go. I'm sorry but I've got to catch my flight."

Dottie stood to leave. She picked up the worn book from the nightstand. "Still reading?" She thumbed through it and landed on the title page, where she had written her name so many years ago. "I wish we could find the answers in here. A real yellow brick road to follow. No worrying over decisions we make in life. No choosing left or right, just a path to follow." She stood on her toes and tapped her heels together. When nothing happened, she put the book down. "Perhaps another day." She walked toward the door. "I'll call you next week to make sure you're okay."

"Wait, Dottie!" Lyle jumped to her feet. "It isn't working. The tattoo. I'm still having nightmares. It isn't keeping them away."

"Of course it isn't working. You never had it finished, Crocodile." She opened the door to leave. "How can you expect it to be strong enough to carry your burden when it still has empty spaces?"

Thirty-Six

Michael drove the truck through the resort, bouncing down the gravel road. The day had started a little cooler than usual, but the sun was streaming in through the windows, warming Lyle's face. She watched as brightly painted buildings went by. She thought of the blond-haired man. "I hope we don't run into Robinson Crusoe again. God, I hope he's not on my flight." She imagined the man sitting next to her on the plane home. Lyle questioned her decision not to report him to the police.

"He'll never touch you again," Michael said quietly.

A salty breeze blew through the open windows. Lyle closed her eyes and inhaled the intoxicating scent.

"What dive site are we going to?" she asked.

"Today is just you and me," said Michael. "I'll pull into the first empty site I see."

They drove past the airport and continued south. Every so often they slowed down to survey the beach. He drove until the pink salt flats could be seen in the distance.

"Can you believe it?" He eased his foot onto the brakes. A bright yellow rock displayed the name *Angel City*.

"Angel City!" said Lyle. "Just waiting for us."

He parked the truck facing the water and removed the key from the ignition. Ripples of water lapped in front of them, with Klein Bonaire on the horizon. They began setting up gear at the tailgate.

Lyle grinned. "Did I ever tell you I grew up in Oz?"

Michael raised an eyebrow. "Oz? As in the wonderful wizard of?"

"Yup, the very one."

"I've got to hear this."

"I grew up in Chittenango, New York. The birthplace of L. Frank Baum. We had an Oz festival every year." Two trucks pulled into the dive site, and her smile faded. "I'm afraid we've been found."

"Shit! Can we never have a second alone? I'm so tired of seeing Rick every time I turn around."

Lyle's friends piled out of their trucks. She touched the back of Michael's hand with the tip of her finger. This would have to be enough. They still had to keep their secret from Rick and Steve.

Rick called from his truck. "We're glad we found you. We should all be together on our last day of diving."

Being in an airplane at high altitude increased their risk of decompression sickness, so they never dove the day before a flight—a safety precaution.

"Are you feeling better?" asked Rick, as he got out of the truck. "We missed you last night. Angela said you were having some woman problems. I'd hate it if you had to miss the last day."

Lyle rolled her eyes then caught Angela with a big grin on her face as she and Victoria joined them.

Victoria's wetsuit hung open around her waist, and water was dripping off her strawberry-blond hair. She spoke in a hushed voice as Rick gathered gear at the back of his truck. "Sorry about this. Angela and I steered them in the wrong direction for as long as we could. Until he saw you here, we had Rick convinced you may still be back in your room. I'm sorry you weren't feeling well last night. I would've come and stayed with you if you needed me."

"Thanks, Victoria. But I wasn't sick, just tired. I wasn't alone either. Dottie stopped by on her way to the airport. We talked for a while, and then I went to bed early."

"Dottie came by?" asked Victoria. "I'm glad she was there for you. It'll be nice diving with you both on our last day. Tomorrow's all sunbathing and souvenir shopping. Then we'll have to leave it all behind."

They assembled their gear in silence. The vacation, as well as their time together, was coming to an end. Lyle fought her deepening melancholy. She refused to mope over their impending separation.

She climbed into the bed of their truck to retrieve an air cylinder. She was surprised to see Rick had joined them. He took the heavy cylinder from her. "I got this, Lyle. Let me help you out since you weren't feeling well."

"I'm feeling much better today. I can do this."

"Nonsense. I'll get it. You should take it easy." Rick proceeded to assemble her gear.

She stood back and watched him, her mouth agape.

"Victoria just told me you saw Dottie again yesterday, on her way to the airport. It's so nice of her to stop by."

Lyle was barely listening to Rick. She saw the frustration on Michael's face while he worked on his own equipment, both his smile and carefree spirit gone.

She pulled on her wetsuit and Rick picked up her BC. She only had to slip her arms into it. He turned her toward him, cinched her cummerbund tightly around her waist, and fastened the Velcro. He snapped the buckles and gave them an extra tug to be sure they were secure. Lyle, feeling very much like a child, half expected Rick to pull out a tissue and wipe her nose.

"There you go. Air is on. Weights are in your pockets. Here's your mask and fins. You're ready to go."

She took her equipment from him and rolled her eyes as she tromped off toward the ocean.

The six of them floated around the buoy marking the reef. They put their masks on, placed their regulators in their mouths, and effortlessly sank below the water. They descended together at an easy pace, the ocean accepting them with quiet calm. Lyle watched her computer until it read fifty feet. They swam weightlessly over the colorful coral in the silence of their hidden world.

Michael mimicked playing a wind instrument when he came upon a trumpet fish floating vertically in a tall branch of sea rod coral. He was able to get close enough to point his finger at the well-disguised fish. He looked back at Lyle as if to say "Look what I found." She played the trumpet herself.

They continued floating along the reef, taking in the spectacular colors of the fish and coral. The sun shone through the water and illuminated the colorful reef to glisten even brighter. She pointed out a school of yellow and white goat fish all resting on the sand. She placed her palms together, then rested her cheek on them, indicating the sleepy fish. He glanced behind them, and not seeing any of the other divers, he ran his hands over her leg and squeezed her ass. She shook her finger at him, indicating he shouldn't push his luck.

They leisurely swam north, taking turns pointing out both the unusual and more common sea life.

After thirty minutes, Lyle checked her computer and gave Michael the signal to turn around. As they did so, a little fish caught her eye.

There, in a protected area of coral, a fish no longer than a few inches, darted in and out of view. She knew immediately what it was: the elusive juvenile yellowtail damselfish. Her favorite. They hovered above the reef and waited for the baby to make another appearance.

Remaining as still as possible, they were rewarded by their patience when the fish swam back into view. It was velvetlike, very dark blue, almost black in color. Speckled all over its body were tiny light blue scales that seemed to glow from within like sapphires. Its bright yellow tail was in stark contrast to the rest of its body. Michael remembered Lyle's description of it all those days ago onboard the *Mi Dushi*. Watching the magnificent creature dart in and out of the coral, he could see now why she searched for this fish with such great resolve.

He remembered her words to his sister: *Anyone can find the big stuff.* She was right. It was the small elusive life that was truly extraordinary. These tiny creatures somehow survived, and thrived, in the vastness of the ocean.

They stayed and watched the yellowtail damselfish until their depleting air supply forced them to head back. They swam to the buoy line where they had descended and followed the line to the surface.

Michael removed his mask. "Awesome fish. I don't even mind owing you the dollar. It was exactly as you described. The scales really do glow like a neon sign."

"I'll take that dollar in cash please."

Only two trucks remained on the beach. Victoria and Angela were removing their gear. Steve and Rick's truck was gone.

Victoria yelled from the beach, "The boys took off to the next site. We're going to go meet them. You two have fun!" Victoria gave a quick wave as she and Angela climbed into their truck.

"I really love them." She brushed the wet hair out of Michael's eyes. His lips were cold, but she liked the salty tang as he kissed her. "You taste like a margarita."

As they made their way out of the water, a truck rolled into the lot. Four men climbed out.

"Hey, Michael Miller," one said. "I heard you were diving on Bonaire. Do you mind if we get a picture?"

The men joined them, carrying their phones. "You did a great job with the John Magnum story."

Michael stood up straight and raised his eyebrows. "That's nice to hear. Thank you."

The man gestured to one of his friends. "Bill and I are both veterans. We appreciated the seriousness of the movie. It wasn't made pretty for Hollywood. It really showed people what can happen over there."

Michael shook hands all around as introductions were made. "Thank you. It was a real honor for me to have been chosen for the role. I'm glad to hear veterans approve of the work. And thank you for your service. You're the true heroes."

Lyle was familiar with her role in these situations. "Would you like me to get some photos?"

They left Angel City and casually drove down the narrow road. Michael slowed the truck when he saw their friends unloading gear at a site. "Do you want to dive with them again?"

"Please? I haven't spent any real time with them in a few days."

He pulled in and backed the truck up even with the others.

"I know you've had it with Rick," said Lyle. "He's annoying me too."

She hopped out of the truck. "Mind if we join you? We're on our last tanks, so this'll be it for us."

Rick smiled. "That'd be great."

They dove as a group and all swam together. As their air pressure got low, they reluctantly ended the dive and left the water.

Victoria looked out over the sparkling ocean. "I hate the last day of diving. It's so sad to have it come to an end. I'm going to miss it so much."

Angela, drying off with a towel, looked at Lyle. "Will you join us for dinner? We thought we'd walk over to Captain Jack's."

"I don't know, I'm kind of—"

"Go, Lyle," said Michael, pulling his shirt over his head. "Enjoy the time with your friends. I need a break from Rick. I'll be fine. I'll get something to eat in town. I won't starve."

"Captain Jack's," she said with apprehension, "I wish you were coming too."

"You're safe now, I promise. Please, no worrying. Enjoy dinner with your friends."

She was grateful for his reassuring words but couldn't help but question the certainty of the promise.

Once back at the resort, Lyle was surprised when Michael climbed the stairs to her room with her. He took her key, unlocked her door, and pushed it open. She took a step inside, but he didn't follow.

He held up the key. "I'm keeping this. I don't want to be locked out again. I'll be waiting for you when you get back."

Thirty-Seven

Lyle finished the last bite of her crab stuffed ravioli. Then she mopped a piece of garlic bread over her plate and gathered the remaining sauce. She washed it down with a smooth pinot noir. She shared a chocolate mousse with Angela. The rich, creamy texture was heavenly.

Lyle was disappointed that Michael hadn't joined them. Now that dinner was finished, she was anxious to get back to him.

Their table at Captain Jack's was littered with empty glasses and dirty napkins. The sun had set long ago, and a lazy atmosphere had set in.

Steve broke up the party when he stood. "I guess we sleep in tomorrow. I'm sure I'll be up at five. If you see me heading toward the dock in the dark, please stop me and send me back to my room."

They began the easy walk back to the resort.

Victoria caught up to Lyle and Angela. She squeezed in between them and draped her arms over their shoulders. "Who's up for souvenir shopping tomorrow? I want to take some Bonaire sea salt home." When she got no response, she continued. "Or we can go on a kayaking tour of the mangroves." Silence. "How about snorkeling at the salt pier? Or we can take a tour of the caves?" She yelled over her shoulder, "Rick, how about the mangroves tomorrow?"

"Or we can try windsurfing down at Lac Bai," said Rick.

"I'll stop by the reception desk tonight and get some information on all our options. We can look through them and then decide." Victoria said.

And with that, tomorrow's activities were being planned.

Lyle had envisioned herself sitting on a lounge chair near the ocean. She thought she would let the sun blanket her while she drank something frozen. In a matter of minutes, her relaxing plans were cast aside.

They said good night and went their separate ways.

She climbed the stairs with a hop in her step and a smile on her face. She came to her door and realized she didn't have a key. She felt silly knocking on her own door. She had barely enough time to put her hand back down when the door swung open. Michael's hair was still wet from the shower. She took a moment to admire the way his muscles cut in behind his briefs. He shut the door and pulled her to him. She inhaled his flowery smell. He had used her body wash and shampoo but hadn't bothered to shave.

"Finally." He kissed her neck. He found her lips and tasted chocolate and wine. "You had a good dinner. Let me taste again." He kissed her and urgently opened the buttons on her shirt.

She leaned her head back and let him explore her body. He put his hands on the back of her thighs and drove them up under her skirt. She grinned like a Cheshire cat when he found the frilly white thong she had chosen for tonight.

"Shit, Lyle, you know how to drive me crazy." He groped her ass. "I'm glad I didn't know you were wearing these tonight. I never would've let you go to dinner."

He released himself from his now too-tight briefs and frantically pushed her skirt up to her hips. He backed her onto the edge of the bed and moved her thong to the side. With her rear end barely on the edge of the bed, he moved swiftly and immediately his need was satisfied. He fell forward breathing heavily. "I'm so sorry. I couldn't wait any longer."

"No need to apologize." She ran her fingers through his damp hair. "I understand."

She removed her remaining clothes and the two of them climbed into bed. They pushed the comforter to the floor and laid under the cool sheets. They were close to sleep when they heard a knock at the door.

"It's Victoria," said Lyle. "She was going to find information about activities for tomorrow." They untangled themselves from the sheets, and Lyle yelled toward the door. "Give me a second, I'm coming." She found her skirt and top and hastily threw them on.

Michael slid into his jeans. "I thought we just practiced our activity for tomorrow."

She opened the door. "Rick, I...I thought you were Victoria." She was suddenly hyperaware of her disheveled clothes and hair.

Rick looked past her to Michael, bare-chested in jeans and untangling himself from the comforter they'd pushed to the floor.

Rick's face went icy. "What the hell? You're sleeping with him? Are you kidding me? What the hell are you doing?" His eyes fixed on Michael. He pushed past Lyle and stopped inches in front of him. "What is this? Some sick kind of Oedipus complex?"

She held the door open. "Rick, get out! Get out of here now!"

He turned toward her. "You're sleeping with the famous Michael Miller? You're a teenaged groupie now?"

Michael grabbed Rick by his shirt. A thud sounded as he pushed him up against the wall. He drew his arm back and let loose, his fist connecting with Rick's face. Rick's head whipped to the side. He held his hands up in front of himself and waited for the next blow. Michael struck him in the ribcage. A rush of air came from his lungs as he bent forward. But Rick was unwilling to fight back.

Michael felt Lyle pull on his arm. At her touch he immediately stopped the assault. Rick wrapped his arm around his ribs. Cringing, he slid down the wall and sat on the floor.

"Oh God, Rick, are you okay?" Lyle shouted over her shoulder, "Michael, get out of here! What're you thinking? Are you crazy? Get out of here, you lunatic!"

Michael grabbed his shirt and bolted out the door barefooted.

"Can you stand? Let me help you up." She put her arm around his back and helped him to the bed. He slumped on it and sat holding his head in his hands.

"I'm going for some ice," Lyle said as her pulse thudded.

She ran out the door and down the stairs. The only ice machine she knew of was at the reception desk. She arrived there out of breath and could only say "Ice?"

She filled a bucket and slammed the lid closed. She took the stairs back to her room two at a time. She caught her toe on the top step and fell to her knees. Ice spilled everywhere. "Fuck me." She scooped up as much as she could, trying to leave the bits of dirt and gravel behind. She walked, shaking, toward her room.

Lyle grabbed a washcloth from the bathroom and wrapped several ice cubes in. She then gently placed the washcloth under Rick's left eye. Her hand trembled and she couldn't keep the ice in place. She placed his hand on the washcloth. "Hold this here. Let me see what I have in my carry-on." She pulled it out of the closet and started riffling through it. She found a bottle of ibuprofen and got a glass of water from the bathroom.

"Here, take these. Do you need a doctor? I can drive you to the hospital."

"You're going to completely ruin my reputation if you make me see a doctor after a little scuffle. I'm going to be fine, really." He stood up and noticed the stress on her face. "You look worse than I feel. Are you okay?"

"I'm so sorry. I thought you were Victoria at the door. I never would've wanted you to find out this way."

Holding the ice on his eye, he walked toward the door. "I'm going to go lay down. We can talk in the morning. Please don't beat yourself up over this. Everything's going to be fine."

She held the door open. "This is all my fault. Dottie told me to end it. She said to end it if I thought there was any chance the relationship could blow up on me. I never thought I was putting anyone in danger."

"Dottie's a smart girl. You should listen to her."

Thirty-Eight

It was still dark outside when Lyle got out of bed and used the bathroom. She picked up her phone and checked the time: 4:45 a.m. She remembered Steve's comment at dinner the night before and wondered who else was up this early.

She hadn't slept well; her head was foggy. She forced herself back into bed, pulled the comforter up to her shoulders, and closed her eyes. Before she could worry about Rick and Michael and the long day she had ahead of her, she was fast asleep.

When she awoke again, the sun was shining and she felt much more rested. For a moment, all was right with the world. She rolled onto her back and stretched her arms over her head. She pointed her toes and stretched her legs as well. The memories of the previous night hit her. She put her hands on her face trying to block them out.

There was a quiet knock at her door, and she padded over to open it.

Rick's voice was dry with sleep. "Good morning. I hope I didn't wake you."

"Good morning. You look like shit. Your left eye is swollen shut." She motioned for him to come in.

He held two cups of coffee and offered one to her. "Cream and sugar, just the way you like it."

"How do you feel?"

"I imagine I feel as good as I look. I think you'll be kayaking and snorkeling without me today." They sat by the balcony doors and sipped their coffees. "I know you'll find this hard to believe, but I'm sorry about what happened last night. I realize I put you in a bad position. Your friend and your...boyfriend, fighting."

"The last thing you need to worry about is how this affects me. Do you think we should take you to an urgent care?"

"No, no doctor. What I need now is time to heal."

"Why didn't you defend yourself? You put your hands up in front of you, but you didn't try to stop him or hit him back." He didn't answer, and a realization hit her. "You wanted me to see what he was capable of doing."

"I had my suspicions after the other night in your room. He has a short fuse, to put it mildly. And you tend to have that same short fuse. It might be a bad combination."

Lyle remembered kicking Michael in the shin and throwing a glass against her wall. She'd sent his sister's sunhat flying out to sea. Rick's assessment was fair.

"I'm so sorry you found out about us this way. I would've gladly gone to my grave with my dark secret than have anything bad happen to you."

"It wasn't your fault. I should've known something was up. You've been talking to Dottie a lot. I'm upset with myself for not seeing what was going on right in front of my eyes."

"You should've defended yourself. You could've been hurt even worse."

"Somehow the son of a bitch has become friends with everyone." He smiled. "Angela would kill me if I hit Michael Miller. Besides, when I was his age, I would've reacted the same way. I'm not a complete idiot, Lyle. I knew what would happen when I said those things last night. I'd seen his temper before. I knew what buttons to push. I'm just as guilty for provoking the fight as he is for landing the punches."

"I need to go see him."

"Let me talk to him first." He stood to leave. "Let me straighten things out with Michael. Then the two of you can talk this through and we can all get back to enjoying what's left of our vacation."

Lyle's plans for a day by the water were now back on track. She put on her emerald-green two-piece suit, her favorite. It had a strapless top with a golden anchor between the breasts. The boy shorts covered her enough to be modestly seen in public. She was determined to get rid of her wetsuit tan lines and covered herself in sunscreen.

She was grateful for the cheerful atmosphere at the waterfront. Island music was piped in from hidden speakers among the vegetation. Guests in brightly colored bathing suits laid in rows on chaise lounges, tanning, chatting, and enjoying beverages with little umbrellas and fresh fruit.

She found an available spot not far down the beach and laid her towel on the chair. She slipped off her sandals, scrolled down her list of music, and put her earbuds in. The brilliant sun had yet to reach its peak. She hit Play and rested back in the warm sun.

The old trailer was the most wonderful home Lyle could have imagined. She was glad to leave the cold tent behind her and grateful for solid walls and floors.

It was a cool fall day when two men knocked on the front door. Roy was out, so she ran to her mother's bedroom and woke her. "Mama, someone is knocking on the door for us."

The workers introduced themselves to Lyle's mother, pointing at the four loose steps at their feet. Roy would always say "Mind the gap" as they hopped over the space between the top stair and the trailer door.

Lyle observed the exchange between her mother and the men. After a few minutes of talking, her mother went to the kitchen and picked up her pack of cigarettes. She lit one and shook the match until the flame went out then tossed it into the sink. Her hair was braided down her back but was frizzy around her face. She stood with one hand on her hip, smoking, as she watched the men outside.

The men ran extension cords out the door to their power tools. They used sledgehammers, and in a few minutes Lyle saw the old steps give way and fall from the trailer.

"Mama, how will we get outside?"

With fresh wood in hand, the men completed a new set of steps for the trailer.

As they gathered their tools, another car arrived. Two women got out carrying several bags of groceries.

Lyle's mother begrudgingly invited all four of them inside. They put the grocery bags down in the kitchen. She dug through the bags and looked up at the visitors. "Are you from the state? Are we on a list somewhere?"

One of the men said, "No, we're not from the state. We're from Catholic Charities." He was jovial when he added, "We like helping people who might be in need. It was brought to our attention that the steps to your trailer weren't safe. Do you mind if we stay and chat for a while?" He gestured toward the card table and four folding chairs.

They gave Lyle's mother a brochure, pointed out some information, and explained to her what the brochure didn't. Lyle had lost interest and had gone to play in her room.

"Lyle, come out here," her mother called out after talking with the group for several minutes.

One of the men, with gray curls and a receding hairline, bent down on his knee to talk directly to Lyle. His thick glasses made his eyes look too big for his face. "How would you like to attend Saint Mary's school?"

Lyle thought he was creepy and didn't know who Saint Mary was. She looked to her mother for guidance and wished Roy was home. He would know what this was all about and would have told Lyle what to say.

Her mother forced a smile. "Lyle, these people are going to see to it that you get a good education at a fancy school." She ran her hand over her frizzy hair. "You should say thank you." She squeezed Lyle's shoulder trying to get a response.

"Thank you," she said in a tiny voice.

She wanted them to leave so she could open the bags of groceries. There wasn't always food in the trailer and Lyle thought she saw peanut butter.

She heard a faraway voice: "Lyle, are you awake? She kept her eyes closed and turned her head away from the intrusion. She was hungry and wanted to open the peanut butter she knew was in the paper bag.

"Come on, wake up," Michael said softly.

She squinted and lifted her arm to her forehead.

"We need to talk, but it can't be here." He was standing above her, his ball cap pulled down low. "You need to get out of the sun, baby."

She sat up and waited for the fog of sleep to clear. She thought briefly of the men that came to her trailer that day and said a silent prayer of thanks. "All right, just give me a second." She was uncomfortably thirsty but didn't dare tell Michael she was out in the heat with no water again. "Did Rick find you? He wanted to talk to you." She was having a hard time waking up. She thought she smelled cigarette smoke and looked around to see who was smoking. The scent vanished. She stood to gather her things. "I can't find my phone."

"You need to wake up some more." He picked up the phone from the sand. "And yes, he did find me. We spent the better part of the morning together." He handed her the phone. "Let's go. We need to get you some water."

"How did he look? Is he feeling okay?"

"He looked like he'd gotten punched by a lunatic. I'm afraid I really did a number on his eye. He claims he feels fine."

"I'm sorry. I shouldn't have called you a lunatic. I was so upset."

"Baby, you called it like you saw it."

They walked to the pool bar and sat at a table hidden around the back. Michael went to the bar and returned with a pitcher full of ice water and two glasses.

"I'm sorry you had to see that last night. I feel horrible about it." He paused, hoping she would respond, but she didn't. "My temper took over when he started talking shit about us."

"This is twice now I've watched you fight. It's going to get you into real trouble sometime. And it scared me."

"Rick has forgiven me. We talked it out. Now I need you to forgive me. We only have this last day together," he said, desperation in his voice now. "It can't end like this."

He looked beyond her, raised his eyebrows, and put a pleasant smile on his face. Lyle knew that smile and prepared to take pictures for the woman who approached them.

The woman went on about how nice Michael was and how his mother must have raised him right. Lyle rolled her eyes only to be caught by him.

"I'm sorry I scared you. It won't happen again. Please, Lyle."

She remembered Rick's words from that morning. He admitted to egging Michael on with the comments he made. Perhaps the fight really was partially Rick's fault. Maybe it wasn't strictly Michael's doing. "I'll forgive you, but last night won't be forgotten for a long time."

Michael visibly relaxed. "I think it's safe to say none of us will forget last night for a very long time. Go put on some clothes and meet me at the reception desk. I have a surprise for you." He started toward his room and called over his shoulder, "Wear sneakers."

Thirty-Nine

Lyle put on a pair of shorts and a pale green tank top. She got to the reception desk in time to see Michael wheeling out a bike from the rack. He had changed out of his swim trunks and was wearing shorts and a sleeveless T-shirt.

"Not the bike again." She remembered their last ride together and moved cautiously toward it. "How far are we going? Last time it was really wobbly."

Michael was glad to see her humor had returned, even if it was at his expense. "Be a sport and trust me, will you?" He patted the seat. "Come on, climb up. You remember how, don't you? We're not going too far."

They rode out of the resort and headed north. He pumped the peddles, and the bike glided over the narrow street. Lyle held onto his waist and enjoyed the breeze and view.

He turned off the main road into the donkey sanctuary. Small herds dotted the landscape in the distance. A flamboyance of pink flamingos was wading nearby in a salt lake.

"This is your surprise." The bike came to a stop and Michael held it steady as Lyle climbed down. "I really wanted to take you to one of the spas on the island. You know, have a couple's massage and champagne. Maybe a nice dinner and then spend the night in the honeymoon suite. Then I remembered who I was trying to impress and decided on the donkeys instead."

"The donkey sanctuary is the perfect surprise. And you're right. I would choose it over a spa any day."

"Why do I think you're not kidding?"

They went inside a brightly painted shelter, where an older man with salt and pepper hair sat behind a counter. Michael paid the small admission fee and bought two bags of carrots from the man, who handed him some information about the sanctuary and pointed them in the right direction.

As they walked, Michael read from the pamphlet. "According to this, donkeys have been living wild on Bonaire since the seventeenth century. Originally they were brought over from Spain and used for hard labor. Once they were no longer needed, they were set free. They still roam about the island in small groups." He turned the page. "There are over four hundred donkeys in the sanctuary. We better get started if we're going to meet them all. I think we should start up this way." He jutted his chin toward the right, indicating a dirt road that wound up a small embankment toward a field of donkeys. A van filled with schoolchildren crept passed them.

"I think we're supposed to drive through the park," said Lyle. "Maybe we should've taken a truck up here."

Michael took her hand. "We could drive the truck, but what fun would that be?" He kissed her cheek. "I always preferred walking through the donkey sanctuaries back home." She narrowed her eyes. He lifted his nose into the air. "Besides, we may not be able to fully appreciate the aroma if we were in the truck."

They walked hand in hand and followed the dusty road deeper into the sanctuary. She rested her head on his arm and felt contented being close to him again.

They saw a herd of donkeys hanging their heads over a fence. The animals brayed as they watched them approach. The donkeys were light brown, almost gray in color, and their gentle dark eyes stood out above their soft muzzles. Their oversized ears perked up as the two got closer.

Lyle tore open a bag of carrots and the braying intensified. She spoke in a baby's voice, "How did you know we brought carrots?" She handed several to Michael. "Watch your fingers. We want to leave here with ten each."

They put bits of carrots on their palms and fed the donkeys until a bagful was eaten. Michael wiped his palm on his shorts and put the empty bag in his pocket.

They continued toward another field of donkeys. As they walked up the incline, the ocean came into view, and they slowed their pace.

"What time is your flight out in the morning?" He took the second bag of carrots from her and tore it open.

"Early. The resort's van leaves for the airport at six. What about you? What time do you go?" She wondered if they would be on the same flight to Atlanta.

"I'm flying through Houston in the afternoon."

They followed the dusty road and endless fence line.

"Catherine, my manager, texted me about reading a new script. I told her not now. I'm unplugged—no business, no internet. I'll see it soon enough."

"You know that by reading her text you totally broke the unplugged rule."

They came to a group of mares with their young foals. Lyle snapped the carrots into bite sized pieces and fed them to the babies. Their muzzles were soft on her hand, and she giggled at the sensation. She couldn't feed the carrots fast enough. Michael laughed at her as she tried to keep up with demand

"I should've bought more bags. You're making a lot of friends with those carrots," he said.

They said goodbye to the foals and ambled through the sanctuary until they could see the brightly painted shelter ahead.

"I knew I wanted to know you that first day we spoke on the dock. I made you so mad you tossed Natalie's hat into the water. Man, you were furious. Somehow there you were the next day, like magic." He smiled. "Angela in that red bikini. My warning signals were at DEFCON 5. You were so cool I was sure you didn't know who I was. Come to find out you knew exactly who I was but wouldn't give me the time of day. I knew I had my work cut out for me. Is it possible that was only two weeks ago?"

Lyle felt a lump form in her throat. "Did you bring me here to say goodbye?"

They stopped walking and released their hands.

"I can't say goodbye to you," she said, her face falling. "Let's simply fade away."

"Rick said there was a farewell dinner at the resort tonight," said Michael. "He said it's a tradition with you guys, and it sounded like we're expected to be there. I wanted a little time with you today, alone, to say good—"

"No," she interrupted. "No goodbyes. I don't want to be sad today. We both know what's coming. I think we both know there's been an expiration date on our relationship since the very beginning."

"We can keep in touch," he pleaded. "This doesn't have to be the end for us. We can see each other again. People do the long-distance thing all the time. Or… you could move to the West Coast. You could be with me."

Being with Michael could never be a conventional relationship. At least, not for the foreseeable future. They would never hold hands in public. She would constantly worry over being found out. Her intuition was telling her to let him go.

"What exactly are you offering me? A love that needs to be hidden, denied even, in order to survive? More of the hide and seek we've had to play already? There are too many obstacles in our way to move forward. The odds of us succeeding are poor at best. You're young and full of optimism. It all looks easy to you."

"Baby, we can make this work. I can…"

"Michael, there's something about Bonaire. It's magical. It brought us together. If we end it now, it ends perfectly. Let's do that. Let's fade into the sunset at the end of our fairy tale."

He could see there was no persuading her. Perhaps he had read her wrong. The inconvenience of being with him was too much for her. He let the subject drop. Lyle was right. They deserved the happy ending.

Forty

Lyle stole some time away from Michael to pack for the trip home. She emptied her locker at the dock then meticulously cleaned her gear and carried it all back to her room. She set her equipment on the balcony to dry while she folded clothes and placed them in neat piles on the bed. She collected her personal items from the bathroom. She draped her jeans and white blouse over the chair for the flight home and fit the folded clothes into her luggage.

The room was suddenly empty. All signs that anyone had lived there for the past two weeks were packed away.

In the morning it would all come rushing back. The news, the internet. She would turn on her phone and check her email. She thought of her coworkers and wondered how things had gone at the office while she was away.

After a long rest, she dressed for dinner. In the mirror, she was surprised to see the sad look on her face. She touched the small laugh lines at the corners of her eyes and forced herself to smile. She lifted her eyebrows, trying to brighten her face. The resulting look was worse, so she put her sad face back on. She placed her key in her pocket, pulled the door to her room shut, and followed the tree-covered path to the pool bar. She stopped near the entrance and scanned the outdoor restaurant. Mookie was setting up his equipment, and the place was starting to fill up with guests. She recognized divers and fans who had stood for photos and asked for autographs. She realized a lot of the fans were older men and women. Michael's appeal wasn't bound by age, something she knew firsthand.

Failing to see any of her friends, Lyle took a seat at the bar, where she could enjoy the view of the ocean while she waited for them. The sun was low in the sky, its golden glow perfectly reflected in the glass-like water.

She ordered the resort special. Once served, she took a sip of the potent cocktail—rum and lime juice with banana liqueur. She looked at the bartender and blew air out of her pursed lips. That was the reaction he was waiting for. He smiled and went to serve a couple at the end of the bar.

She then felt something soft at her feet and looked down to see Calypso's wet nose and dark eyes looking up. Captain Maartin slid onto the barstool next to her. His dark eyes were still bright as a child's. He wore a single gold hoop in one ear, and Lyle found it fascinating that this real-life pirate could blend in so seamlessly at the sleek resort. When he spoke, it was in his familiar dry voice and his fading Dutch accent.

"Good evening, Lyle. I didn't see you on my boat after I had to ground you and your friend. I hope you're not holding it against me. I've come to apologize if I've insulted you." He caught the eye of the bartender and gestured toward the beer taps. He pulled the captain a draft and placed the cool, foaming drink in front of him. "My main concern is always for the safety of the divers on my vessel. Sometimes I'm forced to make tough decisions." He took a long drink of the sparkling draft. "Honestly, Lyle, after talking with Peter, the decision to ground you was an easy one to make."

"Captain Maartin, you did me a gigantic favor keeping me out of the water that day. Looking back, I realize I had no business diving. I want you to understand it was lack of sleep that had me in that stupor." She lowered her voice. "I know Peter thought I was under the influence of something, but really, I wasn't. I want to be sure you know that." She ran her finger around the rim of her drink. "I was so tired that day. I had a nightmare, or maybe it was a daydream, I don't know. I lost track of my dive buddies and lost track of time and my depth. I'm not sure exactly what happened, but I do know I owe Peter a huge amount of gratitude for getting me back to the boat safely." She spoke sincerely. "I need to thank you too for looking out for us, both of us."

Captain Maartin leaned in close. "Michael Miller may not be a good choice for you."

She straightened at the change of subject, not quite believing what she heard. "I don't know what you're talking about. Michael and I are just—"

"I've seen you two together on my boat twice now and here at the resort for the last two weeks. I know you work to keep your affair private, but it hasn't escaped me." He took another drink of his beer and wiped some foam from his graying mustache. "I know this is none of my business, but I must tell you, I see it all the time." He lifted his chin to the setting sun. "Our island, it's magic. Our sun has the strength to reawaken one's spirit, and the salt in the air will cure your heart. People's souls are healed, and their lives pulled back together by the power of our ocean. All you have to do is allow it to happen." He lowered his voice and continued in an ominous tone. "The problem comes when you leave this island. Sometimes the magic stays here, but it will wait for you and will be here when you return again."

Captain Maartin drank the last of his beer, patted Lyle on her back, and walked away. Calypso followed at his side.

Lyle stared at the empty mug. The captain's peculiar words ran through her. *Sometimes the magic stays here.*

"Hey! There you are!" Victoria called out to her, and Captain Maartin's strange words were forgotten. "We found a table around the side, by the pool." She put her arm around her and gave her a quick hug. "Come on. We're waiting for Angela and Michael to join us."

Lyle left some money on the bar and picked up her cocktail. "How was the kayaking today?"

"It was wonderful. Our tour guide was a student from the University of Amsterdam. She's running the mangrove tours as a summer internship. Why didn't I think of that when I was in school? Kayaking in the Caribbean. I interned at a law firm. My office didn't even have a window."

Rick and Steve were seated at a large round table, disagreeing about politics. Victoria put her hand on Rick's shoulder. "Please, no political talk at least until tomorrow. We still have one night to pretend it all doesn't exist. I'd hate to have to give you a second black eye." She kissed Rick on the cheek and sat down. "How're you feeling? Do we need to separate you and Michael for dinner tonight?" She grinned as Michael joined them.

"Don't worry, Victoria," Michael said. "I'm on my best behavior tonight. I'm lucky Rick didn't let loose on me last night."

Michael sat next to Lyle and touched her on the back, saying hello in their secret way.

"How do you feel, Rick?" Lyle asked quietly.

"I hate to break it to all of you, but his black eye is a major chick magnet. Women love a bad boy," he said jokingly.

Lyle was thankful for the lightheartedness. She was even more thankful that Rick and Michael had seemed to put the incident behind them. They did it for her and she felt filled with love.

"And please," Michael continued, "remind me to thank you for making me clean everyone's gear this morning. I feel I've completed my penitence."

Everyone thanked him for cleaning all their equipment and helping them carry it back to the rooms.

"He didn't clean mine," Lyle said disapprovingly. "I had to do my own this afternoon."

"We didn't have your locker key and we couldn't find you," Victoria explained. "You weren't in your room. We knocked several times."

"I fell asleep in a lounge chair by the water. But if I had known, I would've made sure you had my locker key."

A cheerful voice sang out, "I'm here!" Angela, in full makeup, pin-straight hair to her chin, arrived at the table. She wore a burnt red sundress with a plunging neckline. She circled the table, greeting everyone with a kiss and hug, dangerously testing the limits of her bodice. "Our last night, shit. I always hate the last night. It's so sad to have to leave." She sat next to Victoria. "Nice job with my gear Michael, thanks. Feel free to beat up my friend Rick anytime." She picked up her menu as the waiter approached the table for drink orders. "We'd like two pitchers of Island Mule. We're in the Caribbean for our last night. I think we should drink rum."

Lyle smiled and lifted her half-full glass. "I agree. Let's drink rum."

The waiter brought two pitchers of the dark amber drink and placed glasses around the table. Rick gave him their dinner orders without consulting anyone. He passed the pitchers to his friends.

Victoria lifted her glass and waited for her friends to do the same. "La vie Bohéme!"

They all touched glasses and repeated, "La vie Bohéme!"

Michael arched an eyebrow questioning the toast.

"Roughly translated, we're drinking to a long, Bohemian life," Lyle explained.

Michael raised his glass. "Well then, hear, hear!"

Conversation turned to past trips and dives and detailing what made them most memorable. They had told the same stories time and time again, but Michael hadn't heard them yet, so they would be repeated for him tonight.

Lyle talked about her first dive trip to the Florida springs, where she had earned her certification. She talked about her surprise at diving at Devil's Den.

"We drove up and parked in the middle of a huge field. There wasn't a drop of water in sight, but there we were with our cars full of gear. We hiked toward this small group of trees where we saw a stone stairwell, so we went down the narrow set of stairs, ducking our heads so we wouldn't bump into rocks, and entered an incredible underground cavern. The water was so clear. We swam with snakes, turtles, and large catfish. We even saw some bats hanging on the walls. There's a stone statue that looks like the devil hidden in the water among the sunken caves, but I didn't find him. I'll have to go back sometime and look for it again."

Rick told of a dive off the coast of North Carolina when the weather had turned bad. Lyle had heard this one before but enjoyed hearing his over-the-top retelling.

It warmed Lyle's heart to know that this trip, these dives, and this very dinner would be archived to be told again in the future. They would talk about the year they met Michael Miller. They would laugh and try to recall the details. She was sure this vacation, these two weeks on Bonaire, would be among her favorite memories.

Forty-One

The waiter arrived with dinner and was instructed to put the entrées anywhere on the table.

"Michael, let me apologize in advance for the lies I'm going to tell my friends about you," Angela teased. "I hope you don't mind if I elaborate on the romantic vacation we spent together."

Michael would miss Angela's free spirit and her no-nonsense way of expressing herself. "Lie away, Angela, do your worst. If they don't believe you, have them call me. I'll verify every sordid detail."

They leisurely finished dinner. Lyle was thankful that the sun had finally set. Darkness would help keep Michael hidden from his fans.

Steve stood and put his hand out to her. "How about one more trip around the dance floor?"

She was happy to be asked and took Steve's hand just as a familiar face approached the table. She spoke quietly to Angela: "I think an old friend has returned." And she left with Steve.

Cameron smiled sweetly at Angela. "Care to dance?" They held hands as they left the table.

The waiter returned to clear the empty dinner plates. "Shall I bring two more pitchers of drinks? Or perhaps a nice brandy."

"Thanks, but I'll have a coffee. Make it decaffeinated. I have to get up early tomorrow," said Rick.

Victoria slumped back in her chair. "Vacation really is over. I'll have the same."

"Make that three," Michael added.

The three sat quietly listening to the music coming from the dance floor. They caught glimpses of their friends off in the distance. The waiter returned with mugs and a large pot of coffee.

Rick lifted his cup. "Here's to us. Making it to the end of one wild dive trip."

"This is one for the record books," said Victoria, as she sipped her coffee.

"Hey, I'm sorry things got so out of hand," Michael said. "I know this wasn't your typical vacation. But in all honesty, I never thought I'd meet someone I'm so excited about." He pushed his hair out of his eyes. Rick and Victoria exchanged a knowing look. "I never planned to start any kind of a relationship. I came here with my sister to get away from it all." He asked warily, "Any advice on how to convince Lyle to see me again once we're back in the states? She's being stubborn. She's dead set that this is the end for us."

"Tell him, Rick. He deserves to know."

"Victoria," said Rick, mouth in a straight line, "let it go. We're all going home tomorrow."

"What if this isn't the end? What if he convinces her to see him again?"

Michael looked from Rick to Victoria. "What're you two talking about?"

Rick leaned back in his chair. "Nothing, Michael. We're not talking about anything." He muttered at Victoria. "Just let it go."

"He's come this far with her. I don't want—"

"Stop! Stop whatever this is!" Michael said. "What the hell are you two talking about? What is it I don't know?"

"If you don't tell him, I will." Victoria said calmly. "We both know it'll sound better coming from you."

Rick dropped his head, defeated, then looked up. "I don't know how much Lyle has confided in you. I mean, regarding her mother and her upbringing."

Michael chuckled and leaned back in his chair. "Oh, don't worry. She's told me all about her mother. The drug use, the bad childhood. She told me you two helped her mom with some food assistance plan or something. That you guys keep in touch with her mom more than she does." He took a sip of his coffee. "We've gotten close over the past two weeks. She's also told me about her friend Dottie, how they grew up together."

"Yes, Dottie," Rick said quietly.

"I'd love to meet her. What was she thinking talking Lyle into getting that tattoo? She must be a really good friend for Lyle to trust her that much."

Victoria and Rick exchanged an uncomfortable look. She encouraged him to go on.

"What you don't know, and what Lyle doesn't know, is that her mother shared some information with us. Information about Lyle."

Victoria's voice was gentle. "We understand that Lyle can never forgive her mother for what she put her through growing up. Her mom is doing pretty well. She's been clean and sober for several years now. She holds down a part time job and tries to take care of herself."

"What's all this about information she shared with you regarding Lyle?" Michael asked.

"Lyles made some strange decisions. Including that tattoo," said Victoria. "We've noticed she has trouble focusing on day-to-day life. She seems to be haunted by memories from her childhood. We're trying to be good friends. We're trying to help her."

Rick continued, "According to Lyle's mother, there is no Dottie. Lyle created her when she was very young."

Forty-Two

"W hat?" said Michael.

"Lyle needed someone strong to be by her side. Since she didn't have anyone, she made someone up." Rick paused and let the information sink in. "Her mother thinks Dottie is actually Dorothy from *The Wonderful Wizard of Oz*."

"No, no, no," said Michael, slamming his palms onto the table, "Fuck this! You're making this up. This can't possibly be true." His anger faded. "I know her. I love her."

"According to her mother, the inscription on the first page of her book, *Dottie* written in crayon, was written by Lyle. When her mother realized what was going on, she asked her school to intervene. Lyle suffers from post-traumatic stress disorder. There are triggers that bring back memories of the trauma she suffered as a kid. She was in therapy for a little while during elementary school. Her mom thinks she was able to beat the system. Apparently, she convinced her therapist she was cured."

Michael's heart paused for a beat. "No, this can't be true. You're making this up to get rid of me."

"When life gets hard to handle, Dottie shows up to help," Victoria explained. "She gives Lyle advice. Tells her she's strong and that she's going to be okay. When Lyle told us Dottie was at Captain Jack's last week, we knew she was having an episode."

"She'd been attacked in the ladies' room," Michael explained. "It was that drunk guy from the dive site. I showed up just in time. I beat the shit out of him."

"I guess I owe you an apology," said Rick. "I thought you were the one bringing on her trauma. Damn, Lyle. Why didn't she tell us about the attack?"

When no one answered Michael offered, "She can be a little stubborn."

They grinned at his remark.

"Lyle's been stressed over her relationship with you. Your popularity and the age difference," Victoria said. "Dottie supposedly visited her in her room recently and gave her advice. Which of course, was only Lyle talking herself into staying with you until the end of the vacation."

"Michael, I know you don't think much of me," said Rick. "I'm a contradiction—I broke up with Lyle but obviously I'm still in love with her. I had to make a hard decision. It became clear I could take better care of her as a friend. I could be more objective. I do love her. It pains me to have to be her father figure when, in fact, I want to be her lover."

"Shit, Rick," Michael said. "I had no idea. I never could figure out why you'd left her. I could see you still love her. It didn't make any sense. Until now."

"Then off she went with you," Rick continued. "With no one to keep an eye on her. After Captain Maartin pulled you two from diving, I lost it. She needs me" –he nodded at Victoria—"us, to watch after her."

"I'm glad I know. I can watch out for her. I can make her better. I can love her even more." Michael whispered, "I know how to keep her safe."

Victoria took Michael's hand. "You do love her. I can see that. You want what's best for her. I'm proud to call you my friend, Michael. Please, enjoy tonight. Enjoy tonight and say goodbye in the morning."

Forty-Three

Michael leaned the bike up against the small tree at the sandy beach. They slid off their shoes and he removed his wallet from his pocket. He slipped his hand in Lyle's skirt and took her key from her. He placed the items in his shoe and put them under the pedals.

The evening was still warm. The moon was bright over the dark water. The sky was dotted with stars, and the night was perfectly quiet. He put his arms around her.

Thoughts of the conversation at dinner haunted him. His heart ached and the pressure felt too great to be contained in his chest. He thought he might burst open and his pain and despair would spill out and cascade to the sand at his feet. But this was it. Their time was up. Tonight was their last evening together. The tough discussion with Lyle would wait. "You know what they say. The last one in—"

"Is a rotten egg!" She took off running toward the water. She didn't get far before he grabbed her around her waist, lifted her, and carried her over his shoulder. "This isn't fair! I would've won in a fair race." She slapped his butt as he walked.

Michael stepped into the ocean and continued walking until he was waist-deep. He lifted Lyle off his shoulder, holding her tightly as she slid down in front of him. He had been waiting for this time alone with her since they sat down to dinner. His lips were soft and slow as they kissed.

She wrapped her arms around his neck and her legs around his waist. She returned each tender kiss. She ran her fingers up and down the back of his neck and into his hair. They were content to simply kiss under the star-filled sky.

He brushed his lips under her chin and down her neck. She nibbled on his ear, teasing him with her heavy breathing. He looked down at her. They didn't speak. They held on to each moment, knowing it was their last. He watched her expression change as she buried her sorrow and pulled strength from deep inside.

How could this be the same person who relied on an imaginary friend to pull her through? He felt a twist inside and his heartache grew. So many thoughts clouded Michael's mind. He wanted to scream at her, to shake her and tell her she didn't need Dottie. She had him now. How could she be weak and yet so strong? He dropped his head. He didn't want her to see his pain.

Lyle gazed up at the sky and spoke in a quiet voice. "There's Orion's Belt." She put her index finger under his chin and lifted it gently to see the sky. She pointed out the constellation. "It's the easiest one for me to find. Three bright stars lined in a row. Right above it, to the left"—She moved her finger to the star, knowing it was pointless—"that's Betelgeuse, one of the brightest stars in the sky."

But Michael wasn't looking at the stars. He was watching Lyle while she gazed up with wonder.

She caught him watching her, his face filled with sadness. She turned her attention again to the sky. "Follow to the east of Betelgeuse, and it's easy to find Bellatrix."

He barely breathed, mesmerized by the sing-song voice of his lover. All thoughts of Dottie and Lyle's internal pain were gone. They were here now. Alone once again in the warm ocean water.

"Impressed?" she whispered. "The truth is I can't find the Big Dipper to save my life."

Michael remained quiet. He didn't want this moment to end. Lyle leisurely unbuttoned her blouse. She slid her top off her shoulders and let it float in the water around them.

Her wet skin glowed in the moonlight. He lifted her to lick the salty water at her breasts. She watched him as he moved his tongue over her tender skin, her skirt floating around her waist. He ran his hands up her thighs and pulled at her panties. She responded by helping to remove them.

Michael unzipped his jeans and pulled them down off his hips. The deep water lapped against their skin. He positioned her as he wanted and took her there in the warm, dark water, moving together easily in rhythm.

His gentle touch turned aggressive, and soon Lyle let out a low groan. She wrapped her arms around his neck and pulled herself closer. She moved with him as her body climbed with anticipation. Mercifully, a thrumming wave exploded in her and she held on to Michael for dear life.

His arms tightened around Lyle and a single tear fell from his cheek to the water below.

They refused to let each other go and slept entangled in Lyle's bed. Michael stirred around three in the morning and ran his hands over her. She awakened and responded willingly to his touch. They made love in the dim glow of the bedside lamp, hoping to remember every inch of each other.

Fully satiated, they again let sleep overcome them.

Lyle awoke to the alarm and quickly silenced it. She would let him sleep. Last night had been a beautiful farewell. She didn't want to suffer a final send off this morning. Having to say goodbye to Michael would be a wretched ending to a glorious two weeks.

She put on her jeans and blouse and pushed her feet into her shoes. She pulled the laces tight and then gathered up her bags.

She stood over the bed, admiring the face of her lover. Her friend.

Michael slept peacefully, his hair tossed about the pillow. She listened to his quiet breathing and watched his chest rise and fall. She studied that face, hoping to burn it into her memory. Not the face he used with his fans, but the natural face he saved for his family, his friends, and for Lyle.

She placed a folded piece of paper on her pillow, opened the door, and quietly left Bon Adventure.

She had written *When I die and go to heaven, I will be swimming with you at Angel City.*

Epilogue

"We hope you've enjoyed your flight. We will be arriving at Raleigh Durham International Airport in twenty minutes. Weather is a cool sixty-five degrees with a light drizzle."

Lyle blinked, trying to bring herself back to the here and now. Her friends were scattered throughout the plane. The hungover teenager sleeping next to her was no company at all. She put her book into her bag under the seat and readied herself for the plane to land. Rain pelted the cabin window. A truly gloomy day in Raleigh.

Once on the tarmac, she heard several phones dinging and ringing with texts and emails. She dug her phone out of her carry-on and connected to the internet for the first time in two weeks. She had mostly spam emails and no phone or text messages, as everyone knew she was away.

As she checked the headlines, a familiar face caught her eye. This couldn't be true. She must be only half awake. For a moment, she watched the girl next to her fight to get her carry-on out from under the seat.

She turned her attention back to her phone.

The blond-haired man stared back at her from her screen. She knew it was him. She would never forget that face and all that hair. The man who attacked her all those days ago. Only it wasn't his face that was most disturbing. It was the headline *Man Murdered on Bonaire*.

Chills ran through Lyle as a possibility occurred to her.

Lyle, baby, I really need to talk to you. I have something to tell you, but I couldn't raise you from your sleep. Don't worry about him. I won't let him get near you again. You're safe with me. Why don't we stay behind today? I have something I need to talk to you about.

The plane's door opened, and a high-pitched bell rang. A mass of people shuffled to get their bags and depart the plane. Lyle sat frozen. She tried to sort out the probability.

Her phone rang.

"Hi, Dottie. I'm so glad you called."

Acknowledgments

For the people of Bonaire. As a writer I found it impossible to capture the magic of your island in words. Please accept my attempt to do so.

For the reader. I hoped to express to you the fairy-tale wonders of Bonaire and inspire you to love the ocean and the magical creatures found there.

A note from Anne

Time is a precious thing. I've come to realize that reading is a luxury. When I find time to read, I feel very fortunate. It means I've left the office, dinner was made, laundry and family were taken care of. Then, comes our time. I'm sure several of you would agree. I want to sincerely thank you for the time you took to read On Bonaire.

If you enjoyed following Lyle and her friends as they explored Bonaire, I would love it if you let your friends know so they can experience the magic of Lyle, Michael, and Bonaire as well.

Please leave a review for *On Bonaire A Lyle Cooper Story* on the site from which you purchased the book. It will go a long way in helping others to find my story. And I would love to read it! Email me the link at onbonairebook@gmail.com. I read and respond to all e-mails.

You can stay up to date on upcoming releases by joining my mailing list: www.annebennettauthor.com

Be the first to preorder: *Back to Bonaire A Lyle Cooper Story* available online 2023.

Back to Bonaire
A Lyle Cooper Story

Lyle and Michael sat at a table on a patio overlooking the docks. He pulled down the brim of his hat to block the encroaching sun. It was a clear morning on Bonaire, not a cloud in sight. Their empty plates had been cleared away, and crumbs from breakfast dotted the white tablecloth. A single Gerbera daisy in a clear vase offered them a bit of cheer, tempering the tense atmosphere.

Lyle slid her sunglasses from the top of her head to the bridge of her nose. People milled about the deck below, their excited voices trailing off with the breeze. They had already discussed this meeting many times. There was nothing left to say so they sat quietly while they awaited his arrival. Michael drummed his fingers incessantly on the table. He hadn't said a word and was lost in his thoughts. The constant beat he played elevated the tension and Lyle glanced at the time. A minute later, she checked again.

"Are you sure this is a good idea?" He asked her for the third time.

"No. I'm not sure. Please stop asking me that. This could totally blow up in my face."

"Baby, it's not *you* I'm worried about. Should I have a backup plan? I mean, in case this goes south and I need to get out of here fast."

"Backup plan? Like in a movie? No, there's no backup plan. Let's just see how this works out."

She felt him before she saw him; there was something in the air. The other diners stirred. Or was that only in her imagination? She and Michael turned at the same time. She sensed that the entire restaurant was looking too.

There stood Grey.

No longer in the pink shirt he had worn the previous night. He was once again dressed in all black, as Lyle knew he would be. Not even a pair of shorts—jeans and heavy leather boots.

He raised his chin and scanned the crowd, searching for Lyle. He was a grizzly bear on its hind legs, hoping to appear even bigger. The effort was working.

"Holy shit, Lyle. Is that him? Michael looked from Lyle back to Grey. "I definitely need that backup plan." He peered over the railing and judged the distance to the deck below. If he had to jump, he might get away with a bruise or two, or he may not walk away at all. "Maybe we should do this later. Tomorrow, maybe."

"It's going to be fine." She raised her arm and caught Grey's attention. "It has to be fine," she added under her breath.

Like smoke, Grey billowed through the dining area. Darkness crept between the white tablecloths and yellow daisies. The bright sapphire sky and the sparkling blue ocean seemed more brilliant next to him. He moved forward as the rest of the world stood still.

Grey reached their table and stood in silence. He looked from Michael to Lyle and back again. He stood next to her and held her cheek in his hand. He lifted her jaw and kissed her deeply.

"Good morning," Grey said. "I missed you last night."

Lyle put her sunglasses on the table and plastered a huge grin on her face, masking her nervousness. "Grey Locklear, this is Michael Miller. Michael, this is Grey."

As Michael stood, his chair squeaked across the tile floor. He craned his neck and squinted up at the massive man. "I've heard a lot about you."

"I'm sure you have." Grey gripped Michael's hand like a vise and shook it. "You have a lot of nerve coming here." He released his hand and sat.

"Nerve has nothing to do with it. Lyle wants me here." Michael sat back down.

"You abandoned her when she needed support, but here you are on vacation."

"Buddy, you are way off base. You have no idea—"

Lyle's grin faltered. "Michael, please. Let's not start this."

"Mr. Hollywood conveniently has a movie to make when you need him, but he finds the time to show up on Bonaire."

"Grey," she warned.

Michael's voice shot up and octave: "You know nothing about me." Realizing he was attracting attention, he adjusted his hat then slumped back in his chair.

"Guys, please."

"Do you even know what she's been going through?" asked Grey. "All the hard work she's doing, trying to get better?"

"Guys." Lyle's voice was now stern.

"Yes, yes, I do. I've been here for her a lot longer than you have. I know exactly what she's been through, and I've been supportive of her."

Grey glared at Michael. He was done talking.

"Okay, take a break and relax. You're here to meet each other, not to lay blame. No one is to blame for anything. Neither one of you is right or wrong. Let's take some time and see if we can work this out." They listened. "The truth is, you've both been instrumental in my recovery. Michael, you were with me during the crazy days." With a wince of anguish, she continued. "I was hallucinating even, but you never judged me. You saw me through rose-colored glasses and loved me despite knowing the truth about me."

"Grey, you knew I wasn't right from the start. On the first day we met you knew my reason for getting my tattoo was delusional, and although my thoughts were irrational, you chose to go on this journey with me, eyes wide open. You helped me come out the other side. I love you for that."

She took each of their hands in hers. "I love you. Both of you. Because of some wild coincidences, the two of you are joined, through me. I know neither of you asked for this, but here we are. I can't pick one or the other. Not now, not yet. Please don't ask me to. It would kill me to have to choose."

The table was silent. She stood and put her hand on Grey's shoulder. "I'll get you coffee and make you a plate. I'll give you guys a chance to talk. Where we go from here is up to the two of you." She left them on their own.

"Shit," Grey grumbled.

"Fuck." Michael watched Lyle as she took her time at the breakfast buffet.

"We can't undo what she's done," said Grey. "I mean, her healing, her progress. I won't stress her out when she's come so far, not over this. We can't pressure her into choosing. She obviously needs us both right now."

"I agree. When she's ready, she'll decide," said Michael. "I hope you won't be too distraught over getting dumped."

"Like hell. She loves me," said Grey. "What are you doing here? I know who you are. The famous Michael Miller. Lyle tells me you're dating a model and yet, here you are."

"I'm here because I love her," said Michael. "I need her and she needs me. Since we can't be together full time, we have an agreement, which, quite frankly, sitting here with you has me questioning its logic."

As she strolled through the buffet line, Lyle stole glances at them. She hoped it was a good sign that they were talking. She returned with a steaming cup of coffee and a plate filled with eggs, toast, and bacon and put it down in front of Grey.

"Thanks, Crocodile. This smells really good."

Michael was thrown by the nickname, so he threw in his own. "Baby, we agreed that you should have as much time as you need.

Romeo here thinks you'll choose him," he winked at Lyle, "let him dream."

Grey picked up his fork. "Michael, do you windsurf?"

"No. I haven't had the time to learn."

"Good, neither of us will have an unfair advantage. Let's go windsurfing at Lac Bai tomorrow. We'll see which one of us comes out alive."

Lyle rolled her eyes. "This isn't a competition. You're here to get to know each other."

"No baby, you're wrong. It's definitely a competition," said Michael.

"Windsurfing tomorrow does sound like fun," said Lyle. "But I'm also hoping for some rest and relaxation during this vacation."

"Rest and relaxation?" Michael grimaced at Grey. "What've you done to her?"

"Oh, a whole lot of things. I've done a whole lot of things to her."

Lyle held her head in her hands. At least they were talking.

Made in the USA
Middletown, DE
19 April 2023

29098921R00139